Spitfire Sunrise

A Battle of Britain Novel

D.H. Olsen

Order this book online at www.trafford.com
or email orders@trafford.com

Most Trafford titles are also available at major online book retailers.

Printed in the United States of America.

ISBN : 978-1-4269-4099-6 (sc)
ISBN : 978-1-4269-4100-9 (e)

Our mission is to efficiently provide the world's finest, most comprehensive book publishing service, enabling every author to experience success. To find out how to publish your book, your way, and have it available worldwide, visit us online at www.trafford.com

Trafford rev. 08/18/2010

www.trafford.com

North America & international
toll-free: 1 888 232 4444 (USA & Canada)
phone: 250 383 6864 • fax: 812 355 4082

1

*

27 May 1940

"Tally Ho! Bandits nine o'clock low. Got them all sections?"

"Roger." the terse responses echoed in sequence through the crackling static of the R/T.

Twelve Supermarine Spitfires, throttles to the gate, steeped turned in formation executing a maneuver that would place the deadly fighters up sun. Below them, hugging the puffy white undercast, thirty Dornier 17s droned straight and level, sporadically disappearing into the towering cloud tops. Voracious birds of prey speeding to the chaotic feeding grounds at Dunkirk.

"Red and Blue port attack, yellow and green starboard," Squadron Leader Barnes, flying Red one, ordered in calm, cultured Cambridge tones.

The British aircraft, arranged in four V-shaped groupings or 'vics' of three, spread out quickly as they dove toward the unsuspecting enemy.

Several seconds later the Spitfires of Yellow section selected individual targets, deliberately holding their fire until they were within two-hundred yards of the Do 17s—nicknamed the *Fliegender Bleistiff* or 'Flying Pencil' by German aircrews. Pilot Officer Andrew James Duncan, positioned as yellow two, behind and above his leader, had mentally reviewed the check list etched into his brain—gun button on, prop to higher revs, reflector sight on, seat lowered, Sutton harness tight.

Closing to the attack, red tracers from the Dornier directly in front of Andy whipsawed menacingly over his Spit. Reflexively the young Canadian pilot pressed the firing tit on the spade-like control column. In less than a microsecond, eight browning machine guns mounted in the wings of the English fighter came alive, causing the Spitfire to stagger slightly in the air.

A vicious four second burst of .303 de Wilde incendiary rounds tore into the doomed twin engined enemy bomber, moments before yellow two rocketed below the flaming Dornier.

Recovering from the steep dive, Pilot Officer Duncan climbed at full power through the cloying mist that had swallowed him whole. Me 109s had joined the tumbling dogfight and one of the snappers flew right in front of Andrew's aircraft as he emerged from the cotton candy cloud layer. A short well placed deflection burst clobbered the Messerschmitt. The German fighter changed instantly from a flying machine into a roiling black-orange fireball—chunks of metal and well-done flesh scattered like buck shot about an impartial atmosphere.

"Break right Dunc." Billy Allison, in yellow three, shouted over the radio.

The warning came a second split too late. Following a violent explosion, hissing ropes of white glycol steam erupted from the throaty Rolls-Royce Merlin. Several 20 mm canon shells had pulverized the radiator and the engine would over heat quickly. Andy threw the wounded Spitfire into a steep right turn desperately trying to rid himself of the 109 glued to his tail. His Spit cut through the air, like an up-right knife rotating on its handle, barely staying ahead of the Jerry fighters firing window.

Judging the moment to be right, Andy flicked the Spit into a half-roll, then pushed the shuddering aircraft into a full throttle dive. Within a heart beat the nimble fighter was wrapped in fluffy layers of cloud that hid it from the enemy.

The needle on the temperature gauge had jammed itself past the red line and the engine, a white hot thing on its way to meltdown, howled in screeching protest—eleven-hundred horsepower about to die.

Andy broke through the overcast at ten thousand feet, the English coastline looked a long way off. He adjusted the elevator trim wheel for the best angle of glide, then watched helplessly as the altimeter wound down.

He could see from the rippling waves on the surface of the grey, green Channel that the wind was from the west. It would be a close run thing. Two minutes later, Andy blasted the cramped cockpit of the Spit with an ear piercing whoop of joy. RAF Manston, code named 'Charlie 3', lay directly ahead.

"Charlie 3 control, Yellow two, do you read?" he croaked into the microphone nestled in the oxygen mask.

"Roger Yellow two, go ahead."

"I'm dead stick and request a straight in."

"Understood Yellow two. Manston to all aircraft, clear the circuit immediately."

The timing had to be perfect and the landing gear couldn't be lowered until he was sure of making the field. Wheels down would cause extra drag, robbing the Mark 1 Spitfire of precious altitude. Perspiring heavily, he drew in large breaths trying desperately to quell the panic that rose up in his throat.

All the cockpit checks were complete and praying that he had it right, Andy frantically worked the wobble pump handle that would deploy his landing gear. At the same time he delicately applied pressure to stick and rudder pedals.

Realizing the Spit was still too high, he put the aircraft into a side slip to bleed off excess altitude. The maneuver was successful and now past the threshold of the grass runway he kicked the elliptical winged fighter straight with rudder and eased back gently on the stick. The Spit bounced once but stayed down. Pilot Officer Andrew James Duncan had completed his first combat mission and had lived to tell the tale.

Unable to move, after the Spitfire rolled to a full stop, Andy sat perfectly still, his hands shaking uncontrollably as nervous tension drained away. Two German aircraft had been destroyed by his guns but he felt no elation, only relief that the sortie was over. Andrew snapped back to reality when an erk pounded on the side of the aircraft.

For some reason the ground personnel who worked on the fighters and bombers were called erks by the British pilots. Andy made a mental note to find out why.

"Sir, we've got to get the kite off the runway, " a red faced Flight Sergeant yelled, as a dozen airmen began to guide the Spit away from the landing path.

When the fighter was safely off to the side Andy pushed back the bullet proof canopy, unlatched the folding cockpit door, and climbed out onto the wingroot. The NCO who'd hammered on the stressed aluminum skin of the Spit, now stood by the trailing edge of the port wing. "I see your gun covers are gone sir, nail any of the bastards," the erk beamed, as Pilot Officer Duncan stepped on to *terra firma*.

"A 109 and a Dornier, but they're not confirmed," Andy squeaked, realizing how dry his throat was and how tired he felt.

"Jolly good show sir." the Flight Sergeant smiled, while motioning for a Lorry to hook on to the Spit.

"The Merlin's fried and the cooler got shot all to hell, but the rest of the crate's good for parts." Andy stated optimistically.

"Sir, with a touch of the magic brush the chaps at Civilian Repair will 'ave this 'ere poor darlin' mended like dad's old boot before you can say Bob's me uncle."

"Well then Flight, it's a good thing I got her down in one piece." Andy exchanged salutes with the Sergeant before double timing it over to the Nissen hut, where an Intelligence Officer would be waiting for a post action report.

Manston, an all-grass airfield in south-east England, was the forward most of RAF stations and damaged aircraft used it to good advantage. The owl faced I/O nodded curtly when Andy entered the debriefing room. Pilot Officer Andrew James Duncan—a well-built twenty-one-year-old, tall and trim, with a jutting jaw, alert brown eyes, and a full head of black curly hair—patiently answered all the questions put to him by the pot bellied score keeper before filling out a written report.

Andy was then given a travel warrant that would get him back to RAF Stonecroft where 689 Squadron was stationed.

The first part of his journey was a pleasant and memorable one, as he managed to hitch a ride in a NAAFI—Navy Army Air Force Institute—van that was going as far as Dover. The van provided refreshments, mainly tea and biscuits, to the pilots and ground crew of the various airfields in the area. It was the driver of the vehicle who was responsible for the pleasant and memorable part of Andy's trip to the white cliffs.

She wore the uniform of a WAAF—Women's Auxiliary Air Force—Corporal and her name was Emily Smith-Barton. She was a young, buxom, blue eyed, stawberry blonde with a peaches and cream complexation. Andy thought that Emily was the most beautiful creature in the world. He was captivated by her loveliness and completely tongue tied. They drove along in silence for several minutes before Emily asked, "What part of the great Dominion sir?" She'd spotted the shoulder flashes on his uniform.

Andrew was taken a back by the sir part, "My friends call me Andy,"he grinned. "and I'm from the west coast of Canada, a place called Campbell River on Vancouver Island."

"You're an officer sir, and I must obey King's regulations," she retorted testily to the first part of his answer. "and from what I've read you live in a very beautiful part of your country." she instantly mellowed.

"It's still pretty wild up-Island, but the mountains, ocean, rivers bursting with salmon, and the endless stands of tall timber do get in your blood."

"That sounds marvelous sir!" she burbled, momentarily fixing her gaze on Andy's handsome features.

"And if it isn't contrary to Kings regulations, may I ask your name Miss."

"Quite proper sir, Corporal Smith-Barton," she smiled coyly.

Andy chuckled softly, "Is there anything before the double barreled last one."

"Why yes sir, I was Christened Emily."

They drove on in silence for what seemed like an eternity to the young pilot officer. Andy wanted to know more but his mind had shifted to the vicious dogfight in the skies over Dunkirk. Early that morning Six-Eighty-Nine Squadron had been ordered, by Air Vice-Marshall Keith Park, commander of 11 Group Fighter Command, to provide top cover for Operation Dynamo. The cobbled together plan was a desperate attempt to rescue the British Expeditionary Force from General Heinz Guderian's marauding Pancers that had pushed the English army into the sea. A sudden jolt from a large pothole on the left side of the road rocked Andy back to the present.

Not able to think of anything clever to say he stammered, "H-How long have you been a NAAFI driver?"

"For just about thirty minutes now Pilot Officer Andy," she laughed mischievously, while glancing at her wrist watch.

He absentmindedly scratched the back of his head before saying,"Okay you've got me on that one. Any chance of an explanation?"

"Well sir, it's not an official secret and after all you are on our side." she replied in a teasing voice. "I'm stationed at the Chain Home RDF in Dover"

"A radio boffin! So why're we sitting in this van together?" he grinned, finally beginning to relax and enjoy himself.

"I was visiting Mummy at Foreness and when I checked in at Manston on the way back, they asked me to ferry this old bus to Dover. It needs a new clutch."

Andy knew that Foreness was a seaside town on a point of land even closer to France than Dover. A radar facility was located there, or as the British called it, an RDF—Radio Direction Finding—station.

"Why Dover? When you could be stationed right at home," he asked, his curiosity aroused.

"Good question sir, but have you ever known anything that the Brass do to make sense."

Andy snorted appreciatively, "Good answer Corporal Emily.

"You've given me your first one sir, were you by any chance granted a last one?"

"Yes indeed I was, and I'll throw in the middle one as a bonus. Andrew James Duncan at your service Miss Emily Smith-Barton."

"I've an uncle whose name's Andrew but everyone in the family calls him Drew. I think that's how I shall address you as well." she added playfully.

"Do you think King George will mind Emily?"

"Not at all sir," she purred seductively.

*

The contended pair chatted non-stop until they reached the Great Eastern Railway station where Andy boarded the 2:15 for London. He told Emily that he was on Spits at RAF Stonecroft and would like to take her out to dinner if she ever got up to town. WAAF Corporal Smith-Barton thought that Pilot Officer Duncan's offer of sustenance on a given evening in the capital of the Empire was well within His Royal Majesty's rules of conduct and promised to ring him up the next time she visited the city on the Thames.

2

*

As the coal fired, steam driven locomotive chuffed its way west from the sea, Andy had time in the crowded passenger car to reflect on the events of the past year. He'd graduated with a Bachelor of Science degree from Victoria College in the spring of 1939. His long term plans were to attend Medical school at the University of British Columbia in Vancouver, then come back to the Island and set up a practice in his home town.

During that summer he flew floats commercially for a bush outfit in Campbell River. His father, James Angus Duncan a World War One fighter ace, had taught his son how to fly. James Duncan, a civil engineer, ran a consulting firm with offices in Campbelton. Jimmy, as his friends called him, had purchased a Fairchild KR-31 in 1935 and kept it on floats at a marina near the mouth of the river. Andy as a teenager worked for his father and was paid in flying lessons—former Royal Flying Corp Major James Angus Duncan acting as the instructor. Andrew was a fast learner and soon qualified for a commercial ticket. Andy was thrilled when he landed the job as a bush pilot.

Andrew was restless during the summer of '39. The papers were full of sabre rattling from continental Europe. Everyone believed that war with Nazi Germany was inevitable. When Poland was attacked in September, and war was officially declared by the Canadian Government, Andy decided he had to get involved. With his father's blessing, Jimmy had done the same thing in 1917, Andrew James crossed the Atlantic on an ocean liner and joined the Royal Air Force. He figured it would take too long for the Royal Canadian Air Force to become operational.

Because Andrew was an experienced pilot and a university graduate, he was offered a Short Service Commission and sent to an Elementary Flying Training School. He had to start from scratch on Tigers Moths and Miles Magisters.

Oddly enough this was the first time he'd flown an aircraft on wheels and also the first time he'd been able to do aerobatics. When the course ended, he was rated an above average pilot. Shortly thereafter, he was transferred to a Service Flying Training School.

At the SFTS Andy flew the Hawker Fury, a biplane powered by a Rolls-Royce Kestrel engine. The Fury would cruise at two-hundred and twenty miles per hour and was armed with two Vickers Mark IV machine guns. It was faster than the Sopwith Camel his father had flown in the Great War, but its armament was the same. Andrew learned the art of aerial gunnery and scored top marks for his deflection shooting. He had exceptional eyesight, and was able to picture in his minds eye where the target and tracer rounds would meet. His instructors again rated him above average in all categories and he was passed on to No. 2 Operational Training Unit.

Andy was hoping to be put on Spitfires or Hurricanes right away but the aircraft that was available at 2 OTU was the Gloster Gauntlet MK II. It was heavier than the Fury but not much faster, even though it was powered by a Bristol Mercury six-hundred and forty-five horsepower radial engine. It too was armed with twin Vickers. After mastering the Gauntlet he was sent to No. 6 OTU where he graduated to Hurricanes. The Hawker aircraft, designed by Sydney Camm, was light years ahead of anything that Andy had flown. It was a modern eight gun fighter and also a monoplane. The eleven-hundred hp, V-12, Rolls-Royce power plant gave the sturdy machine a maximum speed of 330 mph. Pilots who'd flown the Hurricane in France, following the German invasion, said it was an extremely stable gun platform. It could also sustain a great deal of punishment and still get you home. For that reason, combat experienced pilots had given the fighter the nickname of Hurri-back or simply the Hurri. Again, Andrew's outstanding flying skills and marksmanship caught the eye of several senior officers and he was given the opportunity to convert to Spitfires.

Pilot Officer Andrew James Duncan and the elegant Spit—the brain child of Reginald Mitchell—became fast friends. He found it incredibly responsive to light touches of rudder, elevator and aileron. The most amazing thing was its remarkably short turning radius. The Spit would knife edge through the air like a top and you could hold it rock steady in a vertical banked attitude. As a leather lunged Flight Leader from Glasgow, so aptly put it, "The wee lassies turns are tighter than a Scotsmen's sporran." The Rolls-Royce, eleven-hundred horse, supercharged PV 1200 Merlin would provide a top speed of 355 miles per hour and the Supermarine fighter's eight Browning .303 machine guns, each loaded with 350 rounds, could make mincemeat out of a Luftwaffe fighter.

Having accumulated forty hours on Spits, Andy was declared operational and assigned to Six-Eighty-Nine Squadron at Stonecroft. The aerodrome, a Sector Headquarters, was located on the eastern fringes of London.

*

Andrew came out of his reverie just as the train from Dover pulled into Charing Cross station. The travel weary pilot took the tube to Ash Park, then transferred to a double decker that deposited him at the airbase. He was welcomed back at the officer's mess shortly thereafter.

Billy Allison, a freckle faced, redheaded, five-six, barrel chested American jumped to his feet when he saw Andy enter the room. "Dunc, you old fart, I thought you'd gone for a Burton."

"I was lucky, and managed a daisy cutter at Manston Billy," Andy winked, remembering that his landing had been a hard one and not faultless. "The engine was fried but an erk said the kite could be glued back together."

"You nailed two of those Nazi bastards Dunc. I got a good look at the Dornier as it flamed into the scud and that was some light show with the Me.

"Are they confirmed Alley?" Andy asked, unconsciously holding his breath.

"Sure as hell are! I reported to the I/O right after we pancaked, three more and presto, you're an ace Andrew James." Billy snapped his fingers to emphasize the point.

Squadron Leader Barnes came up behind Andy and patted him on the back, "Good to have you back old chap and congratulations on the brace of Hun's," Barnes smiled broadly while shaking Andy's hand, then trying to maintain a serious expression, he said, "We're on again at first light. Pity, that only leaves us time for ten or twelve pints. Ale for the multitudes my good man." the popular officer shouted in the direction of a Corporal, who'd begun to pump up bitter from the kegs in the basement.

Andy carelessly wiped the foam from his upper lip onto the sleeve of a well worn, battle dress blue jacket. Looking around and beginning to relax he bugled in Billy Allisons direction, "Where the hell's old Corky? He's always first in line for a free pint." The pilots at the bar suddenly went silent. Alley had to clear his throat before speaking, but managed to rasp in guppy-like bursts, "Corky bought the farm on the way back. A snapper got on his tail and blew the Spit apart. He didn't have a chance."

Flying Officer Charles Corkrell was a section leader and well liked by everyone. He was also the first member of the Squadron to be killed in combat. Andrew James, stunned by the news, blinked several times in an attempt to stop the tear drops that leaked slowly from the corners of his eyes.

Squadron Leader Robbie Barnes a stocky, sandy haired, mustached graduate of Cambridge, not wanting the pilots to become morose and frightened, briefly inspected his nicotine stained fingers, inhaled one last puff, grabbed an ashtray then stubbed out a half-smoked Woodbine. The well liked and well respected Squadron Leader, who'd been given the nickname Burnsey, addressed his fellow officers in a hoarse, halting voice. "Corky was a good one chaps and he was doing what he loved best. It's a cruel thing to say, but we must forget him for now. We've got a big job to do and we'll have to carry on in spite of our losses."

Robert Daniel Barnes raised his glass and shouted, "Corky you old bugger, you're with the angels now, and the rest of us poor bastards will be glad to drink a pint in honour of your promotion."

Polite laughter rippled musically on the air. Mugs were drained, then refilled, and the fighter boys of 689 or Panther Squadron, the code name assigned to it by sector control, began to discuss their three favorite topics, women, the fairer sex and popsies. They would all remember Corky in quiet, private moments, but tomorrow would bring gut twisting patrols over the beaches and like the Great War—beware the Hun in the sun.

3

*

As promised, the Panthers took to the air at first light. The ruby red horizon looked inviting but Andy kept thinking, "red sky in the morning sailor take warning." The squadron was on an easterly track that would lead the British fighters to Dunkirk. Each aircraft adjusted throttle and boost for maximum rate of climb—a Spitfire sunrise, battering against the white, blinding bolts hurled earthwards by a life giving star.

East of the war torn beaches Flight Lieutenant Woodston, the leader of A flight, spotted twenty-four Heinkel 111s ahead of, and slightly below the twelve Supermarine fighters. Banking sharply to get the sun at their backs, the Spits soared swiftly into an attack position. Thirty seconds later, amidst a whirlwind of defensive fire, ninety-six Browning machine guns sprayed the German bombers with a chattering mist of death.

Andy waited until he could clearly read the squadron markings on the twin engined Heinkel he'd selected, before pressing the firing button on the joystick. As the Spit dove below the 111 he could see that both engines were belching an expanding column of oily, black smoke. Andrew James yanked back on the control column to pull the Spitfire out of its vertical dive, then climbed like a home-sick angel back up to the fight. This time he picked a bomber that was rapidly descending to reach a protective bank of cloud. Anxious to get the He 111 before it disappeared into the white blanket below, Andy let loose a prolonged burst before he was close enough for the cone of .303 rounds to be effective. Just as his Spit came into killing range all he could hear was a hiss of compressed air coming from the direction of the gun ports. Pilot Officer Duncan was out of ammunition.

The rear gunner of the Heinkel, however, continued to send a blazing stream of metal at the Spitfire, scoring a multitude of direct hits on the fuselage of the nimble fighter.

The whining chucks of high velocity lead ripped apart the steel cables running to the rudder and elevators. Like a wing shot goose, the battered Spit tumbled uncontrollably from the unforgiving skies.

Andy was muddled by the top-like motion—vicious G forces pinning him to the pilots seat. Panic numbed his brain. He fought desperately to open the canopy and unlatch the small folding door. Unbridled terror provided him with the super human strength needed to force the hood to slide back and the door to open. Pilot officer Andrew James Duncan, pushed hard against the cockpit floor and propelled himself into space, narrowly missing the tail plane.

He was now in free fall and clear of the aircraft. Andrew, still in cloud, was completely disoriented but quickly regained his senses. He grabbed the 'D' ring on the parachute and gave it a frantic tug, but his screaming descent remained unchecked. Looking up, Andy saw that the lines were tangled. Grabbing the straps above his head he worked the snarled shrouds like a dog shaking a rabbit by the neck. Several seconds later there was a loud pop as the harness tightened vice-like about his upper thighs and shoulders. Now below the cloud, he could see the checkerboard farmland of France dancing below the toes of his shearling lined flight boots.

Being shot down on his second combat mission caused Andrew James to hang his head in dejection. There was the real possibility that he'd be taken prisoner and spend the rest of the war in a Stalag.These thoughts, however, were shoved to the sidelines as the ground accelerated towards him at brake neck speed. Andy rolled on contact with mother earth and felt fortunate that nothing was sprained or injured. He'd landed on the edge of a large pasture, hard against a mature hedge row. Pilot Officer Duncan hurriedly gathered up his chute and ran like a frightened deer into the tangle that bordered the gently rolling meadow.

He folded the parachute into a neat bundle and hid it behind a fallen tree.

Andy stayed put for thirty minutes, then moved cautiously across the open field. He soon found a dirt road that ran east and west. Keeping the sun at his back, Andrew James walked slowly along the shady country route that he hoped would lead him closer to the sea. Several miles down the road he was able to make out black, roiling smoke on the horizon and figured that this was likely the burning fuel storage depot located near the beaches at Dunkirk. His heart leapt into his throat when he heard the screeching sound of tank treads ahead. Andy jumped over a stone wall that ran parallel to the road, then baby crawled to a small rise where he'd be able to get a better view.

Having reached his objective, he carefully raised his head and peeked over the top of a gigantic rounded rock. At a distance of one-hundred yards, Andy spotted thirty grey clad soldiers, Mauser rifles slung across their shoulders, standing next to a tank with black crosses stenciled on its heavily armored side panels. Andrew James immediately ducked down, his pulse racing and mouth desert dry. He'd have to wait for the cover of darkness to go any further.

For the remainder of the daylight hours Andy watched the German troops and concluded that they, along with the tank, were guarding a road junction directly in front of where he was hiding. From the sound of gun fire and the periodic crump of high explosives Andrew judged that he was very near the beaches. It seemed like an eternity before it was dark enough for him to move. A ground fog had settled in over the area providing Andy with the cover he needed to move forward. He proceeded in the direction of the soldiers voices and estimating time and distance moved away from where he judged the tank to be. Hoping he had it right, and guessing at a direction that would lead him to the Channel, Andy changed course.

As if someone had pulled back a curtain, the protective mist suddenly lifted, stars now sparkling brightly in a diamond studded sky. Andy stopped breathing when he saw a soldier directly in front of him.

He panicked and started to run. A rifle shot whistled over his head and a loud guttural voice split the air behind him. He continued to sprint into the inky darkness not knowing where he was going, unchained fear driving him onwards. Three sharp reports echoed in the night just as the moon came out. Andy dove to the ground and started to crawl on his belly. A powerful spotlight, mounted on the turret of the tank, threw a focused, blinding beam in his direction but he was now beyond its effective range. Andrew James cautiously slithered towards the charnel house that was Dunkirk.

Two hours later the shadowy images of trees and a large building appeared directly ahead of him, as the gun metal glow of dawn began to illuminate the western edges of France. Andy thought of duck hunting with his father back in Campbell River and figured that it was about a half hour before sunrise. Shooting light was what James Duncan called it. Andy grimaced at the irony of the memory because he was now the hunted. As the sky brightened, he identified a dozen soldiers standing in front of what looked like an old barn.

Andy breathed a sigh of relief when he spotted the Great War style steel helmets on their heads. They had to be British infantry. Slowly, he rose to his feet and walked at a snails pace towards the small band of Tommies. One of the Privates, who'd detected the motion, shouldered his Lee-Enfield and fired a shot that whined over Andy's head. The startled pilot froze in his tracks but managed to yell, "Hold your fire you trigger happy bastards. I'm RAF."

A gruff voice answered back, "Might as well shoot you then for the all the bloody good you're doing."

Andy was bewildered by the reply. He'd been risking his life for the past two days to protect the army and now they wanted to kill him.

"Hands up old boy until we know who you are for sure," the bulldog voice rasped again.

Pilot Officer Andrew James Duncan did as he was told and carefully approached the small group of men, his arms hoisted towards the heavens.

The soldier who'd given the orders turned out to be a Captain. He gave the young pilot a withering look as he inspected the identification card that Andy had removed from his wallet.

"So how do I know you didn't take this, and that uniform off of one our pilots?" the hostile officer growled menacingly, his Webley Mk VI .45 calibre pistol pointed directly at Andy's chest.

After being shot down and fired at by both sides Andy blew like a tiny volcano, "Listen to me you shit for brains limey son-of-a-bitch. I'm a Can/RAF Spitfire pilot and I've been up there trying to keep those assholes who work for Hitler off your backs. Now show me the way to the fucking beaches."

The open-eyed captain, stepped to within half a foot of Andrew. He suddenly holstered his sidearm, stuck his head back and started to laugh. "Well old sport, you sure as hell ain't a Jerry. Only a Johnny Canuck could swear like that."

The tension slowly drained away as Andrew James unballed his fists. "S-Sorry sir," he sputtered. "It's been a rough twenty-four hours and I'm dog tired."

"We haven't been sleeping properly either" the British officer yawned openly, "and I meant it about the useless Air Force."

Andy tried to explain that the air battles were going on at higher altitudes and quite often above cloud cover,"You see sir, we intercept the bombers and Stukas before they get to the front, many get through but it would be a lot worse if we weren't up there."

"Maybe so, but the chappie on the ground is still at the sharp end of the stick."

4
*

Andy spotted the serpentine lines of frightened men, stretching from the sand dunes to the water's edge, as he walked cautiously along a grassy knoll east of the Channel. A heavy cloud of desperation hung ominously below the lead streaked skies but the well trained soldiers, waiting to be carried back to England, stoically maintained a semblance of order amidst the chaos that surrounded them.

Pilot Officer Andrew James Duncan worked his way to a makeshift causeway where a destroyer was moored. He broke into a run when he heard the command to cast off coming from an officer on the fore deck. Halfway to his goal a blimp sized Major ordered him to halt.

"Where in the devil do you think you're going?" the field grade officer bellowed.

"Sir, I'm a fighter pilot and I have to get back to my squadron."

"Bloody RAF eh? In that case, back of the line."

Andy was about to push the enraged Major aside when he saw the 109 on its strafing run. Acting instinctively, he went in low and tackled the British officer who had his back to the aircraft. They hit the rough, planked surface hard, but just in time to avoid a hosing of lead, that whistled menacingly, inches above their heads. The porcine Major, winded by the fall, lay gasping for breath as Andy quickly got to his feet.

"It's been swell meeting you sir, but I really have to go."

The startled officer tried to get up but collapsed back in a heap. He gave Andy a dismissive wave before rolling over onto his stomach.

Andrew James reached the rope netting just as it was being raised, but managed to grab hold and scramble his way aboard. Following a brief interview with the officer of the deck he was taken to the wardroom where a glacial reception awaited him. The stony silence of the Army officers gathered there said it all. Andy backed slowly towards the door.

"Bugger off RAF!" was the fond farewell that echoed in his ears.

When he arrived topside Andy encountered a Naval Officer who asked him to help with aircraft identification on the aft gun deck. It proved to be wise request by the young RN lieutenant as the ack-ack crew had just opened up on what they thought was a Ju 88. Andy shouted at them to cease fire because they were shooting at a Blenheim bomber. Seconds later he spotted a German twin engined fighter and ordered the guns to fire on an Me 110 that was beginning its dive towards the ship. Pilot Officer Duncan stayed at his adopted station until the destroyer reached the safety of Dover.

The docks were alive with a milling band of disheveled, churlish troops—tattered remnants of the once proud British Expeditionary Force—most of them were without rifles. Their armor, transport vehicles and artillery lay abandoned on the beaches at Dunkirk. England had lost the battle and defeat weighed heavily on the Island Kingdom. Leaving the crowded wharf behind, Andy walked briskly towards the centre of town, where he found a pub called the Oak and Carriage.

He'd been fed a hardtack biscuit and a scalding cup of tea on board the destroyer, his only meal during the past thirty-six hours. His stomach started to imitate the growling sounds of a hungry cougar as he anticipated being fed a king sized helping of shepherd's pie, or whatever the Inn had to offer. Andy carried a ten pound note in his wallet for emergency situations and the gnawing pangs of hunger qualified as a red alert.

He was able to find a table at the rear of the public house where a florid faced barmaid took his order. Several minutes later she came back with the special of the day—a large plate overflowing with eggs, bacon and chips.

"A flyboy are you sir?" the barmaid crooned.

"Why yes miss, I'm on Spits at Stonecroft."

"Better watch out for the squaddies then love, they don't think very much of the RAF."

"So I've been told.," Andrew James nodded ruefully.

He managed to avoid a confrontation with a disgruntled Army sergeant when he got up to leave and made it safely out the door. Andy had been given directions by the barmaid and easily found his way to the railway station. The passenger cars were filled to overflowing with troops wanting to get home and he was told transport to London was out of the question until tomorrow. Again the attitude seemed to be: "Screw the RAF!"

Andy was about to return to the Oak and Carriage to see if he could get a room for the night, when he recognized a voice from behind that made him melt in his tracks.

"Drew, what on earth are you doing here?"

"Well Corporal Emily, he improvised after turning around, "I thought I'd come down to Dover and look you up." he smiled, his heart beat going off scale.

"Judging by your uniform and two days growth, I'd say Pilot Officer Andy that you're quite a story teller."

"Can we get out of here and go somewhere quiet for a drink," he asked, while admiring her cerulean blue eyes and well formed chest.

"I think regulations would permit that kind sir, since I'm off duty."

"And where might you suggest we partake of this libation? The pubs are packed solid and the Army thinks that the RAF has done nothing at Dunkirk. Every place around here seems like enemy territory."

"Yes, I've heard the complaints from Generals down to Privates. We've had you on our screens and I know the odds you've been facing up there. I've tried to explain it to anyone who'd listen but the fact is; they only believe what they see with their own eyes."

"I can understand that, but after being shot down, fired at by our own side and cursed by everyone wearing a wooly brown suit I'm getting a little gun shy."

"In that case Drew, the best place for us to have that quiet drink would be my flat. My roommate's gone up to town, I was just seeing her off."

She paused for a moment as the shrill whistle of a departing locomotive pierced the air, then with a mischievous twinkle in her eye she said, "I don't believe the King will mind if we aren't chaperoned."

"Emily, if I'm dreaming, please don't wake me." he gulped, a new kind of hunger beginning to grow slightly south of his belt line.

Her flat, as she called it, turned out to be a two-up, two-down several blocks from the harbour. She showed Andy into the tiny parlor, then disappeared in the direction of the kitchen. Several minutes later Emily returned with a bottle of single malt scotch, a small pitcher of water and two glasses.

"I like mine neat," she smiled "but I suspect you'd prefer yours with water."

"I'm not much for the hard stuff, but since this is for purely medicinal purposes, I'll have mine straight as well." he grinned, while reaching for a tumbler half-filled with whiskey.

"Watch out for this Highland nectar then Drew. My father says, it'll put hair on your chest."

"Here's to a fury rib cage," he chuckled, raising his glass in salute.

They were sitting on an over stuffed couch that faced a small bay window. It was a pleasant evening and the room was comfortably warm. Emily was wearing a light blue cardigan, white blouse and navy blue skirt which, even off duty, gave her a military appearance. Andy, stars in his eyes, thought she was the best looking Corporal in the world.

"It's a little stuffy in here." Emily sighed, as she removed her coat sweater.

Andy had managed to wash up in the restroom at the pub, but he still felt grubby wearing a uniform that was stained, and had literally been through the wars. He too was feeling the heat from the room and the scotch.

"Do you mind if I take off my tunic?" he asked, moving closer to her on the sofa.

"By all means Drew. Make yourself at home."

He placed his drink on the walnut coffee table that was directly in front of them and turned towards her. Emily had set her glass on the floor and with one smooth motion she shifted his way, put her arms around his neck and kissed him full on the lips. Andy was startled at first but was soon caught up to her rising passion. Open mouths and probing tongues slowly led to soft caresses and moans of sheer delight as their highly inflamed bodies pressed together.

"Come with me Darling Drew," she whispered in his ear as they got up from the couch. Emily then led him, by the hand, upstairs to her bedroom.

It was a strange first time for Andy. He'd been out on many dates back home but necking and petting were the limit of his experience. Now here he was with a beautiful woman, clearly the aggressor, and far more sophisticated than anyone he'd ever met.

They'd undressed each other and were completely naked under the covers. Fully aroused, after several minutes of tantalizing fore play, Emily cast the sheets aside and swiftly straddled Andy. She rode him like a fine stallion, a sensual rocking motion that led them to a land far beyond paradise.

"I know you'll think this is crazy Drew, but I fell in love with you the moment you got into that old Humber van with the fractured clutch." she cooed softly, several minutes later, as they lay entwined in each others arms.

"Emily, believe it not, I felt the same way when I met you. I kept on telling myself that love at first sight only happens in the movies but I was dead wrong."

At the word dead she pushed away from him and in a tremulous voice began to speak, choosing her words carefully, "I do have one confession to make, I was married before the war started but my husband was killed in '38."

Andy was stunned by the revelation but recovering quickly he stammered,"D-Do you want to talk about it or is that too painful?"

"Drew you are the sweetest man and thank you for being so considerate. Roger was in the RAF and a fighter pilot. You are so much like him in many ways," she paused to get the tightness out of her throat, "but you are also very different. His squadron was on Gauntlets at the time and he had a mid-air while practicing formation aerobatics. The other pilot bailed out and landed safely but Roger went in with the aircraft."

"Emily I'm extremely sorry for your loss, but I'm also extremely grateful to have found you. Are you sure about getting involved with another fighter pilot?"

"Sure as shootin' cowboy," she declared, in a sultry Mae West whisper.

This broke the tension and they laughed until their sides hurt. With tears of joy in her lovely blue eyes she initiated a series of soft kisses at his chest then slowly worked her way downwards. Emily had things well in hand before tantalizingly rolling over on to her back. Andy didn't need to be told what was expected of him next.

5

*

They awoke before dawn and dressed quickly. Andrew James could have gladly stayed in Dover for the rest of the war but that was just a pipe dream. Without stopping for breakfast they hurried to the railway station where Andy was able to get a ticket for the 6:04 to London. This left them five minutes together before the gargantuan, gun metal blue, steam locomotive departed for the capital of the Empire.

"This is so unfair Drew,"Emily murmured as they stood beside the door of a first class coach.

"I hate to go, but I'll be expected to fly tomorrow."

"I can make it to town on my next leave and we can have that supper date we talked about the last time I said good-bye to you."

"That would be wizard Corporal Smith-Barton," he grinned lovingly.

A screeching whistle announced the train's imminent departure. Andy kissed Emily one more time then reluctantly boarded the Great Eastern Express. She waved him out of sight before returning to her flat. She would be on duty at the Chain Home Low RDF station later that day.

*

The compartment was full. All the occupants except Andy were Army officers. A Captain sitting opposite unloaded shortly after the train began to move.

"So where was the bloody Air Force when we needed them?" he all but shouted to a Lieutenant that was sitting next to him.

"Out having tea I suspect sir." the junior officer snickered.

Andy was about to get up and airmail a knuckle sandwich when the brass hat sitting next to him grabbed the Canadian pilots arm. Andrew James turned toward the new threat and was startled to see that the hand was attached to a Colonel.

"Before this goes any further, I want you Captain and you Lieutenant, and everyone in this compartment to listen closely."

The Colonel took a deep breath before continuing, "I've just been given a report from Army Intelligence that is extremely interesting. It seems that the RAF have been very succesful in keeping the bombers and Stukas from reaching the beaches.To date, one-hundred and twenty-six German aircraft have been shot down. This has cost us forty-six Hurricanes and Spitfires and the lives of thirty pilots. I would suggest then gentleman, that from this point on, you treat the Royal Air Force with due respect."

Apologies came in rapid succession from the Captain and Lieutenant. For the remainder of the journey Andy was left alone.

Pilot Officer Andrew James Duncan entered the 689 officers mess just before supper was served.

"My God Duncan you've risen again."Burnsey gasped, as Andy took his usual spot at the dinner table.

"It was a shaky do sir, but here I am ready for another go at the Hun."

"Jeez Dunc, it's great to see your ugly mug, the uniform's a disaster but you look like a million bucks." Billy Allison snorted, while shaking his friends hand.

During the meal Andy provided the attentive pilots with a brief summary of his adventures in France, as well as the trip across the channel. He discreetly left out the bit about Emily and the overnighter in Dover. They were all shocked when he told them about the attitude of the Army but Flight Lieutenant Knobby Clark, a broad shouldered, lank haired, keen eyed giant from Australia grunted before saying, "Well mate, what did you expect from a bunch of Pommie brown jobs."

Panther Squadron flew three patrols a day until June 4th when Operation Dynamo was concluded.

Over three-hundred-thousand troops had been rescued by nearly a thousand boats. Pleasure craft, freighters, sailboats, tugboats, trawlers, lifeboats and paddle wheelers had been used along with a multitude of Royal Navy vessels. It was being called the miracle of Dunkirk.

The British Prime Minister had been told of the friction between the Army and the RAF and attempted to set things straight in a speech before Parliament on the 4th. Later that evening he repeated part of his speech on BBC radio. In addition Winston Churchill intended to rally the British people and send a very clear message to Hitler.

The pilots of 689 had just gathered around the Metropolitan-Vickers mess radio when the resonant, halting tones of the Prime Minister flooded the airwaves.

"Wars are not won by evacuations. But there was a victory inside this deliverance. It was gained by the Royal Air Force. Many of the soldiers underrate its achievements. This was a great trial of strength between the British and German air forces. Can you conceive a greater objective for the Germans in the air than to make evacuation impossible? I will pay tribute to these young airmen. May it not also be that the cause of civilization itself will be defended by the skill and devotion of a few thousand airmen."

Winston Spencer Churchill then paused for a moment before clearly stating his expectations for the British people:

"Even though large tracts of Europe may fall into the grip of the Gestapo and all the odious apparatus of Nazi rule, we shall not flag or fail. We shall defend our island, we shall fight on the beaches, we shall fight on the landing grounds, we shall fight in the fields and in the streets, we shall fight in the hills; we shall never surrender."

There was dead silence at the mess bar and surrounding tables for several seconds before Robbie Barnes shouted, "What do you say chaps? Three cheers for the P.M."
The entire room erupted into a rousing chorus of, "Hip-hip hoorays!!

6
*

Andy was called into the Wing Commander Steven's office the next day. The Wingco told the young Pilot Officer to stand at ease before dropping his bombshell, "I've just received an order from Group. You're to be detached here and temporarily assigned to 242 Squadron at Biggin Hill."

"T-That's the all Canadian outfit isn't it sir?" Andy stammered, his head spinning from the effect of the unexpected news.

"Spot on Duncan, they've lost several pilots in this French cock-up and you're to be one of the replacements."

"And I take it sir that I'm the token Canuck from the mob here at Stonecroft."

"I am afraid so. I hate to lose you old chap but orders are orders."

*

Two-four-two had been formed in the autumn of 1939. The pilots were a collection of 'wild colonial boys' from the Great Dominion who'd been serving in the RAF. With the blessing of the MacKenzie King government and the British Air Ministry an all Canadian unit would be in place long before a properly trained Royal Canadian Air Force fighter squadron could be put together. This, everyone hoped, would be an effective propaganda tool and encourage the continued participation of Canada in the air war.

*

"Now let me get this straight," Billy Allison mused, as Andy stuffed his club bag. "the brass are putting you on Hurricanes at Biggy Bluff despite the fact that you're a super hot shot on Spits."

"I don't like it anymore than you Alley but I did have time on the Hurri at 6 OTU and you know, it's a pretty fair kite."

"Well then Andrew James, lets get cracking. I got the short straw, so it's up to me to ferry you over to 242 in the Wingo's Miles Magister. God, I love to fly the Maggie. How I love ya, how I love ya! My dear old Maggie." Billy crooned.

It was a short flight and after saying good-bye to Billy, Andy bumped into a pilot he'd met in a London pub just before being posted to 689.

"Hey Willie, how the hell are you?"

"Jeez, look at what the cat dragged in," William McKnight, an energetic, solidly built, black, wavy haired, five foot-eight Albertan shouted as he pumped the hand of Pilot Officer Andrew James Duncan.

"I hear you guys got pretty beat up across the ditch eh?"

"Lost eight of our best," Willie croaked."T-There are several Brits in with us now but we're still mostly Can/RAF. Come on Dunc, I'll take you over to see the old man."

Several minutes later Andy presented his orders to Squadron Leader Fowler Morgan Gobeil. F.M. Gobeil, an RCAF officer and a native of Ottawa, had been chosen to lead the all Canadian 242. He was also the first RCAF pilot to shoot down an enemy aircraft. On May 25th, while leading a patrol near Calais, he destroyed an Me 110.

"You're not by any chance related to Major James Duncan are you Andy?" Gobeil asked, after salutes were exchanged.

"He's my dad," Andy stated proudly.

"Sir, if you'll excuse me, I need to talk to the Flight Sergeant," McKnight interjected.

"Off you go then Willie," Gobeil smiled, then turning towards Andy he continued, "Your father was a hero to me Duncan. Right up there with Bishop and Collishaw."

"Pop never talked about the war sir, and what I know of his Royal Flying Corp days I got from history books."

"Yes, I can understand that. Many of the Vets that I've met clam up if you ask them about their years on the western front."

"That describes my dad perfectly sir, but he did teach me how to fly."

"Well, he must have done something right. I see by the file attached to your orders that you've got three confirmed."

"Just plain luck sir."

"Luck or not, you've made a good start."

"Thank you sir." Andy accepted the compliment gracefully.

"How many hours on Hurricanes?" Gobeil asked abruptly, getting back to business.

"Twenty-five in all sir, but none in combat."

"If you can fly a Spit as well as your file suggests then you shouldn't have any problems. I'll have McKnight run you through a cockpit check, then you can do some airwork together."

"Is Willie as good as they say sir?"

"Let's put it this way Duncan. He's already an ace and will be awarded a gong by the King two days from now. The citation's for a Distinguished Flying Cross." Gobeil beamed, displaying a paternal pride in the accomplishments of one of his pilots.

"Sounds like another Billy Barker in the making sir."

"If he's half as good as Barker then he'll be sensational. Too bad Billy got killed in that plane crash." Gobeil paused for a moment remembering the terrible day in 1931 when Canada's fourth highest scoring Great War ace, William George Barker VC, met an untimely end while testing a Fairchild KR-21 at Ottawa's Uplands airport. "Okay, off you go then Duncan and pay attention to what McKnight tells you. It might just save your hide."

"Yes sir!" Andy came to attention and saluted smartly before executing a perfect parade ground about face. He then marched briskly out of Squadron Leader Gobeil's office.

Later that day Andy sat in the cockpit of a Hawker Hurricane and listened carefully as P/O William L. McKnight reviewed the changes that had been made to the sturdy eight gun fighter since Andrew James had last flown one.

"This kite's factory new Dunc and has the Merlin III engine. It runs on 100 octane and is supercharged. It'll give you about five minutes of overboost and increase your airspeed by 35 miles per hour. You probably noticed the 3 bladed Rotol constant speed prop which adds a little more zip to things as well. The wings are stressed aluminum now and that sure cuts down on drag."

"All good ones Willie. Ready for a round of tail chasing?" Andy grinned at McKnight.

"You're on Dunc. We'll try easy stuff first then aerobatics in a loose formation of a 200 feet. We've found the old wingtip and ribbon routine doesn't work worth a damn in combat. After that, shake me off your tail if you can."

"You got it Ace." Andy chuckled.

They took off line astern and ascended steadily to twenty-thousand feet. Andy noticed, that compared to the Spit, the rate of climb and airspeed were much slower. After reaching altitude they started with steep turns followed by loops, stall turns, flick rolls and spins. Andy was amazed at how fast he was able to adapt to the Hurricane. He thought he'd be rusty but the previous hours on type had paid off.

During the climb up from a high speed dive, Willie McKnight had maneuvered behind Andy. Before takeoff they had designated each other as Red One and Red Two.

"Now Red Two!" Willie shouted over the radio.

Andy immediately rammed his fighter into a vertical turn and half way around he spun the aircraft. Looking into his rear view mirror he could see that McKnight was right behind him. After recovering from the spin the kid from the big island pulled the plug for overboost and looped the Hurricane, hoping to catch Willie by surprise and come out on the Albertan's tail. P/O William L. McKnight was still behind him.

"Boy this guy really is good!" Andy murmured into his oxygen mask.

In sheer desperation Andy power dived, twisting and turning as he rapidly descended. Five seconds later he was playing pussy inside a puffy white cloud bank. He'd shaken Willie but he knew, that a least once, the Ace from Calgary would have torn him apart with a killing burst.

Emerging from the scud Andrew James was able to quickly locate McKnight's aircraft and this time Andy was the hound to Willie's fox.

The match turned out to be a draw as Andy managed to mimic McKnight's every move. Andrew James knew that in a real dogfight he would have scored one solid hit when the Hurricane in front of him was centered in the reflector gunsight. Several minutes later, low on fuel, the two fighters headed for Biggin Hill. The cockpit of the Spit and Hurricane were not heated. It had been freezing cold at angels twenty, but Andy was wringing wet under his fleece lined leather flying jacket. A mock dogfight was hard work and Andy felt like he'd just played an all out period of hockey.

"Well Dunc what do you think?" Willie McKnight asked as they sat at a table in the officers bar.

"She can turn like a Spit but the crate's slower and less responsive on the controls."

"I'll tell you one thing though," McKnight paused to take a sip of bitter. "She doesn't bounce around as much when the Brownings are fired."

"A stable gun platform sounds like a good thing to me." Andy smiled.

"You'll find out tomorrow cowboy because we're taking a flip over to the range at Sorchester and you can blast away to your hearts content."

"As our Wingco would say Willie. That old sport, will be a damned fine show."

Cardboard targets representing trucks, tanks and ground troops were scattered about the Sorchester range. Willie made his pass first, followed closely by Andy acting as McKnight's wingman. The hurricanes, spewing sparkling rivers of hot lead, obliterated the flimsy silhouettes, then climbed away at full throttle before doing an airshow wingover. They carried out two more attacks but could not complete a fourth—their guns had run dry.

"Return to base Red Two," Willie's booming voice crackled over the R/T.

"Wilco Red One." was Andy's concise reply.

When their scores were relayed to Biggin Hill, Squadron Leader Gobeil went looking for Andy and Willie.

He found them on the flight line talking to a pair of plumbers—as the armorers were called—who were carefully filling the Hurricane's gun boxes with fresh belts of .303 rounds.

"Look a this Willie, or should I call you two guys Dead Eye and Buffalo Bill." Gobeil grinned openly as he handed the startled twenty-one-year-old Pilot Officer a sheet of yellow signal paper.

"The best score on record!" Andy whooped as he read part of the document over Willie's shoulder.

"Well sir, what did you expect, after all, we are from the wild west." Willie quipped.

"The Huns won't stand a chance when we get to France sir." Andy added.

"You must own a crystal ball Duncan. Along with this gunnery report I've just received orders that we're to return to France in two days. Well, if you'll excuse me gentleman there's work to be done." While shaking hands with the two beaming fighter pilots, Gobeil offered his sincere congratulations. He then marched smartly towards his office.

*

The next day, 7 June 1940, Willie was awarded the DFC by his Royal Majesty King George VI. The citation read:

McKnight, William Lidstone (41937) - Distinguished Flying Cross - No. 242 Squadron.

On the 28th of May, this officer destroyed a Messerschmitt 109. On the following day, whilst on patrol with his squadron, he shot down three more enemy aircraft. The last one of the three enemy aircraft was destroyed after a long chase over enemy territory. On his return flight he used his remaining ammunition and caused many casualties in a low-flying attack on a railway along which the enemy was bringing up heavy guns. Pilot Officer McKnight has shown exceptional courage and skill as a fighter pilot.

7
*

8 June 1940

Twelve Hawker Hurricanes, taking off in pairs, departed Biggin Hill in the growing light of a clear, cool morning. After refueling at RAF Christchurch the fighters, grouped loosely in three finger fours, proceeded across the Channel, down the Cherbourg peninsula, then overland to Le Mans. On final approach Andy was shocked to see the charred remains of a Hurri, scattered about a scorched circle of grass, two-hundred yards short of the north-south runway.

*

Pilot Officer Andrew James Duncan was directed to a revetment adjacent to the taxiway and several seconds later he pulled the mixture control to full lean. The powerful Merlin III crackled and popped several times before the three bladed Rotol propellor clattered to a grinding halt. After pushing back the bullet proof canopy Andy was greeted by a freckled faced, carrot topped Flight Sergeant.

"Welcome to France Sir." the pint sized NCO grinned as Andy unbuckled.

"Thanks Flight, who pranged the kite?" Andy pointed towards the end of the active runway.

"It was Cobber Kain sir, so it was," the erk, a native of Carrickfergus in Northern Ireland, grimaced as he jumped down from the wingroot.

"The Kiwi ace?" Andy rasped, astonished by the news.

"Caught a wingtip on a naught feet flick roll, so he did. The poor sod bought the farm before a blood wagon could get to him."

"What a waste." Andy shuddered, imagining the thunderous impact that must have accompanied the crash.

Flying Officer Edgar James Kain, a highly skilled fighter pilot from Hastings New Zealand, was the first RAF ace of World War II and had been credited with sixteen confirmed before his untimely death.

Orders had come from 67 Wing headquarters to leave the smashed Hurricane where it was. The brass hoped that this would act as a warning to others who might consider a low level beat up of the aerodrome. A bold, aggressive fighter pilot was a desired characteristic but a dead, bold aggressive fighter pilot was of no use to anyone.

When refueling was completed, 242 Squadron departed for Chateaudun airfield northwest of Orleans. Ground crew, ferried to France in several Bristol Bombays, arrived later that afternoon.Two divisions of the British Expeditionary Force, and what was left of the French Army, were fighting a desperate battle to keep the Germans north of the Seine River and the boys from Biggin Hill were there to help. Leading elements of the 1st Canadian Division had also been dispatched to the continent. Panic and confusion abounded amidst the steamroller advance of the Nazi Blizkrieg.

The pilots were assigned to a large twelve man bell tent. After hitting the chow line Willie and Andy decided to take a walk to the airfield's main gate. A small guardhouse, resembling a dilapidated pit privy, was located beside a long, five inch pipe that swung from hinges mounted on a black iron post. A tall, grizzled, grey haired man wearing a light blue Great War uniform, festooned with brass buttons, sat on a metal chair beside the barrier that regulated access to the Chateaudun airfield.

Andy and Willie waved at the solitary sentry and he beckoned them to join him.

"*Bonjour les Canadien,*" he shouted, recognizing the moose head badges of 242.

"*Parlez-vous Anglais?*" Andy said in his best high school French.

"*Mais oui*, I-I mean yes," the cadaverous veteran stated proudly. "I was liaison officer with the *Armie* during the last war."

"What kind of rifle is that sir?" Willie inquired, pointing towards the long barreled weapon that rested across the guard's knees.

"It is the Label, or as it is also called, the 1886 *Fusil modele."* the Frenchman smiled, while patting the stock of the sturdy weapon.

"Did you use it in the War?" Andy asked.

"Yes. I kill two Boche with it at Verdun but now if they come, I can kill just one."

"Why's that?" Willie scratched the back of his head.

"Because I have only this." the aging soldier sighed ruefully, while pulling a single 8 mm cartridge from his front pants pocket.

Andy caught Willie's gaze and they knew exactly what the other was thinking. The French were beaten and it's just a matter of time before a surrender is negotiated. They gave the man a bar of chocolate and left him to his memories.

Two day later, Red and Green sections flew a reconnaissance mission north of Evreux. The Germans had crossed the Seine in battalion strength and were advancing towards the port of Le Harve. Squadron Leader Gobeil spotted the motorized column and gun carriages shortly before noon.

"Line of stern attack on my command," he called over the R/T.

Willie and Andy flew in the seventh and eighth positions. The scene they observed on their firing pass was horrific. Billowing plumes of black smoke erupted from the burning troop carriers and bullet riddled grey clad bodies were scattered like rag dolls along the roadside and in the ditches. Horses had been used to pull some of the lighter field guns and their twitching death throes resembled a slaughter house tableau from a demented technicolor nightmare.

Andy waited until he was past the line of wrecked vehicles before pressing the firing tit on his control column. When he released the red button, four more trucks were added to the destroyed list and thirty men lay writhing in agony on the blood soaked earth. Willie spotted a staff car on his pass and managed to spoil the day for several high ranking German Officers.

A good morning's work for the boys from across the pond. Home now James for tea and crumpets.

*

Paris had fallen on the 13th and Panzers, in strength, were crossing the *Seine*. Orders arrived that very same day from Air Marshall Barrett, commander of the RAF in France. All squadrons were to return to England by the 18th. In the mean time, Two-forty-two had been assigned the task of providing air cover for the evacuation port at St. Nazaire. The next morning the squadron took off from Chateaudun for the airfield at Nantes. It turned out to be anything but a milk run.

Pilot Officer Andrew James Duncan, who'd been gifted with exceptional eyesight, was the first to spot the swarm of 109s.

"Red leader, Green two, bandits twelve o'clock low," Andy warned over the R/T, trying to keep the excitement out of his voice.

"Roger Green two," Gobeil acknowledged immediately. "Tally Ho, all sections." he ordered calmly.

Above the enemy aircraft with the sun at their backs was a fighter pilots version of a wet dream. In half a heart beat the twelve Hurricanes were transformed into birds of prey, each pilot selecting an individual target. Moments later the sky erupted into a three dimensional killing ground.

Andy waited until the Messerschmitt in front of him completely filled his reflector gunsight before giving the sleek enemy fighting machine a four second burst. The de Wilde incendiary rounds pulverized the centre fuel tank of the 109 and seconds later the German fighter exploded into a thousands bits of metal and well done flesh.

"Green two break right," Willie's strained voice, echoed over the radio.

Without hesitation Andy threw the Hawker fighter into a vertical turn.

"Round and round she goes and where she stops nobody knows,"Andy kept repeating to himself as he calmly played ring-around-the-rosy with the 109.

The Hurri was slower than the German aircraft but it could turn on a dime. Several seconds later the tables had reversed and Andy was provided with a deflection shot as the snapper tried to dive away from the fight. Firing well ahead of the 109, Andy was able to walk the pyrotechnic rounds into the port wing of the enemy fighter. He watched the stressed aluminum surface evaporate and without thinking, Andrew James Duncan whooped into his microphone, "Gotcha Jerry."

The pilot of the 109 was able to escape from the rotating piece of junk that moments before been a top-of-the-line fighter. Andy watched as an umbrella of silk magically appeared over the falling airman and was tempted to follow him down to finish the kill. He remembered seeing the gunner of a Defiant murdered by the pilot of a twin engined Me 110. It had happened in the closing days of Dynamo and the lifeless body dangling from a parachute harness still haunted his dreams. Andy, however, couldn't do it. In his minds eye, he could picture himself suspended over the French countryside after bailing out of the Spitfire.

*

Having come to his senses, he looked around and found himself alone in the skies. Where had they all gone? One moment the air was filled with twisting, snarling aircraft and now, nothing. In the tumbling chaos of the dogfight Andy had become separated from the other Hurricanes. Andrew James knew he was somewhere over France but that was about it. Looking downward, he spotted what appeared to be a hayfield. Andy decided to make a precautionary landing in order to get a positive fix on his position. It had been reported, before the squadron left Chateaudun, that the German Army was fifty kilometres to the north. A quick departure was ordered, and in the confusion Andy had forgotten his maps.

The hayfield was a short one and he came in slow over a meandering stone fence. His timing was perfect and the aircraft stalled as soon as he was clear of the obstacle. The Hawker fighter hit the ground hard but nothing broke.

Andy stood on the brakes and came to a full stop twenty yards from a drainage ditch at the far end of the gently rolling meadow. He was surprised to see a giant of a man running towards his aircraft. Pilot Officer Andrew James Duncan unstrapped quickly, pushed back the canopy, and climbed out. By the time he'd set foot on the ground, an enormous, rawboned farmer stood directly in front of him, pointing a shotgun at Andy's stomach.

"*Vous estes Boche, vous estes merd*!" the man screamed, spittle running down his unshaven chin.

"I'm not a Hun you damned fool. RAF, RAF." Andy snarled.

The man had no English and assumed that Andy was speaking German. Without hesitation the angry French farmer pulled back both hammers on his double barrelled twelve gauge shotgun.

Andy realized his mistake and hoping that he had it right he stammered. "*J-Je suis Canadien. Une amis, une amis.*"

"*Canadien Francais?*"

"*Non,non Anglais.*"

The mammoth Frenchman looked puzzled for a moment, then he uncocked and lowered the shotgun.

"*Bienvenue!*" the farmer smiled.

After hand shakes were exchanged, Andy was startled to see a young girl running across the field towards them. She stopped beside the farmer and looked Andy in the eye. She was a tall, full breasted, raven haired beauty.

"*Bonjour monseiur.*" she smiled coyly.

"*Parlez-vous Anglais?*" Andy asked, figuring the odds were a million to one.

"*Oui*, I do." she stated firmly. *Ma mère*, she was part English.

"Thank God!" Andy sighed openly. "Would you have a map of the area?"

"No, but if you tell me where it is you are going, I try to help."

"I'd appreciate that miss," he grinned. "I was on my way to the airfield at Nantes."

"That will be easy *monseiur*," she stated in a clear, sweet voice. " You are ten kilometres north of the Loire River. Follow it towards the sea and you will find Nantes."

Andy thanked the girl, then turning to the farmer he once again drew on his high school French, "*Mecri beacoup mon amis et aurevoir.*"

Andy turned to the girl and extended his hand. She stepped towards him, wrapped her arms around his neck and kissed him full on the lips. He could feel her trembling and knew she was terrified. The pale horse of Nazi Germany was riding unchecked and he could sense her desperation. Gently grasping her wrists, he carefully stepped backwards. She let go reluctantly and moved away.There was nothing he could say or do. The Royal Air Force was abandoning the farmer, his daughter and the people of France. Andy felt guilty as he climbed into the cockpit to do his pre-flight checks. Before starting the engine he waved at the girl and shouted, "*Bon chance.*" He could see tears streaming down her high boned cheeks.

The big Merlin caught immediately and Andy wound up the rpms to maximum while standing on the brake pedals. The nose dipped over when he released the binders but he managed to keep the prop from chewing up mounds of turf. The Hurricane rapidly gained speed over the rough terrain but a hedgerow at the end of the field stood green and tall.

Andy held the throbbing aircraft down as long as he dared before yanking back on the stick. The fighter vaulted into the air, barely clearing the tree tops. The Hurricane quickly ran out of ground effect and began to sink. Fortunately the land ahead was flatter than a frozen lake in winter. Pilot Officer Andrew James Duncan flew due south. Five minutes later he was over the broad, winding Loire. As the Rolls-Royce droned steadily at cruise he thought of the 242 motto, "*Toujours prêt*". Andy knew one thing for certain, he might not always be ready, but even after meeting the farmer and his lovely daughter, he sure as hell was ready to leave France. An hours flying time had elapsed when Andy landed at Nantes.

8
*

17 June 1940

The ground crew had been ordered to return to England and were given transport on the Polish ocean liner *Sobieski*. This was part of Operation Ariel—the final evacuation of France. The pilots of 242 had been assigned the task of providing cover for the ships involved in rescuing British civilians and military personnel from, what the English press was calling, the French debacle.

*

Since the erks were homeward bound it was up to the Brylcreem boys to fuel and arm their own aircraft. They were up before first light and worked hard to prepare the Hurricanes for battle. By noon the squadron had completed two missions and were beginning to feel the strain.

"Jeez Willie, I've always liked the fitters, riggers and plumbers but I never appreciated all they do till now."

"Me too Dunc. I'm going to stand my gang to a round when we get back to Jolly Old."

"Yeah, pints for the fellas sounds like a wizard plan."

"Hey Andy, maybe we can grab a little sack time before the next show."

"No way, McKnight me good man. I talked to Gobeil while you were tanking up and we're off again after a sumptuous feast of spam and powdered eggs."

"With or without Daddies sauce?" Willie doubled over pretending to retch.

*

The Cunard Liner RMS *Lancastria* had taken aboard five-thousand souls. She would be carrying double the number of passengers listed on her capacity tables. The ship's captain, concerned about the threat of U-boats, decided to wait for the afternoon to sail. A Royal Navy destroyer would be available by then to escort the Scottish built vessel.

The *Lancastria*, under way at 1:45 p.m., was beginning to gain speed when she was attacked by three Junker 88s. One of the German bombers scored a direct hit and the big liner started an ever accelerating roll to starboard.

*

Willie flying as leader and Andy as his wingman, arrived over St. Nazaire Harbour twenty minutes later. They were horrified to see a large ship hull-up and hundreds of people thrashing about in the calm sea. Fourteen-hundred tons of fuel oil blanketed the ocean's surface and many of the terrified passengers were chocking to death in the creeping, black slick. A pair of Me 110s intent upon strafing the helpless victims with incendiary rounds had set the sea ablaze. The RAF pilots were spared the screams of those being burned alive in the roiling, black-orange conflagration.

"Red leader to red two," Willie rasped into his oxygen mask microphone."Follow me!"

"Roger Red leader."

*

The rear gunner of the twin engined Messerschmitt fired at the Hurricane that had come out of nowhere. Pilot Officer William Lidstone McKnight closed to within seventy-five yards of the 110 and blew it out of the sky. Andy over-flew Willie and launched an attack on a Junkers 88 that had just begun its run in to finish off the capsized ship. The pilot of the bomber had been warned by the rear gunner that a British fighter was on their tail. He panicked and attempted to climb away, prematurely releasing his bomb load well clear of the target.

A stream of red tracers poured over the canopy of Andy's Hurricane as he battle climbed to get underneath the rising Junkers. In his mind's eye, Andrew James pictured the Ju 88 as a large Canada goose attempting to fly away from a number four buckshot spread. The three dimensional puzzle solved itself when the eight gun fighter ripped open the area beneath the cockpit, red hot de Wilde rounds shredding flesh and bone of the helpless German pilot.

The 88 nosed up sharply into a hammer head stall, then slammed into the sea. The enemy bombers and escort, having finished their work, were now safely hidden in the slate grey cloud layer that blocked the sun. Andy searched the skies around him and finally spotted Willie's Hurri.

"Red Leader I will reform with you now."

"Roger, Red two." Willie replied in a combat strained voice.

They could do nothing else to aid the victims struggling for their lives in the fire bright sea. The scenes he'd witnessed would haunt Andy's dreams for weeks to come. The two fighters, gas tanks nearly empty, set a course for the aerodrome at Nantes.

RMS *Lancastria* had been swallowed whole by the cold waters of the Atlantic along with two-thousand-eight-hundred souls ,however, the maritime disaster was not reported in the British press. A wartime measure, refereed to as the D-Notice, allowed the government to control the news published by the English papers. Five weeks passed before an American Journalist got wind of the story and it became front page headlines in most stateside newspapers. The next day several London tabloids printed the details of the sinking.

Twenty-four hours after the *Lancastria* tragedy 242 received the order to return to England. Andy and Willie stretched the endurance of the Hurricane to the limit and landed at RAF Tangmere late in the afternoon. A signal was waiting for Andy that required him to return to Stonecroft and rejoin 689. He would be back on Spits and a factory new Supermarine fighter was ready on the flight line. He would ferry it to his home base as soon as he'd been fed.

"Jeez, Dunc I was kinda hopin' you'd stick with us." Willie grinned. Two-four-two had been posted to 12 Group in order to refit and rest after the beating it took in France.

"Yeah, I was just getting to like the Hurri." Andy sighed, as he shook Willie's hand.

"Look me up if you ever get up to Coltishall."

"Sure thing chum." Andy smiled broadly, as Willie motioned for the ground crew to begin start-up procedures.

Andy watched until the Hawker fighter was just a speck in the sky before returning to the dispersal hut. The Tangmere pilots were gathered around the radio listening to an address by the Prime Minister. His rich, redolent tones once again informed the citizens of the Island Kingdom what lay ahead.

"What General Weygrand called the Battle of France is over, I expect the Battle of Britain is about to begin. Upon this battle depends the survival of Christian civilization. Upon it depends our own British life, and the long continuity of our institutions and our Empire. The whole fury and might of the enemy must very soon be turned upon us. Hitler knows he will have to break us in this island or lose the war. If we can stand up to him, all Europe may be free and the life of the world may move forward into broad, sunlit uplands. But if we fail, then the whole world, including the United States , including all we have known and cared for, will sink into the abyss of a new dark age made more sinister, and perhaps more protracted, by the lights of perverted science."

The British Prime Minister paused dramatically before delivering his concluding statement that would reverberate through the ages: "Let us therefore brace ourselves to our duties, and so bear ourselves that if, the British Empire and its Commonwealth last for a thousand years, men will say, this was their finest hour."

9

*

With Churchill's hard hitting words still rolling around in his tired brain, Andy, parachute draped over his shoulder, walked slowly towards the revetment where his new Spit waited. Half-way to the aircraft he was hailed from behind.

"Hold on a minute will ya Duncan."

Turning around Andrew James spotted a sturdy, dark haired Flying Officer rushing to catch up with him. The F/O was dressed in flight boots, Irivn pants and an unbuttoned beat up, fleece lined, leather jacket that partially covered a well worn RAF tunic.

"What's up sir?" Andy asked as the other pilot approached him.

"Nothing much. Just wanted to say hello to someone from back home. Mark Brown's the name but everyone calls me Hilly."

"A-Are you from BC?" Andy stammered.

"Nope, a little town on the prairies, Greenboro Manitoba."

"Glad to meet you Hilly." Andy grinned as they shook hands.

"I talked to the I/O and he filled me in on who you are."

"Boy it's sure good to back in England. We saw the *Lancastria* go down and it wasn't a pretty sight." Andy grimaced.

Brown's expression changed to a frown and his big toothy smile suddenly disappeared. "Look Andy I don't mean to pull rank but, we've been ordered to say nothing about what happened in France. I suspect you'll get the same message when you land at Stonecroft."

"Thanks for the tip Hilly, I'll keep my big trap shut from here on in."

Mark Brown nervously wiped his coal black mustache and wanting to change the subject he asked. "You a hockey fan?"

"Sure am. My dad and I used to listen to the broadcast from Maple Leaf Gardens every Saturday night."

"I came over in '36 and I've really missed hearing Foster Hewitt calling a game."

"Well Hilly, I can tell you the Leafs lost to the Rangers in six back in April."

"Now, that's a crying shame. I've always cheered for Toronto. We were in France for quite awhile and it was hard to get news. Thanks for giving me the gen on the cup final."

"Red Horner's the Captain of the Leafs now, he had a terrific series, but it wasn't enough. Believe it or not three of the games went into overtime."

"Boy that must have been one hell of a Stanley Cup!"

They'd reached the side of the Spitfire and Andy had to end his conversation with Hilly Brown. Much later he would learn that Flying Officer Mark Henry Brown was Canada's first fighter ace of World War II and at the time of their meeting Hilly had already been credited with a dozen confirmed.

*

The flight back to Stonecroft was uneventful and Andy was thrilled to be back on Spits. The Hurri was a good kite and a very stable gun platform he thought, but you couldn't beat the Supermarine for speed, maneuverability and rate of climb. Given these qualities, it was a far better match for the 109s than the Hawker. The Hurricane, however, had proved to be a very capable aircraft when it came to shooting down twin engined bombers, Me 110s and Stukas.

After landing at Stonecroft Andy reported to the Wing Commander.

"Good to see you back with us Duncan." Stevens smiled, while returning Andy's salute.

"Thank you sir. It was touch and go there for awhile, and I'm glad to be away from the continent.

"I suspect you've been told already, but just in case, orders have come through from Group that pilots are to say nothing about events in France."

"You're right sir. Hilly Brown from No. 1 squadron at Tangmere passed that on to me just before I took off."

"Good show Duncan, I suspect you're anxious to meet with your squadron mates."

"Sure am sir. I've missed the mob here since I was detached to 242."

"On your way then." Stevens waved his hand towards the door and got back to the mountain of paper work that covered his desk.

*

Andy then checked in with the I/O. Following a brief interrogation, he made a beeline for the 689 mess. When Andrew James entered the building everyone was at the bar having a pre-dinner drink.

"Holy cow, look who's risen a third time." Billy Allison shouted. "That's three of your nine lives gone Dunc, or should I start calling you the Cat?"

"Not on your life Alley boy." Andy grinned, as they pounded each other on the back.

"Got the gen on you Ace from the Wingco, he says you're up to six."

"Horseshoes and rabbits feet Alley. Jeez, it's good to be back!"

The other pilots gathered around Andrew James and he told them about the tactics he'd learned from 242.

"They fly in real loose formations. Three groups of finger fours, each fighter separated from the other by 150 yards, give or take, seems to work the best."

"Where did the Can/RAF crowd get that one?" S/L Burnsey Barnes asked.

"From the Jerrys sir. That's how they fly. Learned it in Spain. It sure gives you a lot better chance of seeing the enemy."

"Spot on mate," Knobby Clark interjected. "These tight vics the Air Ministry swears by keep you busier than a bonzer Sheila at a Friday night dance. You're always looking out for your cobbers wingtips."

"Come on Knobby speak English!" Alley chortled, while giving the big Aussie a playful jab on the right shoulder.

"Root you too Yank," Clark laughed, as the pair began to shadow box.

Flight Lieutenant Harry Woodston, a swarthy skinned, squared jawed, South African looked like he'd struck gold. "That's bloody brilliant Andy. What do you think Burnsey?"

"It's a jolly good idea Woody, we'll give it a try tomorrow on convoy patrol."

"They came to the same conclusion as we did about harmonizing our guns at 200 yards or less and getting in close before you squeeze the tit." Andy continued.

"Sounds like we're on the right track then chaps." Burnsey smiled, while acknowledging the Corporal who was beckoning them to the dinner table.

"Anything else to tell us about France Dunc?" Harry Woodston inquired, after they were seated.

"It was a piece of cake Woody." Andy asserted, remembering what Hilly and the Wingco had said.

The ceiling was Angels ten and the Spitfires of 689 stayed well below a smear of grey-black cloud in order to keep the ships of the convoy in sight. The twelve Supermarine aircraft flew in the three groups of four that Andy had described the night before. Each section was further divided into a leader and wingman. Billy Allison acted as Andy's wingman.

The Spits had arranged themselves in a loose arrowhead formation, with Burnsey Barnes leading the forward most group. Andy and Billy were part of Knobby Clark's port finger four while Woody Woodston led the starboard collection of fighters.

Each member of the squadron continually searched the skies above, below and behind for enemy aircraft. At the end of a mission the necks of the pilots were often worn raw because of the constant rotation of the head. Several of the pilots had taken to wearing silk scarves in order to save their necks from chaffing. Alley had gotten the idea from a book he'd been reading about the 1914-18 airwar.

The Panthers had been on convoy patrol for a week but had yet to encounter the *Luftwaffe*. Squadron Leader Barnes was about to give the command for a return to base when the deafening sound of Knobby's voice shook his headphones.

"Bandits, three o'clock low!"
Andy looked to his right and below. His pulse rate increased dramatically when he located fourteen Dornier 17s flying towards the merchant ships.

"Red and Blue, Tally Ho! Green, keep a sharp eye for the escort." Barnes ordered succinctly.

Andy and Billy, in Blue section, were the last to dive on the bombers. Two of the Dorniers, engines spewing oil, spiralled downwards towards the channel. Andy focused on a bomber that was trailing smoke and closed in for the kill on a beam attack. He gave the damaged aircraft a four second burst.

His Spit nearly collided with the flying pencil but at the last moment, stick pulled back and throttle wide open, the British fighter skimmed over the top of the twin engined bomber. Billy was hot on Andy's tail and managed to direct a squirt of blazing lead into one of the Dornier's gas tanks. Moments later he found himself lifted by the searing fireball of the exploding 17. Billy could hear hot fragments of metal pounding like hail stones on the stressed aluminum skin of the Spit's wings. He uttered a frantic prayer, asking God to protect him from the shrapnel that was hammering his aircraft.

Three of the Dorniers had been destroyed and four had been hit hard enough that they were now heading east in a frantic attempt to reach the continent. The rest of the raiders had jettisoned their bomb loads and were on their way back to France.

In the skies above, Green section was locked in a deadly struggle with fifteen Me 110s. Barnes knew that the Spits were low on fuel and could not pursue the bombers into enemy territory. Making a quick decision he toggled the switch on his oxygen mask. "Red and Blue, battle climb to escort."

With their overboosted Merlins roaring like enraged lions, eight Spitfires rocketed towards the grimy cloud layer to meet the Messerschmitts.There was no organization to the rescue, just an all out effort to save Green section.

Andy had learned in France that the *zerstoerer*—German for destroyer—was vulnerable to an attack from behind and below and he had angled his ascent to come up underneath one of the twin engined fighters. As soon as the Me filled the glowing amber crosshairs of his reflector gunsight, he thumbed the red firing button. Andrew James watched as a fiery jet of pyrotechnic rounds collided with the underbelly of the 110. Twenty of the high velocity bullets rammed into the pilot. Travelling upwards, tumbling pieces of burning lead ripped apart liver, kidney, lung, heart and brain tissue. The German aviator never knew what hit him.

From Angels ten, Andy watched as the stricken aircraft violently nosed over and began to spin out of control. The rear gunner of the crippled fighter had kicked open his canopy and tumbled into space. Andrew James felt sick to his stomach when saw that the chute of the gunner had opened but was not filling out. In morbid fascination he watched until the plummeting German airman bashed into the cold waters of the English Channel. Once again Andy found himself alone in a drab gunmetal sky that moments before had been alive with a swarm of twisting, turning fighters. This time, however, he could see the coastline and he set course for RAF Rochford to refuel. Thirty minutes after topping up his tanks he returned to Stonecroft accompanied by Knobby Clark who'd also pancaked at Rochford.

It was a red letter event for the squadron. Everyone had returned, they'd saved the convoy, claimed three bombers and two 110s destroyed, along with a list of probables and damaged. The Intelligence Officer Sherlock Trowbridge, a portly, ruddy faced, balding Oxford don, on leave from the university for the duration, who, the Panthers for obvious reasons called Holmes, smiled like the Cheshire Cat as he recorded the combat reports of the 689 flyboys.

"A great day for the chaps," Holmes bubbled an hour later, when he presented the Wingco with the mission tallies.

"Damned fine show!" Stevens exclaimed loudly, before lighting up his favorite pipe.

10
*

22 June, 1940

The French had surrendered and Hitler was the master of all Western and Northern Europe from Bergen to the towering Swiss Alps. There was a pause in the airwar as the Luffwaffe moved its fighters and bombers to bases in France, Norway, Denmark and the Low Countries. Pilot Officer Andrew James Duncan became a grateful beneficiary of this brief lull in the action. He had been granted a long overdue four day leave. His first act of freedom on the morning of the 23rd was a visit to the local telegraph office. By noon he'd received a reply and was on a train bound for Dover at three o'clock.

*

She was there at the station. A vision of infinite beauty, radiating colour and light in the cavernous, coal smoked terminal that serviced the Great Eastern Railway. Andy's heart stopped for a moment when he spotted her standing at the edge of the arrivals platform. Emily Smith-Barton, he suddenly realized, was his very reason for living.

She looked anxiously as the bright red, highly lacquered doors of the second class compartments began to open. Andy was the first to emerge from the third coach down the tracks from where Emily stood. Without hesitation she ran towards him. The radiant WAAF Corporal slowed down to a snails pace as she covered the last two feet that separated them. They stared a each other for a moment, wonder struck by the overwhelming joy of their closeness. Then, as if in a slow motion dream they fused together as one person, blending magically into each others arms. A passionate embrace that gave promise to the Eden that awaited them.

"I know it for sure now Drew," she murmured into his ear, after a prolonged yet tender kiss.

"Me too," he shivered from the effects of their intimacy.

"It's real, isn't Darling?" Emily whispered.

"My God woman! How I love you."

"Yes Drew, that's it. We both feel the same."

"At first I thought it was the war, being lonely and far away from home, but I was wrong. The truth is Emily, I love you with all my heart and soul and always will."

"That's amazing darling Drew, when you got on that morning train for London a tiny, nagging whisper kept saying, this can't be real, it's moving too fast, then I realized, you'd become the most precious thing in my life."

Dinner was a simple meal of fish and chips at the Pear, a quaint, cosy public house, set solidly on an ancient cobble stone street. Liberal sprinkles of cider vinegar and several pints of a dark local bitter added to their enjoyment of the evening special. There was rum soaked plumb pudding, complete with hard sauce, for desert and before leaving they were treated to a complimentary coffee and brandy.

"Me lad's RAF," the proprietor of the Pear stated proudly, dutifully placing cups, sugar, cream and sniffers on the table in front of them.

"A pilot sir?" Andy nodded respectfully, while taking a sip of the well aged Napoleon.

"Aye, that he is, on Blenheims at Manston."

"Here's to your son then," Emily smiled, raising her glass to eye level.

"God bless us all." the heavy set father wheezed, wiping his brow carefully with a clean white cloth.

The pub owner, who'd introduced himself as Ned Farley, stood and chatted for a short while, then left to tend the bar. Later, when Ned returned to their table, Andy and Emily thanked him for his good cheer and hospitality.

"You're most welcome and it's on the 'ouse tonight." Mr. Farley grinned.

"That's frightfully kind of you." Emily beamed, grabbing Ned's hand.

"You're the one's who'll be saving us from this 'ere wee 'itler' chappie and me 'ats off."

Andy shook hands with Ned and Emily couldn't resist giving the rotund pub owner a peck on the cheek.

It had been a marvelous meal and both of them felt, if Mr. Farley was typical of the British populace, the Nazis would never break the spirit of the English people.

*

Their clothes lay scattered throughout her small bedroom. They were now content, after a prolonged period of love making, to rest in each others arms. Several guttering candles bathed the room with a soft yellow light and the compact double bed had become their refuge from the terrors that would soon be unleashed from across the Channel.

"What are you thinking?" Emily murmured, snuggling in closer and nuzzling his neck.

"Just how happy I am and what an incredible day it's been."

"You won't die will you Drew?" she asked, suddenly afraid and remembering her husbands fate.

"They've tried twice to nail me Em, but I'm still kicking."

"You're invincible then aren't you darling." she brightened.

"Like the Rock of Gibraltar."

"My God, I wish I were a man and could be up there in a Spit."

"I wish you could be up there with me in my Spitfire, then we could try some real aerobatics." he smiled wickedly, before nipping at her erect right nipple.

"I could fly you right now." she whispered, reaching for his burgeoning joystick.

*

All too soon, Andy found himself, once again, on the London platform of the Dover railway station. The leave had been a bitter sweet affair. They knew their time together was metered and used it wisely getting to know each other intimately as well as personally. However, the reality of separation and Andy's return to Stonecroft was a dark, threatening cloud that hung menacingly on the horizon.

"When will I see you again Drew?" Emily's voice quavered, fearing lonely days ahead.

"It's bound to get hectic soon and I doubt they'll grant us leave until things settle down."

"I have an excellent chance for a posting to Fighter Command Headquarters," she offered proudly. "as you know, they've taken over Bentley Priory."

"That would be smashing Em."

"They want someone who's an experienced RDF operator to help process data for the beauty chorus."

Bentley Priory was the heart of the fighter control network. It was also where Air Marshall Hugh Dowding, Commander-in Chief of Fighter Command had his office. All information from radar sites and the Royal Observer Corp was relayed by telephone to the Filter Room at the Priory. German aircraft gathering across the channel were plotted on a large table by a team of WAAF's. The plotters moved coloured wooden blocks—each block representing a *Luftwaffe* formation—around on a large map of southern England that was superimposed upon the table's surface. Since they were an attractive group of young women, beauty chorus had become a part of the RAF lexicon. Information from the Filter Room was passed to Group headquarters, then on to the sector stations where controllers would call for squadron scrambles. The controllers, in contact with the fighters by radio, would then vector the Spitfires and Hurricanes to intercept the enemy aircraft.

"With your looks you should be in the chorus." Andy grinned.

"I'll have to start calling you Prince Charming." she quipped.

Their laughter was cut short when a conductor stepped off the waiting train and shouted, "All aboard!"

"Write me Drew," she cried desperately, as the coach carrying him away from her passed by.

"Every chance I get. I love you Emily!" he yelled through the open window. She strained to hear what he'd said, but his words were drowned out by the harsh steam blasts boiling, backwards from the labouring, gunmetal blue locomotive.

11

*

1 July, 1940

It was still dark when Corporal Nigel White, a slightly built, eagle nosed Cockney, tapped P/O Andrew James Duncan gently on the shoulder. Andy slowly stirred, but wanting to finish a highly erotic dream, featuring the alluring charms of Emily Smith-Barton, he turned over onto his side and fought the upward spiral that would bring him back to the real world. There it was again that annoying knock on his upper arm. Slowly, and with great effort, the sleepy pilot cracked open his left eye.

"Ah, there you be sir, back from the land of nod."

Recognizing the concerned look on White's face, Andy croaked, "What time?"

"The bleedin' cock ain't crowed yet sir, and it's still darker than the insides of the Old Bailey. Quarter past four I'd reckon."

"Ten more Corporal," Andy pleaded.

"Me 'umble regrets sir, but Squadron Leader Barnes requires your pink, powdered arse at dispersal in thirty minutes."

"Thanks Whitey," Andy chuckled, he always enjoyed Nigel's colourful expressions.

"I knows wot'll fix you sir, a nice cuppa char."

While Andy placed his feet on the floor, one at a time, the cheerful Corporal went to the kitchen to get his yawning charge a mug of tea. By the time he'd returned with the steaming orange pekoe—milk, sugar and lemon already added—Andy was putting on his Irvin jacket and trousers. Gloves and and boots had been placed on the foot locker at the end of the bed. Billy Allison, his roommate, had already gone to dispersal.

"Here we goes then sir, just the way you likes it." White grinned, displaying a double row of cavity ridden, tobacco stained teeth.

"Hey, Whitey there's one question I've been meaning to ask. How come the ground crew are called erks?"

"You've come to right source Guv, er-er I begs your pardon sir, an old 'abit from me cab driving days. When a Cockney says aircraftman," he pronounced the word carefully for Andy's benefit. "It comes out erkmun."

"Now I understand, they've just dropped the mun part."

"Gor blimey sir, you've 'it the nail."Whitey lit-up triumphantly.

Before going to dispersal Andy checked his kite. The sun was just starting to apply a pinkish paint to the low scud in the east when he greeted his fitter and rigger.

"Morning, Tucker, morning Harris."

"Good day to you sir," the NCO's replied in unison.

"Could you make sure my chute's on the port wing please."

"Already there sir." Tucker smiled reassuringly.

"Thanks fellas," Andy shot them an appreciative thumbs up before climbing into the cockpit.

He checked the instruments, made sure the gas tanks were full, adjusted the tail trim wheels to neutral, prop to fine pitch and set the directional gyro to the compass heading. Andy then placed his helmet on the reflector gunsight and plugged in the radio and oxygen leads. Feeling confident that his Spit was flight ready, Andrew James made his way to the dispersal hut.

"Well if it ain't sleeping beauty," Alley chuckled as Andy came through the door.

"Right nice of you to join us mate." Knobby Clark grinned.

"Roll me over neath the white cliffs of Dover." Woody quipped.

"Jealous are we gentlemen," Andy chirped, as he put Alley into a playful headlock.

The good natured horseplay and kidding came to an abrupt end when Squadron Leader Barnes and three other pilots entered the room. Flying Officer Sean Riley a short, sandy haired, blue-eyed, native of Belfast, whose nickname was Buzz, spotted Andy and extended his right hand.

"Welcome back boyo, good to see you survived your leave, so it t'is." Riley winked knowingly.

"Jolly good of you to return so soon," Pilot Officer Colin Ducksworth, a tall, thin, squared jawed Londoner chipped in. "I say Duncan, you're awfully lucky to get a four day pass."

"Comes from clean living and straight shooting Duckey." Andy deadpanned

"Aye laddie, and I bet you were a red breasted Mountie before you joined the mob."Pilot Officer Agustus McGregor saluted mockingly.

"Jeez Gus, I didn't know a brown-eyed, red faced, curly haired, reject from the kilt brigade would be that good at things Canadian."

"Sorry to spoil your homecoming old sport," S/L Barnes spoke directly to Andy. "but the chaps at Group have suggested we spend a fun filled day at Manston."

"Scramble ready, is it Burnsey?" Buzz Riley piped up.

"Not to worry Buzz, dear boy, Jerry's likely having a day off over there in frogland." Duckey snickered.

"Unbloody likely." Gus McGregor added mournfully.

"Now chaps, if I could have your attention," Burnsey, a heavy smoker, coughed fitfully before he began. "As you know four of our merry band are on leave, therefore, we'll fly in two sections. I'll lead Red and Woody will take Blue. Knobby you'll be my wingman. Allison and Duncan you're assigned to Red as well. Obviously, Duckey, Buzz and Gus will fly with Woody. Any Questions?"

"I take it the finger four's working out then?" Andy asked, pleased that the tactics he'd learned from 242 were being put to good use.

"Hush is the word Dunc," Burnsey placed his Woodbine into an ashtray. "The Brass still think we're up there in vics. I—uh, somehow forgot to seek approval."

"As me dear Da would say sir, t'is better to beg forgiveness than ask permission."

"Buzz, you're bonnie wee land's clearly a home for philosophers."

The briefing now over, Duckey muttered ruefully,"Once more into the breach." Five minutes later the morning stillness was ruined as eight Spits raced the prevailing wind.

The flight to 'Charlie 3' was short and uneventful. After their aircraft were refueled and inspected by the Manston ground crew, the pilots lounged in deck chairs placed in front of the Nissen hut that acted as a ready room. It promised to be a sunny, but cool day. Andy and Billy had dozed off but came wide awake when the metallic clink of the Tannoy sounded. The public address speaker placed on a fascia board above Woody's head suddenly came alive. "Panther Squadron, scramble!" Chairs overturned and newspapers were hurled aside as eight pairs of legs pumped madly—a stampeding herd on the run to its feeding ground above the clouds.

As soon as Andy reached his aircraft, he grabbed the parachute off the port wing. A fitter had already started the Rolls Royce Merlin and waited on the ground until Andy had settled into the cockpit. The fitter, now on the wingroot, adjacent to the folding door of the Spit, helped Andrew James with the chute and seat straps. By this time Andy had his helmet on and leads plugged in. He waited until the erks pulled the chocks, then advanced the throttle in order to taxi the aircraft. Andrew James was airborne, two minutes after the orderly in the ready room had called for the scramble.

The Spitfires of 689, throttles wide open, climbed in a wide spiral to three thousand feet and formed up into two finger fours.

"Fox-trot control, Panther Squadron at Angels three." Burnsey radioed the sector controller at Stonecroft.

"Panther leader, Fox-trot Control, I have trade for you, vector one-one-zero, ten plus bandits at angels twenty."

"Roger, Fox-trot Control."

The Supermarine fighters, trimmed for maximum rate of climb, reached their assigned altitude seven minutes later. Burnsey had learned that sector control usually underestimated and kept on climbing until the squadron was at twenty-three thousand feet.

Several minutes later, Woody bellowed over the R/T, "Red Leader, bandits at twelve o'clock low."

Directly ahead and below, two reconnaissance Do 17s were flying towards the English coast. "Got them blue leader." Burnsey's voice pierced the static."Red and Blue follow me."

Squadron leader Robbie Barnes led the eight Spits over the Dorniers then ordered a steep turn that would bring them into position behind the German bombers.

"Tally Ho!" Burnsey shouted into his mic."Red, port aircraft, Blue starboard and keep your eyes peeled for the escort."

Barnes and Clark, flying line-astern, attacked the Do 17 from behind and above. One after the other the eight gunned fighters poured a barrage of armor-piercing, incendiary and tracer rounds into the enemy aircraft. In an attempt to avoid defensive fire they dove below the flying pencil. Andy and Billy Allison followed suit firing four seconds bursts at the bomber whose port engine was now ablaze. As the four Spitfires of Red section climbed towards the now burning 17, four chutes appeared below the stricken Dornier. The entire crew had bailed out and would soon plunge into the numbing waters of the Channel. The German airmen, however, would likely survive. They'd been issued self inflating life rafts, and stood an excellent chance of being saved by a float plane or rescue launch. The RAF pilots had only a Mae West life jacket which they had to inflate by blowing into an attached tube.

Andy kept rotating his head and looking into the rear view mirror mounted on the rim of the windscreen frame. A small speck suddenly appeared in the reflective glass just as Alley cried over the radio. "Break Red three."

The Me 110, that had gotten on Andy's tail, fired a short burst a split second before he rammed the Spit into a vertical dive. One of the bullets smashed through the engine cowling and punctured the fuel tank that was directly ahead of the instrument panel. Andy needed both hands on the control column to check his screaming descent. He was horrified when he noticed a growing pool of 100 octane gasoline bathing his flight boots.

Pilot Officer Andrew James Duncan wasted no time in setting course for 'Charlie 3'. The *zerstoerer* had been shot down by Billy Allison.

He knew it would be a race between running out of gas and the real possibility of becoming a flamer. Fifteen miles back of Manston his engine began to smoke. Andy was terrified and immediately switched off. He could bail out but the thought of a watery grave kept him strapped to his seat.

A minute later Andy realized he couldn't glide all the way to the landing field, so he started the big Merlin. This gave him enough power to climb. For a several minutes he thought that everything would be fine, but the engine started to smoke again. Andy switched off quickly and was partially relieved when he judged his height above ground to be sufficient to reach the grass runway.

Once he was sure of making it, Andrew James attempted to lower his landing gear but the left wheel wouldn't come down. It was too late to go around. Andy held his breath as the Spit touched down lightly. The aircraft still had lift and very slowly the port wing started to sink towards the ground. When the wingtip hit, the fighter began to rotate. Andy was able to counteract this by the use of brake on the right wheel and the Spitfire settled into a three point, sideways skid on the good tire, tailwheel and wingtip.

It was like a slow motion movie from Andy's perspective until the Spitfire came to a full stop. Snapping back to reality, he slammed the hood open, booted the folding door and launched himself onto the wingroot.

Now clear, he sprinted head down away from the Spit. Seconds later a violent explosion, followed by a rush of scalding air, drove him to the ground. The fleece lined, leather Irvin jacket protected him from the heat and the cool grass of Manston felt good under his chest. He lay there not wanting to get up. Maybe if he stayed where he was the war would pass him by and he could get on with his life. Suddenly the image of a white hot cockpit and roasting flesh shot across his mind.

The panic attack seemed to last forever, but in real time it was no more than a second. By now his Spitfire was nothing but a metal skeleton, framed within a roiling furnace of black-orange flames. He struggled to his feet, then walked towards a waiting blood wagon.

"You all right sir?" the driver of the ambulance asked, when Andy approached the vehicle.

"Just another day at the office Corporal." Andrew James smiled weakly, hands jammed into the pockets of his flight jacket, so the NCO couldn't see them shaking.

"Jolly good sir, now if you'll hop in, I'll drive you over to the I/O."

Andy found Billy Allison in the tent that had been allocated to the Intelligence Officer.

"I nailed the Jerry that was breathing up your ass Dunc." Alley crowed proudly.

"Thanks Billy, he had me dead to rights. I would've been a goner if you hadn't warned me."

"No problem pardner," Billy grinned. "I see you've pranged another one of his Majesty's kites."

"Yeah, got her down just before she became a bonfire" Andy rasped.

Billy could see the look of raw fear in Andy's eyes and insisted that they go over to the NAAFI van to get a hot chocolate and a strawberry jam tart. Pilot Officer Andrew James Duncan had a hard time holding his mug steady, but the drink and food helped to settle him down.

The rest of 689 landed safely several minutes later. They too reported to the I/O. Billy was given credit for a 110 destroyed and Barnes and Clark shared a confirmed on the Dornier. The other Do 17 was claimed as damaged. The squadron was placed on standby for the rest of the day, but no further scrambles were ordered. Early in the evening the pilots and their aircraft returned to Stonecroft. Andy flew a Spitfire that had been recently repaired by the Manston fitters and riggers. It would be ferried to Kenley the next day.

The mess bar that night was turned into a soccer pitch with a full beer bottle acting as the football. Each time the bottle was kicked between a pair of chairs that represented the goal, everyone was required to down a shot of Scotch. By the time the score stood six to five, Knobby feeling no pain, threw the 'ball' into the air and attempted a header. For his efforts Flight Lieutenant Clark was rewarded with a goose egg—hairline dead centre—and a beer soaked tunic. Burnsey, acting as referee, issued the big Australian a red card for poor form and the destruction of a perfectly good football.

The river of hard liquor numbed Andy's frazzled nerves, and when he finally went to bed, sleep came easily. At three in the morning, however, the incandescent heat consuming flesh and bone in the nightmarish cockpit of a spinning Spitfire forced the sweating pilot to sit bolt upright and slap at the imaginary flames that were turning his exposed arms into glowing lumps of charcoal.

12

*

Thunderous drops of rain rattled on the metal roof of the large Nissen hut that housed several of the 689 pilots. The building had been divided into small cubicles that provided just enough space for two narrow beds, two foot lockers, two tiny closets and two men. It was a duff day and Air Vice-Marshall Keith Park had ordered the Panthers to stand down until the weather cleared.

This allowed the hungover, would-be-footballer's a chance to sleep-in. It also granted the suffering Brylcreem boys the precious time needed to exorcise a rash of heaving gut problems and to pray for relief from an endless supply of world class headaches.

Nigel White allowed his sleeping beauties, Andy and Billy, to remain in the sack until well after the rooster crowed.

"Roll over sirs, daylight in the swamps." was Whitey's cheerful message to the snoring pilots.

Billy, held the bed frame in a death grip, in order to keep the room from spinning, as he reluctantly cracked one eye open.

"Come on Whitey, it must be four in the morning," Billy moaned.

"Quarter past nine sir, by me old time piece."

"Holy cow!" Billy yelled, throwing two bare feet over the side of the bed.

"W-What's going on?" Andy stammered, his heart pounding like a runaway piston.

"Gentlemen please," Whitey soothed. "It's bleedin' cats and dogs out there."

"Are we off the hook Corporal?" Billy half-groaned, collapsing backwards.

"Free as the birds in Trafalgar sir. They won't be needing your royal arses in the Spits till there's enough blue up there to make a sailor's suit." the grinning batman pontificated confidently.

"Praise the Lord and pass the ammunition." Andy beamed.

"However sir, Squadron Leader Barnes 'as called a meeting at eleven."

"Thanks Whitey." Billy Allison waved over his shoulder, towel in hand, walking carefully towards the showers.

Aircraft recognition was the topic of the day when nine of the Panthers gathered in the ready room one hour before noon.

"It's Blenheims," Pilot Officer Glynn Morgan, a diminutive, mousey haired, bug eyed Welshman predicted before S/L Burnsey Barnes had arrived.

"More than likely Taffy, someone's mistaken a Hurri for a snapper again." Flying Officer Edward George Kingsford retorted, running his fingers through a shock of long, curly chestnut hair. For obvious reasons Eddie Kingsford, a scarecrow thin New Zealander, had been dubbed Rex by his squadron mates.

"Could have been Defiants sir," Sergeant Pilot, Harold Blackwell interjected.

"Come on Blackie, everyone can tell the difference between one of those Boulton Paul flying coffins and a bleedin' Hurri or Spit." Percy Armstrong Taylor, the squadrons only other Sergeant Pilot added authoritatively.

"When we want comments from the cheap seats we'll ask." Colin Ducksworth snorted derisively." "You trades people are full of it. Now, mother bless us, you're flaming experts."

"Piss off Duckey," Agustus McGregor piped up. "Blackie and Paddy may just have it right."

"Yeah, give the guys a break," Billy Allison snarled, while clenching his fists.

"From what I hear through the grapevine, in the past week, a Blenheim, Defiant and Hampden have all been shot down by our side." Andy glared directly at Duckey.

Pilot Officer Colin Ducksworth, who'd been reading History at Oxford before the war began, was from the old school and believed that pilots should all be officers. He had no use for Sergeant Pilots in the RAF, especially if they were merely grammar school boys.

He smugly agreed with the Brass, who insisted that officers and those considered to be in the 'ranks' should have their separate messes and not fraternize off duty. There was still a full measure of snobbery and class demarcation in the Royal Air Force.

*

Percy Armstrong Taylor—who'd been nicknamed Paddy because of his initials—along with Blackie, Rex and Taffy had just returned from a short leave. The Squadron would now be able to muster twelve Spits for the their next sortie. Further discussion was brought abruptly to a halt when S/L Barnes and his two Flight Commanders entered the ready room.

"I'm afraid it's silhouette time again chaps," Burnsey smiled weakly, while pulling a bundle of papers from a large, well worn leather satchel. Each of the papers had a black ink impression of an aircraft stenciled on it, some German, some British. The pilots were required to quickly identify the airplane shown on the eight by eleven sheet when it was held up by an instructor.

"Green section, we'll get this done in my office," Woody Woodston ordered while grabbing a stack of file folders from Robbie Barnes. Following like kids grasping a school rope, Taffy, Duckey and Gus dutifully trailed behind Flight Lieutenant Woodston.

"We'll do ours right here mates," Knobby Clark grinned at the members of Blue section ."then it's off to the mess for some tucker." Andy, Billy and Buzz gathered around the big Australian.

"Red, you lucky buggers, may accompany me." Burnsey coughed fitfully, as he collected Paddy, Blackie and Gus.

*

"All right then," Knobby began. "The Blenheim and Hampden could be mistaken for a Ju 88 or a Do 17. As you may have been told, we've recently lost a Blenheim and a Hampden to what the Air Ministry calls friendly fire."

"There ain't no such thing pardner." Alley quipped, testing Knobby's sense of humour.

"Spot on mate. Now let's look at these bleedin' ink blots till we get them straight."

They worked hard for the better part of an hour. Sean Riley, growing restless, groaned loudly, "Come on Knobby we're going to be cross-eyed if you keep this up. I'll be chasing these little darlin's in me sleep, so I will."

"Good on you Buzz. I'm getting tired myself. Off to the mess then my fair dinkum cobbers." Knobby drawled in pure Aussie.

"Do they really talk like that down under," Billy stage whispered to Andy.

"Only if you 're a swagman from the outback mate," Andy winked in Knobby's direction.

*

The rain Gods prevailed and the squadron was off ops for the entire day. That evening the officers of 689 gathered at the White Horse, a pub just down the road from the base. The Sergeant Pilots and ground crew drank at the Red Lion. Even the public houses appeared to be segregated. This of course was not part of the King's regulations but an NCO who dared to enter the 'officer's pub' was made to feel extremely uncomfortable.

The ale flowed like a bubbly, amber river at the ancient oak beamed local. Half-way through the evening the bleary eyed flyboys decided that a rousing game of High Cockalorum was in order. This required the participants to race around the room without touching the floor. The contestants were timed and the pilot who was the quickest would be declared the winner and collect a shilling from each of the losers.

"You have the distinct honour of going first Buzz," Robbie Barnes shouted, above the din of the appreciative audience.

"Watch a master at work me fine boyos," Buzz bellowed, bounding across the bar top like a scalded hare.

The mahogany surface was wet with spilled beer and Buzz slipped just before he reached the folding gate at the end. With a loud thump Flying Officer Sean Riley landed on the rough plank floor.

"What a shame dear boy," Duckey simpered, while extending a hand to help the stunned Irishman to his feet.

"Who's next then," Harry Woodston demanded.

"I'm afraid it's your turn Woody old man," Burnsey grinned, his thumb poised above the stem of a stopwatch.

Woody made it off the bar top, then leaped to a nearby table, but misjudged his jump to a chair that had been placed against the wall. Uttering several unsavory oaths, Flight Lieutenant Woodston staggered to the bar and ordered a double scotch.

"Watch me Dunc, this'll be a piece of cake." Alley boasted, vaulting like a gymnast onto the bar. He'd been drinking heavily and immediately teetered backwards. Luckily Andy was standing right behind him and cushioned his undignified descent. The game went on for another thirty minutes.

Taffy, the last contestant, almost made it to the end of the course but tumbled off a wooden beer case that had been placed close enough to the finishing line for a person to lean forward and touch the brass rail attached to the side of the bar. Knobby Clark declared it a no decision and the coin of the realm, held in trust by one of the barmaids, was used to buy several rounds of the best ale in England.

When the publican called,"Time, gentleman please." There was no argument from the 689 pilots. The head swimming, loudly signing, occasionally belching, darlings of the wild blue yonder departed the White Horse and managed to navigate a weaving course back to the cosy confines of the Stonecroft drome.

13
*

14 July, 1940

"Hey, you've got to listen to this," Billy Allison bugled as he charged out of the ready room at Manston. The squadron was on scramble alert at the forward base.

"I say William old chap, what's all the excitement." Duckey yawned then stretched, getting up slowly from a deck chair.

"Yeah Billy, you're disturbing my beauty sleep," Andy groaned. He'd been laying on his back watching the fluffy clouds pass overhead in the mainly blue sky.

"It's the radio, everyone's inside listening to some hot shot doing a play-by-play of a dogfight over the Channel."

"Holy cow," Andy whooped. "I sure as hell don't want to miss that."

Several seconds later Pilot Officer's Allison, Duncan and Ducksworth had joined the rest of the 689 pilots, who were gathered around a table top wireless, listening to BBC announcer Charles Gardner broadcasting from a car parked along side the white cliffs of Dover.

"The Germans are dive-bombing a convoy out to sea; there are one, two, three, four, five, six, seven German dive-bombers, Junkers 87s. Gardner exclaimed excitedly. "There's one going down on its target now—bombs! No he missed the ship... Now the British fighters are coming up. Here they come..." the radio gave a short burst of static and then Gardner's voice was clear again. "Somebody's hit a German and he's coming down with a long streak—coming down completely out of control—a long streak of smoke—

"Too right mate!" Knobby whistled and stomped his feet as if he were witnessing a goal being scored by his favorite football player.

Gardner took a deep breath before continuing, "The pilot's bailed out by parachute. He's a Junkers 87, and he's going to slap into the sea... By now the entire squadron were on their feet cheering like madmen.

"Smash! A terrific column of water and there was a Junkers 87. Only one man got out by parachute, so presumably there was only a crew of one in it."

"The gunner must have gone in with the kite," Harold Blackwell interjected.

"Very good Blackie, you can actually count to two without using your fingers." Duckey smirked.

Gardner had paused for a moment and once again his frantic tones tickled the ether, "Now then, there's a terrific mix-up over the Channel! It's impossible to tell which are our machines and which are Germans...there are fighters right over our heads...Oh boy! I've never seen anything as good as this."

Without warning,the shrill ring of the ready room phone filled the dispersal hut. The pilot's attention immediately shifted from the radio to the orderly answering the landline. He listened intently for a moment, slammed down the black Bakelite receiver and yelled like a banshee from hell, "Six-Eighty-Nine, scramble!"

Stonecroft sector control vectored the twelve Spitfires to intercept fifty plus bandits at Angels fifteen. Sergeant Pilot Paddy Taylor of Red section was the first to spot the enemy, "Red leader, Red three, Stukas at two o'clock high."

"I see them Red three. All sections follow me." Burnsey modulated smoothly over the R/T.

The Spits continued to climb towards the Ju 87s. An escort of twenty Me 109s hovered above the dive-bombers, but they had not spotted the British aircraft . The Supermarine fighters went straight for the bombers, completely ignoring the snappers.

The formation of Stukas scattered like bird shot fired from a cylinder bore shotgun. Each pair of Spitfires selected a Junkers and the radio came alive with chatter as prey and predator dived, looped, stall turned and rolled in the clear, deadly air.

"He's hit," Woody trumpeted into his mic. The Stuka above him had just begun to trail smoke.

Woodston immediately looked around for his wingman, "Are you still with me Taffy?"

"Roger Green leader, right on your tail."

"Break right Knobby," Buzz shouted, maneuvering frantically to get behind the 109 that had suddenly appeared in front of him.

"I've got the bastard in my sights," Rex cried, before thumbing the red firing button.

"Nailed the bugger!" Duckey exalted, scanning the skies for snappers.

"Take the one on the right, Blue two," Andy bellowed over the radio.

"Sold American," Billy yodelled, throwing his Spit into a vertical turn.

"Behind you Red three," Gus McGregor warned.

"I see him Red two," Blackie rasped, pulling the stick back into his stomach while punching the knob for full emergency boost.

Sergeant Pilot Harold Blackwell couldn't shake the Messerschmitt that had locked itself on his tail. The inexorable German fighter pummelled Blackie's fighter with a barrage of 20 mm cannon rounds. One of the incendiary shells hit the fuel tank behind the cockpit firewall and flames began to envelope Blackie's legs. He tried frantically to push back the hood but it had been damaged and was jammed shut. The trapped pilot groaned in agony as the fire worked its way towards the upper part of his body. Blackie had left the mic switch on and his screams and curses filled the airwaves. All those at sector headquarters and every pilot in the squadron could hear the crazed animal howling coming from the cockpit amidst the distinct sound of sizzling flesh. It was like someone frying bacon in a red-hot skillet. Several seconds later the unmistakable report of a Webley .45 caliber pistol rocked the airwaves. Sergeant Pilot Harold Blackwell had blown his brains out.

There was complete radio silence for a minute. Andy kept rotating his head but was unable to spot any German aircraft.

Since the enemy had hightailed it for home and the British fighters were low on fuel, the Spitfires set a course for Manston instead of chasing the 109s and Stukas. The pilots of 689 desperately wanted to avenge Blackie, but that would have to wait for another day.

*

When his Spit came to a stop, Paddy jumped from the aircraft and crawled around like a baby, vomiting continuously until his stomach ran dry. Billy Allison was the first to reach Paddy and helped him to his feet.

"He was roasted alive," Percy Taylor whimpered, like a dog who'd been hit by a car.

"Blackie ended it himself." Billy stated firmly. "I know that's not much of a comfort, but for Christ sakes Paddy get a hold of yourself, we'll be on cockpit standby in an hour."

Andy had joined Billy and together they walked Sergeant Pilot Percy Armstrong Taylor over to the dispersal hut.

"The world got you down old chap?" Duckey snickered, when the threesome entered the ready room. He'd reported to the I/O and was all by himself.

"Shut the fuck up Ducksworth," Billy exploded. "Blackie was his best friend."

"You see it's absolutely true, these grammar school boys just can't take it." Duckey persisted.

"You heard Billy, lay off!" Andy growled.

"Now isn't that touching, a snot nosed Johnny Canuck riding his dogsled to the rescue, too much Nelson Eddy and Jeanette MacDonald I suspect."

Andy's face took on an expression of dead calm, but his eyes were like points of red hot steel. "Duckey, what say you and I step out behind dispersal and discuss this like gentleman."

"Glad to dear boy," Duckey smiled menacingly.

Everyone knew that P/O Colin Ducksworth's sport at Oxford was boxing and he was the undisputed inter-university middle weight champion.

"Hey, I'm coming too." Billy insisted.

"Stay here and take care of Paddy, Alley. I can handle this."

Moments later, Andy closed the door behind him and turned to face Duckey.

"I'm going to enjoy this Duncan. Someone has to teach you wogs how things are done here in England." Duckey baited, taking up a fighter's stance.

Andy had been taught the fundamentals of boxing by his father as well as the art of hand-to-hand combat and raised his fists in readiness. He waited until Duckey threw a left jab before acting. Stepping inside Ducksworth's punch, Andy held Duckey in a clinch and without warning kneed the unsuspecting Englishman in the crotch. Duckey dropped his guard immediately and Andy followed up with a powerful right hand to the solar plexus. Duckey hit the ground like a sack of flour, his breath coming in short gasps. Instinctively he curled up into a foetal position, hands cupped over his aching genitals. Andy was still seeing red and booted Ducksworth in the rib cage.

"T-That's against the rules you twit." Duckey groaned.

"Hey Ducksworth, there's a war going on. It's been in all the newspapers, or hadn't you noticed. Sorry to inform you old sport," Andy mimicked. "but the first rule in wartime is; there are no rules." Andy left Duckey laying on the ground and slowly made his way to where the Intelligence Officer was holding court.

After entering the Nissen hut, Andy sat down beside Billy who was waiting his turn to report.

"That was quick," Alley looked surprised, but relieved that his friend showed no marks from the fight. "Where's Duckey?"

"Slightly indisposed at the moment." Andy took a ragged deep breath.

"You decked him huh?" Billy beamed, happier than a rooster perched on an open bag of three grain scratch.

"He did hit the ground rather hard." Andy voice cracked slightly, his vocal chords strained to the limit from the effects of air combat and the fight.

One hour later, following a quick lunch of bully beef sandwiches and mugs of lukewarm tea, the pilots of 689 were put on cockpit standby. This required them to sit in their Spitfires, strapped in and plugged in. If the scramble call did come, the fighters would be airborne in under two minutes. In the late afternoon the squadron was stood down and ordered back to Stonecroft. Just before takeoff Duckey passed Andy on the way to the flight line.

"It's not over yet Duncan, " Ducksworth hissed. "I'd watch my back if I were you old sport."

Andy turned sharply but refrained from fanning the fires when he saw the murderous look in Duckey's coal black eyes.

*

This phase of the Battle was referred to as *Kanalkampf* or Channel Battle by the Germans. Hitler had ordered *Reichsmarschall* Herman Goering, Air Minister, and Commander-in-Chief of the Luftwaffe to attack British convoys, Channel Ports and RAF forward airfields. Goering hoped to draw the English fighters up in large numbers. The Nazi brain trust figured they'd be able to easily shoot down the Spitfires and Hurricanes that came to the aid of the ships, naval bases and fighter stations.

Air Chief Marshall Hugh Dowding, C-in-C of Fighter Command, was reluctant to commit his fighters to protect the convoys but Churchill had ordered him to mount standing patrols over the ships. Most of the cargo could have been shipped by rail but the Government was determined not to lose control of the Straits of Dover and the Channel in general. This decision would eventually cost the RAF 151 fighters and 45 pilots. Sergeant Pilot Harold Thomas Blackwell was one of them.

The good news: Churchill, in mid-May, had appointed the Canadian born Lord Beaverbrook as his Minister of Aircraft Production. Beaverbrook, a successful financier and owner of several newspapers, had the ability to cut through red tape and get the job done. In just two months he'd nearly doubled the production of fighters.

On the homeward flight, tired and depressed by the events of he day, Andy worked hard to maintain his position in the finger four. The big Merlin throbbed faithfully and the R/T was quiet. Unable to relax, his right hand wrapped around the control column in a death grip, Andrew James kept on hearing the pitiful cries from Blackie and remembered the tortured appeals he'd made for his mother to help him. The fight with Duckey played like a recurring bad dream, and Andy knew there would be a time of reckoning. He was greatly relieved when Stonecroft appeared on the hazy, blue horizon and shortly thereafter the wheels of the Spitfire kissed the ground in a perfect three point landing.

14

*

Dowding, realizing the near breaking point stress his fighter pilots were forced to endure, had set up a system by which, on a given day, they were off duty eight of the twenty-four. He also insisted that his 'chicks', as the press called them, be granted a one day leave every seven.

This scheme worked in Andy's favour because the next day he was able to meet Emily in London. She'd gotten the posting at Stanmore, northwest of town, where the headquarters of Fighter Command was located. The RAF had taken over Bentley Priory, a former girl's school. This was the nerve centre from which the Battle of Britain was controlled.

Andy had asked Billy, who was also on a twenty-four ticket, to accompany him. Emily wanted the young American, who hailed from Saginaw Michigan, to meet a friend of hers. They met at the Savoy Hotel. The upscale hostelry boasted posh accommodations, a fine dinning room and a state of the art bomb shelter. Emily, who was from a very wealthy family, had booked two rooms at the Savoy. One for herself and one for fellow WAAF, Corporal Margot Cooper. The foursome met in the luxurious piano bar of the hotel shortly after lunch.

When the introductions were completed Emily ordered a large shaker of martinis. Ensconced in a semicircular booth, they chatted away like long lost cousins.

"I'm from Devonshire Billy," Margot cooed, after the second olive had been laid to rest.

"It must be very beautiful in that part of England, just like you." Alley charmed.

"Flattery will get you anywhere," Margot smiled innocently.

"You ain't seen nothing yet doll." Billy grinned, feeling the warm glow of the vermouth and gin.

"I'm ever so glad you two are getting along," Emily interjected. "you never know if these so called blind dates will work out."

"Alley the cat's eyes are wide open by now." Andy quipped.

"Drew, the American expression for that keen observation would be cornball. Isn't that right Billy?"

"More like ham bone," Billy chuckled amiably.

Another shaker appeared at the table and by the time it had disappeared Emily could wait no longer. "Drew remember when I told you about the Trafalgar medal that was presented to my great-great uncle Simon Smith-Barton."

Andy drew a blank for a moment, but recovering quickly he played along. "Yes, indeed I do Corporal Emily."

"Well, Pilot Officer Andy," she smiled coyly. "I just happen to have it up in my room and I thought perhaps."

"I'd love to. You'll excuse us then, won't you my faithful wingman William 'Horatio' Allison and his lovely companion radar expert extraordinaire, Margot, looks-a-lot-like Vivian Leigh, Cooper."

"See, what did I tell you Maggie? He's a born actor." Billy was already on very friendly terms with his 'dim-eyed' date.

"Off to the boudoir you two," Margot winked knowingly, while stroking Alley's thigh under the table.

The room on the fifth floor turned out to be a small suite. Andy managed a glance at the satin covered chair and couch in the sitting area before they entered the bedroom.

Clothes flew in all directions as they raced to become naked. The large double bed was put to good use several times before their seemingly insatiable hunger for each other was appeased.

Resting at last, hands cupped behind his head, Andy stared at the ceiling, reveling in the lingering endorphin rush of their lovemaking.

"I think Billy and Margot hit it off quiet well," Emily murmured.

"Sure thing Em. I'll bet they're in the other room you booked, playing an advanced game of hide the salami."

Emily giggled. "You colonials do have the most unique expressions." she teased.

"How's your new posting?" Andy asked, suddenly becoming serious.

"It's extremely interesting and I've been very impressed with Stuffy."

"Is that some kind of toy animal?"

"No, silly that's Dowding's nickname. He's rather stiff and dour but he's also a genius when it comes to air strategy."

"I'll take your word for it, but most of the time the Jerrys have us heavily outnumbered up there."

"From what I've learned, old Stuffy thinks we can only win the battle as long as the RAF continues to exist, and committing large numbers of fighters at any one time would play right into the German's hands."

"Yeah, our understrength hit the bombers and run tactics are working well, if you can believe the daily scores. We seem to be knocking them down most days two to one."

"Enough about the war," Emily suddenly returned to her playful self. "now let me tell you about Margot."

"You mean Maggie don't you." Andy grinned.

"I like that, and so does Margot, from the look of joy I could see her eyes. She's really all alone in the world, and Billy couldn't have happened along at a better time."

"Sounds like a real tale of woe." Andy sighed.

"Yes it is. Her parents died in a car crash before the war, her grandparents are all gone, her mother was an only child and her father's brothers, he had no sisters, were all killed in the Great War. Apparently she has no living relatives."

"That is a sad one." Andy said, furrowing his brow.

"I'm so lucky I have you Drew." Emily shivered slightly. "I also have a wonderful family. Margot must feel totally abandoned at times."

"She is beautiful though. When you two walked into the piano bar I kept on thinking "Gone With the Wind" and Scarlet O'Hara."

"Yes, the resemblance is striking." she stated flatly, trying her best not to sound jealous.

"Watch out Miss Smith-Barton, your claws are showing."

"I do look rather plain beside her don't I?"

"Emily you're the most gorgeous woman on this planet!"

"In that case Prince Charming I shall allow you to kiss me one more time."

The single kiss turned out to be a tidal wave of pleasure. He started with her sweet mouth, then on to the tips of her fully erect nipples, downwards still to the gentle curve of her stomach and finally the secret places between her thighs. Once again there lovemaking knew no bounds.

Early morning saw the WAAF's and Pilots going in opposite directions. The love struck couples were unusually subdued as they waited above the dimly lit tracks, of Charring Cross station. The tube was definitely the best way get about London.

Margot finally broke the silence. "Billy I'd like it very much if you'd write me." she half-pleaded, while squeezing his hand.

"Maggie I'd do a book for you if I could. Of course I'll drop you a line any chance I get."

"That would make me feel very special." Margot purred.

"I hate to break this up you two," Emily interrupted. "but our train's coming."

Hurried kisses were exchanged and before anyone was really ready the girls were on a subway car heading north. Andy and Billy waved till the red tail lights disappeared into the inky black tunnel. They then crossed over to the eastbound platform and awaited their ride to a transfer point that would eventually get them to Ash Park, the station closest to Stonecroft.

The world suddenly seemed a dark, dangerous place to the sad faced Pilot Officers from across the pond—the nagging uncertainty of air combat once again a grim reality. There was no safe place to hide.

*

The next morning 689 was ordered to RAF Hawkinge, a forward air base near Dover. Manston had been bombed the previous day and the personnel at the grass airstrip were busy filling in craters. They hoped it would be operational in twenty-four hours.

The Squadron didn't have to wait long to be scrambled. Forty minutes after landing at Hawkinge they were vectored to intercept fifteen plus bandits approaching from the southeast. It turned out to be a swarm of 109s on a free range fighter sweep. The dogfight was a short lived affair because the snappers, their red, low-fuel lights blinking, left the air battle before any significant damage could be done by either side. In the brief melee of swooping, darting fighters, Andy again became separated from the rest of the Squadron. He was surprised, however, when Duckey's Spit, clearly identifiable by its squadron markings, formed on him several minutes later. The two fighters flew, in loose formation, towards the English coast at angels 20—twenty thousand feet.

Andy wasn't thrilled to have Ducksworth as his wingman, but two pairs of eyes searching the skies for enemy aircraft were better than one. Several minutes passed before Andy identified Hawkinge directly ahead and started to relax. He momentarily lost track of Duckey's Spit while concentrating on the airfield that had just appeared on the horizon. When he looked to his left Ducksworth was nowhere to be seen. Andy instinctively switched his gaze to the rear view mirror and was startled to see a Spitfire on his tail. A fraction of second later the armor plate behind his seat clanged like an anvil hit by a blacksmith's hammer. Duckey was closing quickly all eight Brownings trained on Andy's fighter.

Ducksworth, impatient for the kill, had opened fire from 400 yards. This gave Andy the split second he needed to shove the Spit into a vertical dive. Pilot Officer Andrew James Duncan frantically worked the stick and rudder pedals in order to keep the Supermarine twisting and turning. Duckey fired several times but the random gyrations of Andy's Spitfire threw him off. He panicked again and kept the red button depressed until his ammo boxes came up empty.

The cold, green waters of the Channel seemed to race upwards at the two fighters. Andy's airspeed indicator showed 480 mph. He tried, with a strength born of sheer animal fear, but couldn't get the stick to pull back.

He was going to crash into the rock wall surface of the Channel if his dive remained unchecked. Andy held the control column firmly in his right hand and began to play in elevator trim. Ever so slowly the nose of the Spit started to raise up. It was a close run thing but fifty feet above, the yawning salt water graveyard, Andy's shuddering Spitfire leveled out. Duckey, in the same predicament hadn't adjusted his tail trim wheel and crashed into the sea—a streaking meteor from hell. The Spit slammed into the water, compressing instantaneously into a crumpled mass of aluminum and steel, as if it had been squeezed between the jaws of giant compactor. Pilot Officer Colin Ducksworth's body was crushed into a amorphous package of bone, skin, fat, and organ tissue that resembled a large blob of red jello.

*

Andy was wringing wet with sweat as he climbed for altitude. He felt no remorse for Duckey, only relief that it was over. Ten minutes later he was on the ground and talking to the I/O.

Three days passed by before Ducksworth was officially reported as missing and presumed dead. Andy said nothing about the attempt on his life. If they ever found Duckey's body and he was buried, Andy fully intended to piss on the miserable bastard's grave.

15

*

In mid-July, Hitler issued Directive No. 16 to: *Reichmarschall* Hermann Goering, C-in-C of the Luftwaffe, Colonel-General Alfred Jodl, Chief of Operations OKW (*Oberkommando der Wehrmacht)* and Grand Admiral Erich Raedar, Commander of the German Navy. The Fuehrer, in general terms, outlined his plans for *Seeloewe*, Operation Sealion, the invasion of England. He made it clear to Goering that, "The English air force must be so reduced morally and physically that it is unable to deliver any significant attack against a German crossing...." Hitler did, however leave himself a weasel clause by saying, "I have decided to prepare a landing operation against England and, if necessary, to carry it out."

Several days later Hitler gave what he called his "appeal to reason" speech. It was broadcast by Radio Berlin in English and many in the Island Kingdom heard it on their short wave wireless sets. German bombers, carrying bundles of leaflets, dropped copies of the speech on many of the larger British cities. One of these copies was brought into the 689 mess by Billy Allison the day after the leaflet drop.

"Hey you guys, listen to this," Billy showboated by jumping up onto a chair and holding a short black comb under his nose. "here's what the Furor, I think that's what they call him, said in Hunland last night. Now remember fella's I'm just quoting old Adolph."

"The struggle, if it continues," Alley began, in a comical German accent. "can only end with the annihilation of one or the other of the two adversaries."

"That would be Jerry I'd suspect old boy." Burnsey guffawed.

"Right on sir," Billy smiled before plunging back into his music hall imitation of der Fuehrer. "Mr. Churchill may believe this will be Germany. I know that it will be Britain." A loud chorus of boo's erupted from the amused pilots.

"Hold on there's more," Billy coughed before continuing.

"In this hour I feel it to be my duty to appeal once more to reason and common sense in Britain. I consider myself in a position to make this appeal since I am not the vanquished begging favors, but the victor speaking in the name of reason. I can see no reason why this war must go on. I am grieved to think of the sacrifices it will claim."

"Root you Hitler," Knobby exploded. "the bleedin' Jerry people will be the poor buggers who'll pay the piper in the end."

"Too right mate," Billy shouted switching accents."and here folks is the conclusion you all tuned in for." Alley cleared his throat before getting back to his Hitler routine. "Possibly Mr. Churchill again will brush aside this statement of mine by saying it is merely born of fear and of doubt in our final victory. In that case, I shall have relieved my conscience in regard to the things to come."

"Alley, good fellow that you are, could you please hand me that piece of paper. Speaking of relieving oneself, I can use it in the bog." Burnsey grabbed the sheet of fine German pulp that would now have an important role to play in the mess toilet.

"Morning at Manston, a bit like, "Moonlight Becomes You", don't you think?" Rex Kingsford wondered out loud as the pilots waited in the dispersal hut.

The forward aerodrome had been repaired and it was business as usual. "More like a bonnie wee day in the Highlands." Gus McGregor snorted.

"Or the fresh clean air of Ballycastle, so it t'is." Buzz Riley waxed poetically.

"You Brits ain't seen anything 'till you've caught the sunrise over the coastals." Andy sighed, seeing in his minds eye the great fiery globe climb slowly above the mainland ranges east of Quadra Island.

"Who're you calling Brits?" Rex, Buzz and Gus called out in unison.

"Sorry fellas," Andy cringed realizing his mistake. "I kinda got carried away with a mental snapshot of home."

Like a church bell sounding an ominous warning, the heart stopping jangle of the telephone brought the dialogue to an end. The orderly swung around in his chair and yelled, "Panthers scramble."

*

"Panther leader, Fox-trot control. I have trade for you at angels fifteen, vector one-three-zero."

"Fox-trot control, Panther leader, Roger." Burnsey affirmed calmly.

The Spits climbing on a southeasterly heading reached eighteen thousand feet six minutes later. Ten pairs of eyes scanned the air underneath them. The clouds below were like rumpled rolls of cotton batten. For a moment, the hypnotizing throb of the Merlin coupled with the azure blue sky above released the mind into a dreamworld of timeless, travel.

"Heinkels, two o'clock low," Paddy Armstrong shouted, into his oxygen mask mic. An ice cold shower that brought everyone back to reality.

"Green stick with me. Blue lookout for the escort." Squadron Leader Barnes ordered.

Billy, Knobby, Andy and Buzz watched as six Spitfires zoomed downwards onto the bombers. Duckey and Blackie had yet to be replaced, so 689 was still under strength. Blue section didn't have time to watch the show. Like avenging angels a dozen Me 110s screamed out of the sun. Andy slammed his Spit into a vertical turn and within seconds his vision darkened from the pressing G forces. When his eyes cleared he found himself behind and below a *zerstoerer*. As soon as the twin engined fighter filled his reflector gunsight, Andy squeezed the firing tit. The Me pulled up sharply, then fell over on its side. Flames erupted from the punctured fuel tanks and two sharp breaths later a brilliant orange light lit up the cloud base. The only evidence that the Messerschmitt had existed was an oily black plume. Billy, Knobby and Buzz had each scored and the remaining 110s steep turned towards the French coast.

Knobby looked at his fuel gauges and judged that Blue Section had enough gas in their tanks to give chase, "Follow me mates," F/L Clark ordered calmly. They trailed behind the Me's and managed to catch up to the fleeing Germans south of Wissant. Knobby, over anxious for another kill, carelessly got behind one of the *zerstoerers* before he realized he was out of ammo. The rear gunner of the Me poured a river of lead into the big Australians Spit, blowing apart the air scoop and radiator.

Trailing white wisps of glycol smoke, the Supermarine fighter began to lose altitude as its engine overheated and eventually stopped. Andy, Buzz and Billy abandoned the chase and followed Knobby down through the clouds. Emerging from the thick strato-cumulus, they could see farm country below them. Flight Lieutenant Clark picked out a long, gently rolling field and made a two bounce dead stick landing. Andy circling above, took a pencil and hurriedly scratched a brief note on an air map. He folded the map around his survival knife, slid back the hood and threw the weighted paper backwards. It bounced harmlessly off the port wing and plummeted to the ground. Andrew James had written: *Stay where you are we'll be back.* Fortunately Knobby's Spit had rolled into a small gully. It was hidden from sight by the depression and the hedge row that grew along a nearby road.

*

After landing at Stonecroft, the anxious trio rushed up to Wing Commander Stevens' office. Andy, slightly out of breath, explained what had happened and their plan to rescue Knobby.

"Sir, if you'd let us use that new Miles Master we just got from Training Command. I could fly it over there and pick up Knobby."

"And sir," Billy jumped in. "Buzz and I'll go along to protect Andy."

"It'd be a grand thing if you'd let us try sir, so it would." Buzz added hopefully.

Stevens knew the risks involved and was tempted to say no. Jeopardizing three aircraft and three experienced pilots to save one man just didn't make sense.

"I suspect, I'll get the chop from Group if you fail, but if it were me over there I'd be damned glad to see someone from home. Permission granted." Stevens nodded grimly, as he ushered them to the door.

The Miles Master was a two seat advanced trainer and looked like a cross between a Spitfire and Hurricane, though the canopy resembled a discard from a Harvard. It was powered by a Rolls-Royce Kestrel engine and had a top speed of 260 mph. Its armament consisted of one Vickers .303 machine gun.

The three pilots of Blue section were airborne twenty minutes after clearing things with the Wingco. The Spits had to throttle back to keep station with the Miles which had a much slower cruise. Two hours after leaving the area where Knobby force landed, the three aircraft were closing rapidly on their objective. Just west of the field ,however, they were bounced by a pair of 109s who'd spotted Knobby's downed fighter.

"Land and get him Blue one," Billy called out over the radio. "we'll take care of the snappers."

Andy lowered the landing gear of the Master, deployed the flaps and quickly set up his approach to the meadow where Knobby waited. He had judged things perfectly and came to a halt 50 yards from the edge of the gully where the big Australian was standing.

"Want a ride mate?" Andy bellowed, after he'd opened the bulky hood of the trainer.

"G'day cobber," Knobby yelled over the idling engine. "I'd love a lift in your bonzer kite."

The jovial giant from down under sprinted towards the Miles but instinctively hit the ground when a bullet from a Mauser rifle whined a foot over his head. The 109s, both damaged by Buzz and Billy, had radioed ground troops in the area when they'd spotted the shopworn Spit.

The response had been immediate and three German infantrymen were now rushing across the field in an attempt to capture Knobby. Andy made a split second decision and leaped out of the cockpit. Pulling a .45 Webley pistol from his right flight boot, he slid off the trailing edge of the wing onto the ground. The Huns were now directly in front of him. Holding the revolver in a two handed grip he fired at the leading German who hit the ground like a felled tree. Andy then took careful aim at the second soldier and dropped him in his tracks. The third grey clad figure, seeing his comrades lying dead in the short grass, lost his nerve and ran, head down, towards the hedge row.

Knobby vaulted to his feet, drew a Very pistol from his waste band and fired a flare at the crippled Spit in the gully. Flight Lieutenant Clark had coated the wings with 100 octane gasoline and before he could blink the Supermarine fighter burst into flame. Knobby then raced towards Andy, who was already climbing back into the cockpit. As soon as the Aussie was seated, Andy slammed the hood shut, turned into wind and opened the throttles. Shots rang out from the edge of the field but they flew wide of the accelerating aircraft. The trainer bumped and shuddered as it picked up speed but was able to clear the tall trees at the far end of the undulating meadow. As the Miles climbed towards the orbiting Spits it was attacked by a hedge hopping 110. The *zerstorerer*, on a routine patrol, had been alerted by radio. Its camouflage paint scheme blended in with the ground and it hadn't been spotted by Buzz or Billy. Andy reacted quickly by chopping his throttle and lowering the flaps. The trainer lost air speed quickly and the Me overshot. Full power on and flaps now retracted, Andy thumbed the firing button for the single Vickers. It was a one in a million shot but he hit the rear gunner in the head. With brain tissue and blood from the gunner smeared on the back of his helmet, the pilot of the 110 lost his desire to continue the fight. Several minutes later Andy formed on the two Spitfires and they flew towards the coast of England.

The radar station at Pevensey had spotted them on their cathode ray tubes, but the three aircraft were equipped with IFF transmitters. Pulses from Identification Friend or Foe beacons on board each aircraft told the radar operators that the approaching aeroplanes were indeed British.

*

Shortly after landing at Stonecroft the four pilots reported to Wing Commander Stevens.

"Damned fine show," the Wingo smiled, before getting up from his desk and enthusiastically shaking each pilots hand.

"Dunc, Alley and Buzz deserve a gong for this sir." Knobby began when they were told to stand easy.

"Heck, it wasn't anything special sir." Billy piped up.

"Just doing our duty sir," Andy added.

"It was a fine plan though sir, so it was." Buzz grinned like the Cheshire cat. He could already picture the grandeur of Buckingham Palace and the King presenting him with a DFC.

"Yes, well I'll see what I can do." Stevens stated flatly.

"If you'll excuse us then sir, I'd like to stand these fair dinkum cobbers to a pint."

"Off you go then and have one for me." Stevens licked his lips reflexively, wanting to join them, but the forms piled high on the top on his in-basket would keep him busy for the rest of the day.

Wing Commander Henry Stevens had already decided that the unauthorized rescue might not be appreciated by Group and needed to be kept quiet. He called his orderly and instructed him to get Squadron Leader Barnes on the landline. Flying Officer Sean Riley's fantasy of meeting his Royal Majesty had gone up in smoke, just like Knobby's shot up Spitfire.

16
*

29 July 1940

Panther Squadron had been ordered to RAF Lympne at first light. It was a clear cool morning with the promise of a warm day to come. All was quiet at dispersal until mid-morning when the scramble order came. Sector control vectored the 689 Spitfires to intercept a raid headed in the direction of Dover harbour.

"Red one, Bandits nine o'clock low." Rex Kingford's, high pitched voice broke through the ever present static on the R/T.

"Red one, twenty 109s at twelve o'clock high," Andy added.

"Roger I count thirty Stukas." Burnsey Barnes, coughed once before deciding what to do. "Tally Ho! Red and Green, Blue take the snappers."

Moments later six diving Spits pounded into the Junkers that were intent on attacking the shipping anchored at Dover. It was a slaughter, as four of the Ju 87s splashed into the Channel. Six-Eighty-Nine had been joined by a flight of Hurricanes from Hawkinge and three more Stukas were shot down. The rest of the bombers quickly jettisoned their five-hundred pounders and fled eastward.

Blue was not so lucky. The German fighters had the advantage of height and outnumbered the Spitfires five to one. It was every man for himself when the deadly swarm of Messerschmitts bounced the Supermarines. Andy was fortunate that the two 109s that attacked him had overshot. Without thinking he pulled the plug for emergency overboost and rocketed towards the tail end Me. A four second squirt tore the rudder off the sleek Nazi war machine and it spun unchecked towards the harbour below.

Out of nowhere a second pair of snappers jumped Andy from behind. Machine gun rounds slammed into his engine, followed by a blast of 20mm cannon.

The white hot incendiary rounds punctured, then ignited the gravity tank in front of the cockpit. Smoke rapidly spread over the cockpit floor and Andy could hear the beginning of a roaring fire behind the instrument panel. He undid his straps, unplugged the oxygen and radio leads then frantically pulled at the hood, but it barely cracked open. No matter how hard he tried it wouldn't budge. Andy knew he was trapped and in a matter of seconds the cockpit would become a blazing inferno. He'd decided what to do well in advance and reached for the pistol tucked into his flight boot.

The 109s continued to fire at Andy's Spit, a barrage of machine gun and cannon rounds tearing off his port wing. The Spitfire violently rolled over and Andy crashed into the top of canopy. He'd unbuckled and the force of his upper body hitting the Perspex hood was enough the pop it open. Before the hot licking flames, that had singed his boots, could work their way upwards, Andrew James Duncan became an object in freefall. He was at eighteen thousand feet but opening the chute right away might attract one of the snappers. It was well known that Hun pilots would not hesitate to shoot at someone hanging helpless in a parachute harness.

He tumbled downward like an anvil dropped off a high cliff. At first the water below seemed a long way off and Andy began to enjoy the sensation of terminal velocity. One-hundred and forty-one miles per hour appeared to be a leisurely pace until he reached two-thousand feet. Suddenly the waves below took on shape and seemed to be hurtling towards him. In sheer panic he pulled the ripcord. A silk umbrella billowed above him and his plunge to planet earth was gratefully checked. Andy did have the foresight to start blowing up his Mae West life vest and had it properly inflated when he hit the cold waters of the Channel. He was dragged along for a moment when the wind caught his parachute but this all changed when he hit the release mechanism and the straps and buckles came free. The current was strong and carried him further out to sea.

In the initial excitement of his unscheduled swim he didn't notice the icy chill of the water. Time passed slowly and he was surprised by the numbness in his fingers. No reason to panic, a lifeboat would surely spot him and he'd be saved. Two hours later, unable to fight the effects of hypothermia any longer, he fell asleep. It would only be a matter of time before he became food for the fishes.

Andy was shocked back to life when he felt something pulling at his hair. Then the oddest sensation, a mysterious force was dragging him over a slippery curb. Andrew James knew he was hallucinating, his time had come. This ended with a sharp slap on the face.

"Wake up Englishman, if you sleep all is *kaputt*."

"What the hell," Andy groaned, coughing up a gout of seawater.

"*Achtung*, Englishman stay awake." another slap.

Andy, adrenalin electrifying his body, popped his head up and was astounded to see a German bomber pilot hovering over him. They were in a three man life raft, bobbing like a cork on the rolling swells of the Channel.

"*Sehr gut*, now perhaps you live."

"Y-you're a Jerry," Andy chocked violently.

"*Nein*, my name's Leutnant Karl Whilhelm."

Andy chuckled softly, "That's a good one and I'll bet your friends call you Willie."

"*Wunderbar*, you are a mind reader Englishman?"

"Hey Willie, let's get things straight, I'm Canadian, not a Brit."

"You come all the way across the ocean to fight this war?"

"Look Willie, I've got enough troubles right now, so let's leave politics alone. How'd you learn such good English." Andy asked abruptly.

"*Schule* and also London. *Mein Tante* Frieda has home there."

For the first time Andy noticed that the German officer had a belt strapped tightly around the right leg of his blood soaked pants.

"My God you're wounded," Andy gasped audibly.

"*Ja,* a bullet from a *Spitfeuer,*" Karl Whilhelm grimaced.

Andy suddenly remembered something and reached into the side pocket of his Irvin Jacket to fetch a small metal flask that Emily had given him.

"Here, try some of this Willie," Andy smiled, while handing the leg shot bomber pilot the half-pint hip flask.

The shiny silver container was filled with scotch whiskey and Karl Whilhelm drank greedily, "*Dankeschon mein* Canadian *freund."*

Andy looked down at the rubber floor of the raft and was shocked to see it was red with blood, "Let me have look at that hole in your leg, maybe I can help."

"*Nein,* I have placed a dressing there and that will do," Willie stated authoritatively.

Andy didn't want to argue with the pinched faced German and asked instead, "Where's the rest of your crew."

"*Alle tot,* how you say all dead."

Wanting to change the subject Andy said, "You've called me Englishman and Canadian but my name's Andrew Duncan."

"That's much better than Englishman and I bet they call you *dunkel.*" Willie attempted to smile, his white lips frozen in pain.

"Nope, just plain Dunc."

"*Dunkel* would be *gut* because of your dark hair."

"Oh, I see dunkel means dark."

"*Ja,* just like *gut Deutsch bier."*

"I could sure use a pint of bitter now." Andy's mouth watered at the thought of a mug of beer.

"So *Dunkel,* you are married?"

"Not yet, but I've met the woman who'll be the future Mrs. Duncan." Andy stated confidently.

"You have picture?"

Andy reached inside the breast pocket of his Irvin Jacket and retrieved a small snap that Emily had given him. He then handed it to Willie, "She is *schon,* in English I think the word is beautiful."

"That she is," Andy sighed, wondering if he'd ever see Corporal Smith-Barton again. If a German rescue craft picked them up he'd spend the rest of the war in a prison camp.

"Now I show you my family," Karl Whilhelm, groaned slightly, as he extracted a tiny photograph from the band of his flight cap. The grainy photo showed a lovely woman holding the hand of a three year old boy.

"Your wife and son?" Andy asked gently.

"*Ja,* I am lucky man."

Andy took a long pull from the flask, offered Willie another drink which the German accepted gladly, then put it back into his jacket before yawning loudly. "I'm okay now, I think a little shut eye would do us both good."

"What is this shut eye," Willie looked confused.

"Sleep my friend," Andy stretched stiffly.

"*Jawohl Dunkel."* Willie nodded sluggishly, before leaning back and resting his head on the curved side of the raft.

*

Andy was the first to awaken. A thick sea mist had settled in and he could barely see fifty feet ahead. Andy felt something warm on the calf of his left leg and immediately looked down. It was soaked in blood. His gaze shifted quickly to Willie. The face of the German officer had taken on a waxy, ivory colour and his chest was perfectly still. Karl Whilhelm had hemorrhaged while he slept and bled to death. Andy felt for a pulse but there was none. Much to his amazement Andy wanted to cry. He suddenly realized the enemy were not all fanatical Nazi monsters but simple, ordinary people like himself. A deep sense of grief and guilt filled his soul. He'd been responsible for the death of at least a dozen pilots and air crew. Yes, but this was war and people were paid to carry out acts of violence that in peace time would result in a date with the hangman. If I'm going to survive he thought, then turning soft will make me hesitate in a dogfight and it'll be me lying there instead of Willie.

Andy hated to do it, but he lifted the corpse up gently and slid it over the side.

Tears steaming down his cheeks he quoted from the bible, "I am the resurrection and the life sayeth the Lord. He that believeth in me, though he were dead yet shall he liveth, and whosoever liveth and believeth in me shall never die." It was cold and lonely in the cloying fog.

*

Andy had nodded off for sometime but was brought rudely back to the land of the living when he heard, "Get your hands up you flamin' Hun bastard."

Andrew James knuckled his eyes slowly and looked up. Standing on the bow of a small fishing trawler was a stout, bearded, grey haired man pointing a ten gauge shotgun at Andy's head. "Hold up there chum," Andy croaked. "I'm RAF."

"Like hell you are. That's a Jerry raft, I've seen 'em before."

Andy lost his temper and bellowed like a wounded bull,"Piss off you stupid prick. If I'm a friggin' Fritz, then how come I sound like some dumb shit son-of-a-bitch from across the pond?"

"That you do lad," the fisherman relaxed. "no bleedin' Jerry could be that eloquent with the King's English."

*

They were in the Straits of Dover and the boat was named the Channel Queen, out of Folkestone. The man who'd pointed the shotgun was her Captain Glenn Jacob Snodgrass. Andy had been lifted aboard by Glenn's son David and was now resting comfortably on a small bench in the wheelhouse of the sturdy craft. The father and son team fished for sole in the waters off Dover and had rescued both British and German pilots in the past. Andy was fed a hot bowl of rabbit soup and several cups of scalding tea laced with rum. By the time they'd docked Andy was feeling much better. Glenn had lent him some dry clothes and dressed the way he was, Andy could have passed as a local fisherman. After thanking Glenn and David, Pilot Officer Andrew James Duncan found his way to the railway station. It was well past the dinner hour when he arrived back at Stonecroft.

17
*

31 July, 1940

Several days before Andy bailed out over the Channel the Panthers had been brought up to strength when two new pilots arrived from No. 6 Operational Training Unit. The sprog airmen, recently graduated from an accelerated course, were still learning the ropes. They had yet to fly on ops and needed an experienced pilot to coach them along. Andrew James had been asked by Bursney to take the rookie pilots under his wing.

The Panthers were on a twenty-four hour stand down on the final day of the seventh month and Andy decided to meet with his charges to go over some of the finer points of combat flying. The trio gathered at dispersal shortly after breakfast. It was a duff day, unlimited quantities of a driving drizzle filling the air beneath a three hundred foot ceiling. Sergeant Pilots Robin Alesworth and Charles Goodhue got up quickly, each presenting a parade ground salute, when Andy entered the room.

"Relax fellas," Andy smiled warmly, "we're not that formal here."

"We'd get proper 'ell at 6 OTU if we failed to recognize an officer sir," Birdie Alesworth, a slightly built, ginger haired, hazel eyed nineteen-year-old chirped nervously.

"You'll get used to it Birdie," Andy grinned reassuringly.

"Recovered from your swim sir?" Charlie Goodhue asked, looking concerned.

"No more high diving into the Channel for me Goody." Andy quipped, trying to make light of his latest escape from the Grim Reaper, but the sprogs could see the fleeting look of terror in their mentor's dark brown eyes.

Charles Goodhue, a handsome, stocky, fair haired, blue eyed son of a Sheffield steel worker, stammered apologetically, "I-I guess that's one you'd rather forget then sir?"

"Sure as hell is Goody," Andy stated firmly, "now here are several tips for staying alive up there. "One," Andy began counting on his fingers, "never fly straight and level in the combat zone for more than twenty seconds. Two, get in close, one-hundred and fifty yards or less before pressing the tit."

"I'd crash into to Jerry if I got in that tight sir," Robin Alesworth gulped reflexively.

"How many hours on Spits?" Andy inquired tartly, annoyed by the interruption.

"As of yesterday sir, I've racked up thirteen." Birdie affirmed proudly,

"And I'm up to twelve now sir," Goody volunteered.

Andy shook his head in disgust but said nothing to the Sergeants, "Three," he continued. "never stop searching the sky around you and don't forget your rear view mirror, that speck the size of a fly is probably a 109. And remember, it's kill or be killed up there, so forget all this knights of the air crap."

"We'll try to keep that in mind sir." Birdie grinned sheepishly.

"How much gunnery practice did you guys get at No. 6?"

"Got to fire them twice into the sea sir," Goody answered for both of them.

"Hit anything?" was out of Andy's mouth before he could stop it.

"A couple of sharks and a whale by my reckoning," Birdie shot back.

"Hey, you're pretty quick Alesworth." Andy chuckled

"A regular George Formby, I'd say sir." Goody added to the light banter.

"Very clever Charlie." Andy laughed easily. "Now, if you need to use your brolly, and I seem to be an expert there, remember to unplug your oxygen and radio leads before hitting the silk."

"I imagine sir, it would be a good idea if you had your parachute strapped on as well." Birdie smiled innocently.

"Not again Alesworth." Goody groaned loudly.

"You know Birdie you may just qualify as the station comedian. Now one more thing, be aware of the position of the sun because that's likely where they'll come from."

"The Hun in the sun bit again is it sir?" Birdie jumped in again.

"It's an oldie but goodie," Andy winked at Sergeant Pilot Goodhue.

"No disrespect intended sir, but I think Birdie's starting to rub off on you."

Andy was glad that he was getting along with the new Sergeant Pilots. He figured if they liked him they'd listen and that might just save their lives. "No problem Goodhue I just couldn't resist. Okay, one more thing, if Fritz gets on your tail, he'll expect you to break left and be ready for a deflection shot. If you don't dive away then a vertical right turn might fool him. As you know the Spit can out turn anything that Jerry has and you may be able to get him in your sights."

The two nineteen-year-old Sergeant Pilots, the replacements for Duckey and Blackie, and the twenty-one-year-old Pilot Officer from Vancouver Island talked flying and tactics until it was time for them to go to their respective messes. It would never do to the let the ranks enter the hallowed halls of the commissioned officers dining room. Most of the NCO's didn't mind, because they figured the food was better and more plentiful where they sat down to supper.

Squadron Leader Robbie Barnes had given Andy and Billy Allison permission to leave the base for the afternoon and evening. He reminded the beaming young pilots that he'd expect them to be back at Stonecroft by midnight. Andy had received word from Emily that she was on a twenty-four hour pass and had invited him and Alley to join her and Margot Cooper at the townhouse that her father had rented in London. Lord Anthony Smith-Barton had made a fortune in gold and diamonds in South Africa after the Great War.

He was one of the wealthiest men in England and a tireless behind the scenes backer for the Baldwin Government. His wealth and political connections had netted him a peerage in the early thirty's. Tony Smith-Barton was very proud of his only daughter, he also had a son Richard who was on Wellingtons with Bomber Command, and realized they'd need a place to escape to whenever leave came their way. He'd therefore given his children the keys to the townhouse and made sure it was cleaned on a regular basis. He'd also left instructions with the rental agency to have the kitchen stocked with food and the bar well supplied with beer, wine and liquor. Lord Anthony knew about Pilot Officer Andrew James Duncan and was pleased that Emily had found someone to love after the tragedy of her RAF husband's death.

"Hey, get a load of this joint." Billy paused, before they climbed the short set of stairs that led to the entrance of the brownstone end unit.

"I sure wasn't expecting this." Andy mumbled, thunderstruck by the smell of real money.

"The dame must be rolling in the green stuff."

"Watch your mouth Alley." Andy snarled. "She's it, as far as I'm concerned and Emily's no dame."

"Jeez Dunc, I was only kidding. Friends right?" Billy punched Andy playfully in the shoulder.

"S-Sorry Alley, that swim in the Channel's got me a little edgy."

"Let's see how the two best looking broads in the universe are doing." Billy smiled contritely, while hammering the polished brass door knocker.

Emily and Margot greeted them and proceeded to guide the open mouthed Pilot Officers on a brief tour of the finely decorated, luxuriously furnished, nine room dwelling. The two bathrooms, complete with gold plated faucets, were magnificent. The three bedrooms were palace quality. The kitchen and adjoining laundry room were small but functional.

The living room and dinning room, however, definitely came under the heading: nothing-but-the-best.

"T-This is your father's place?" Andy stammered, when they'd settled in at the wet bar that stood adjacent to an antique, ten place oak table.

"He's just renting it." Emily's voice quavered slightly when she saw the look in Andy's eyes. "Perhaps we should have a word in private darling." The lovely WAAF Corporal took the hand of the stunned Pilot Officer and led him upstairs to her bedroom.

"I guess I should've caught on at the Savoy when you said that the rooms were complementary because your father did business there."

"That was true Drew, but I omitted to tell you that daddy has a twenty percent interest in the hotel."

"Okay keep it going." Andy made a beckoning motion with his right hand.

"I wanted to tell you everything from the start Drew, but I was afraid it might scare you off. My father's Lord Anthony Smith-Barton and he does have a shilling of two stored away safely in the Bank of England."

Andy chortled softly before saying, "All right then, I'm still listening."

"Whenever I met someone, after Roger was killed, he'd change as soon as he found out about my family. I was never treated like a normal person after that. All they could see was a rich heiress and their interest switched from me to the money."

Andy's heart melted when he saw the anguish in her eyes. Acting instinctively, he held his arms wide open. Stepping forward, Andrew James enfolded her in a loving bear hug and whispered. "Rich or poor Corporal Emily, I really don't care, it's you I love, end of story."

"You are the sweetest man Pilot Officer Andy," she cried softly as he stoked her long strawberry blonde hair. "I was sure I'd lose you if you found out, I know it sounds silly but I love you so much it hurts."

"Relax babe," Andy showboated, doing a perfect imitation of Billy Allison. "we'll be as happy as pigs in shit on that little farm back in Saginaw."

Emily sighed in relief and started to giggle, "You sure know how to charm a lady flyboy."

"Holy cow, Lords and Ladies! Are you one of those?"

"Mummy's Lady Smith-Barton and according to protocol I'm accorded the title as well, but I hate it. I refuse to let our butler and maids use it."

"Must be nice though, with the servants and all. Hey wait a minute, did your old man have anything to do with the posting to Bentley Priory?"

"Well, he and Winston are friends, but I'm rather good with radar."

"You mean Winston as in Churchill?" Andy looked dumbfounded.

"Yes of course darling, he and Daddy often shoot grouse together."

"And what does your father do when he's not out hunting with the Prime Minister."

"He's a special assistant to Lord Beaverbrook at the Ministry of Aircraft Production. He and the Beaver get along famously."

Emily became upset when she saw the way Andy was looking , "It's happening already, you now see me as a spoiled little rich girl don't you."

Andrew James realized that all she'd revealed didn't matter in the least. He loved her for her and to hell with the money. Andy smiled wickedly, and said the first thing that popped into his head, "You may be wealthy, but you're still the best piece of ass in the Empire."

Emily laughed until the tears ran down her cheeks. Finally regaining her composure she rasped, "That's perhaps the nicest thing anyone's ever said to me."

"Look Em, my feelings are for you, not for your father's bank account, or his position."

"Speaking of positions cowboy," she cooed seductively.

Emily looked him straight in the eye and purred, "I don't think we've tried horse style yet."

Before he could reply, Lady Smith-Barton grabbed Pilot Officer Andrew James Duncan by the belt and pulled him firmly towards the large four poster that dominated the room.

*

Well before the bewitching hour the RAF gold plated coach turned into a pumpkin. Andy and Billy, reeking of perfume and post coital euphoria, bade their fair damsels adieu and headed for the tube. The Panthers would be on alert at first light and be responsible for protecting the airbase.

18
*

1 August, 1940

Füehrerdirectiv No. 17

"In order to establish the necessary conditions for the final conquest of England, the Luftwaffe will overpower the English air force with all the forces at its command, in the shortest possible time. Attacks to be directed primarily against flying units, the ground installations and their supply organizations, also against the aircraft industry.

In view of our own forthcoming operations, air attacks on shipping could meanwhile be reduced, but at anytime the Luftwaffe must be ready to support naval operations and take part, in full force, in Operation Sealion. I reserve to myself the right to decide on terror attacks as a measure of reprisals."

Reichsmarschall Herman Goering, Air Minister and Commander-in-Chief of the Luffwaffe was delighted with the directive. At last he would be able to show everyone in the *Wehrmacht* and that dammed *Kreigsmarine* who was really going to win the war. The grossly overweight Great War flying ace, called the Fat Man behind his back, immediately decided on the code names for the next phase of the airwar against England. The operation would be called *Adlerangriff*—Eagle Attack and opening of the attacks would be *Adlertag*—Eagle Day. Goering had been ordered to start his knockout blow, weather permitting, on or before August the 5th. The pale horse of the Nazi war machine was about to hurl its enormous power directly against the Royal Air Force.

*

It was a grey dull morning but the meteorological boffins had predicted a clear afternoon. Birdie had taken Duckey's place in Green section and Goody had replaced Blackie in Red.

Shortly after lunch the Panthers received the scramble order and were vectored by sector control to intercept a raid approaching from the southwest. This time they had adequate time to gain altitude and north of Tunbridge Wells, the R/T erupted into a series of excited exchanges between the English fighters.

"Red one, bandits at nine o'clock low," Gus bellowed into his microphone.

Andy spotted them immediately. Thirty Do 17s escorted by an equal number of Me 109s.

"Tally Ho! Red and Green. Blue take the snappers." Burnsey shouted, his usual cool manner abandoned in the heat of the moment.

The Spits dove on the thundering pack of German aircraft below. Red and Green ripped into the bomber formation and within seconds two Dorniers were trailing smoke. Blue raced towards the 109s and picked out individual targets.

"Behind you Buzz," Knobby warned as an Me glued itself to the Irishman's rudder.

Buzz gave the Messerschmitt in front a three second burst before diving away.

The Me behind overshot and Buzz escaped unharmed. Meanwhile Andy had launched a head-on attack against another 109. The snapper turned away just before the two aircraft were about to collide. Andy reacted quickly by throwing his Spit into a near blackout vertical turn. He came out behind the Me and blasted the German with all eight Brownings. Smoke pouring out of its Daimler-Benz engine, the damaged 109 rolled over and dived inverted towards the undercast. In the blink of an eye another Me passed directly in front of Andy. The three dimensional jigsaw puzzle for a deflection shot was solved instantaneously in Andy's brain and he hosed the snapper with a long burst. The sleek enemy fighter, belching white vapor, spun out of control towards the cloud layer below.

"Behind you Dunc!" Billy screamed over the radio. Without thinking Andy chopped his throttle.

In the blink of an eye, the 109 dove past the slowed down Spit. Andy fired at long range but quickly ran out of ammunition. Throttle at the gate, Andrew James followed the snapper to ground level. The two fighters began a southwest hedge hop, narrowly avoiding power lines and tall trees. Inexplicability the Me reduced speed and Andy was able to draw alongside. Pilot Officer Duncan, bluffing as if he were in poker game, pointed downward signalling for the German to land. The pilot ignored the gesture and started to turn away. Andy still bluffing initiated a fake quarter attack, pulling up and over the enemy fighter at the last moment. He then drew level with the 109, once again pointing towards the ground. The German aviator dropped his wheels and attempted a landing in a wheat field, close to the town of Lewes. He clipped the trees at the end of the field and tore off the landing gear. The snapper slid on its belly, cutting a wide swath, before finally coming to rest. Andy circled the downed 109 and was pleased to see a small group of Home Guard, rifles and shotguns at high port, charging through the tall grain. The Hun pilot raised his hands as soon as the five elderly soldiers, puffing from their sprint across the field, reached the downed Messerschmitt. Andy showing off, for the benefit of the Home Guard, did a victory roll before setting course for Stonecroft.

*

"You forced him to land old chap?" Sherlock Trowbridge stared at Andy in amazement.

"Yep, that's about it Holmes," Andy grinned winningly at the I/O

"The two 109s that were trailing smoke, did you see them crash?"

"Nope, I was too busy watching my ass to notice what happened to the Me's."

"Please don't take this personally Dunc, but I can only give you credit for three damaged."

"But the Jerry at Lewes was a write off Holmes."

"I agree dear boy, but you didn't actually shoot him down."

"Well someone else must have seen the snappers I did shoot at."

"Yes indeed they did, but no one saw them hit the ground."

"Maybe the army will find the wrecks then."

"That's possible but unfortunately Andy, they won't have your name on them."

"Jeez Holmes, you can't win for losing in this lousy war."

"Too true Andy, now be a good fellow and get a nice cup of tea and a jam tart at the NAAFI."

Andy would have preferred a stiff Scotch but they were still on scramble alert. For now, he could only dream of a trip to the White Horse or several pre-dinner drinks at the officer's mess.

On his way to a get a cuppa and something to eat Andy met the Squadron Adjutant. In the Royal Air Force, by tradition, the Adjutant was usually addressed as Uncle.

"I say Duncan, you look a little down in the mouth." Basil Lewis, a rotund, balding, slightly stooped, Flying Officer of medium height, wheezed noticeably

"No justice Uncle," Andy growled, as he proceed to explain the claims that had gone unrecognized.

"If this were the Great War you'd have been credited with three victories, two driven-down-out-of-control and one forced to land." Basil puffed, while cleaning a pair of horn rimmed bifocal glasses.

"You were in the RFC?" Andy seemed surprised.

"That I was old sport, a scout pilot on SE5a's."

"No guff Uncle, my dad flew Camels."

"Why yes, your father and I were stationed at the same aerodrome."

"Holy mackerel, you're the first person I've met who knew Pop during the war."

"How is the Major?" Basil asked tentatively.

"He's just fine now, from what I heard, Pop had a rough time at first but that all changed, according to my mom, when we moved up-Island to Campbell River."

"Now that you mention it, I recall that your father was from a little town in the Cowichan Valley called Cobble Hill."

"Boy, you've got a good memory Uncle."

"Why did your family move Dunc?"

"Pop was too well known, the war hero bit and all. He got fed up with not being able to be, just plain old Jimmy Duncan."

"He was a great pilot Andy, and perhaps the best natural shot I've ever seen."

"Yeah, that's my father all right. He taught me to fly and to shoot as well."

"Does the wound still bother him?"

"Dad says it wasn't much, just a scratch and I haven't noticed it holding him back."

"He was in the hospital for several months Dunc and just about lost his arm."

"God, the things you don't know about yours parents."

"It may help you if I tell you more. Shortly after the armistice your father's fiance died of the Spanish flu. Her loss just about destroyed him."

Andrew James was thunderstruck, "Y-You mean he was engaged to someone over here!"

"Her name was Lady Sarah Atherley."

Andy was speechless for the moment, as he thought of Emily. He was stunned by the parallel events of his life and those of his father's. The revelation of a lost love was likely the underlying tension he'd sensed between his parents. Basil's words had explained many things.

"Holy smoke Uncle, you've told me more about Pop than I've learned in twenty-one years."

"He's an exceptional man from where I stand old boy. We British owe him a lot. Please remember me to him in one of your letters home."

"I sure will Uncle, you can count on that."

They'd reached the NAAFI van and Flying Officer Basil Lewis, the kindly Adjutant of Panther Squadron, excused himself saying he needed to catch up on some paper work.

19
*

Adlertag

13 August, 1940

In a state of unbridled euphoria *Reichsmarschall* Hermann Goering sent, what he considered an inspirational message to his three *Luftflotten* commanders: *Generalfeldmarschall* Albert Kesselring, *Luftfotte* 2, *Generalfeldmarschall* Hugo Sperrle, *Luftflotte* 3 and *Generaloberst* Hans Jurgen-Stumpff, *Luftfoltte* 5.

From Hermann Goering to all units of airfleets 2,3 and 5. Operation Eagle.
"Within a short period you will wipe the British Air Force from the sky. Heil Hitler!"

The sun tried its best to penetrate the fog surrounding the German airfields in western France but with no great success. Across the Channel in south-eastern England a persistent drizzle, which Gus McGregor claimed was in fact a Scotch mist, wet the summer countryside under low cloud. Goering having read the weather reports, relayed to his headquarters by reconnaissance aircraft, decided to postpone the *Adlerangriff—Eagle* Attack—zero hour to 2 p.m.

A group of fifty-five Dornier 17s, whose radios had been provided with the wrong crystals, failed to get the recall signal after they took off at 5:30 a.m. The sixty Me 110s that were to escort them did receive the cancellation message and returned to base. The Do 17s droned on without the protection of the *zerstoerers.*

*

The raid was spotted by British radar as the German bombers formed over *Gap Gris Nez*. It was plotted at Bentley Priory, the Control Centre of Fighter Command.

The information was then passed on to Uxbridge, Group 11 headquarters. By this time the sky had cleared to the east, and Air-Vice Marshall Keith Park dispatched three squadrons to meet the threat. One of these was 689.

"Scramble!" the ready room orderly yelled.

After dropping books, cards, newspapers, and chess pieces the twelve pilots of Panther Squadron sprinted towards their Spitfires. Two minutes later they were airborne. Several additional minutes ticked off the clock as the Supermarine fighters gained altitude and formed into three finger fours.

*

"Fox-trot Control, Panther leader at Angels four." Burnsey called over the R/T.

"Panther leader, Fox-trot Control, we have trade for you, vector one-zero-zero, forty plus bandits at Angels fifteen."

"Roger Control. Red leader to all sections battle climb to Angels eighteen." Robbie Barnes was still in the habit of adding three-thousand feet to the altitude given by control.

Seventy-four Squadron, flying Hurricanes and led by the South African ace 'Sailor' Milan, were the first to intercept the Dorniers, however, 74 was unable to break up the formation and the German bombers pounded the Coastal Command station at Eastchurch. Several hangers suffered direct hits and five Blenheims were destroyed on the ground. Faulty German intelligence had reported that Eastchurch was a Fighter Command base.The Dorniers had just pointed their noses towards France when the Panthers arrived on the scene.

Birdie Alesworth was the first spot the Do 17s. "Red Leader, Green three, bandits at three o'clock low."

"Roger Green three, I've got them, does anyone see the escort?" Burnsey suppressed a cough as he spoke into the microphone.

"Red Leader, Blue two," Andy toggled his mic switch."Skies above are clear, there is no escort."

Robert Daniel Burns scanned the air around him and took a long deep breath before commiting the sqaudron.

"Tally Ho! all sections. Pick your own targets." Burnsey ordered calmly.

Andy and Billy roared downwards, then pulled up underneath an unsuspecting Dornier that was flying straight and level. Andy gave the twin engined bomber a four second squirt before turning away sharply. By banking steeply, he was able to avoid accurate return fire from the Do 17. Billy was right behind Andy's Spit and he too blasted the Jerry kite that was now trailing ribbons of black smoke. Woody and Taffy in a line astern attack killed the ventral gunner of a second Dornier before regrouping.

*

Charlie Goodhue wasn't as lucky. He was hammered by the cross fire from five bombers and had to bail out. Andy saw him jump clear and offered up a silent prayer for the sprog pilot. The Spitfires and Hurricanes harassed the fleeing bombers until their fighters were either out of ammunition, or dangerously low on fuel. Four Do 17s had been destroyed and five more severely damaged. *Der Dickie*, the Fat Man, would not be pleased with the initial results of *Adlerangriff*.

*

The Panthers refueled at Hawkinge but did not return to Stonecroft. Instead they'd been ordered to Tangmere as backup to the squadrons based there. After landing the pilots were fed bully beef sandwiches while sitting in their cockpits. Further raids were expected and there was no time for a proper lunch. An hour later the haggard Brylcreem boys were allowed a much needed break. Andy headed straight for the latrines. It had been a long morning.

He was walking back to dispersal when he heard a familiar voice, "Any news from back home Dunc?" Flying Officer Mark Henry Brown, smiled while extending his hand.

"No hockey if that's what you mean Hilly," Andy chuckled.

"Yeah, it sure is the wrong time of the year for that. I'd probably be looking at the baseball scores in the local rag if I were back in Greenboro."

"You a Yankee's fan?" Andy asked, the morning's combat tension beginning to fade away.

"Hey, how'd you know that?"

"Somehow I figured if you cheered for the Leafs, you'd root for the Bronx Bombers."

"Maybe you should get out of this fighter pilot racket and become a mind reader." Hilly quipped.

"Probably pay a lot better too. Hey speaking of money, Joe DiMaggio's making over thirty grand a season."

"Boy, imagine that, just for playing baseball." Hilly emitted a low soft whistle.

"The last time I looked at an American newspaper, my buddy Billy Allison's from Saginaw, 'Jumpin' Joe was hitting three-fifty or better, he's the best in the bigs eh?."

"Joe's got my vote Dunc. Since we've talking about the Yanks, do you think the guys from the States will ever come in with us?"

"From what I've heard, as long as bozo's like Lucky Lindy and Joe Kennedy have their way, you'd best not hold your breath." Andy frowned.

"Yeah, I hear that old Joe quakes in his boots every time a Heinkel flies overhead."

Their escape from the war was brought to an abrupt halt when a Flight Sergeant approached them. After salutes were exchanged the middle aged NCO, sweating profusely in the August sun, stammered nervously, "B-Beggin' your pardon sir, but Squadron Leader Harris would like a word with you."

"Sure thing Flight," Mark Henry Brown sighed."Good luck then Dunc, and it was nice bumpin' into you."

"Happy landings Hilly, remember to fly low and slow eh?." Andy joked, before shaking the hand of the Manitobin Flying Officer.

In the late afternoon 689 was scrambled again. This time they were vectored, along with 152 and 238 squadrons, to intercept a raid converging on the Isle of Wight.

"Red leader, Green two," Gus barked into his mic. "Stukas at twelve o'clock low."

They were above the enemy aircraft with the sun at their backs.

"I see them Green two, all sections Tally Ho!" Burnsey ordered. Two-three-eight Squadron had arrived first and were engaging the escorting 109s and 110s.

"Get the one on the left Alley," Andy shouted over the R/T.

"He's all mine pardner," Billy shouted back.

Radio discipline had been abandoned in the heat of the moment and the airwaves were full of miscellaneous chatter.

"Bulls eye," Billy cried, as the Ju 87 below him erupted into flames.

"Stuka pulling up," Woody screamed at his wingman."

"Piece of cake," Taffy replied, the staccato rattle of the Brownings chopping his words. Seconds later a Ju 87 left the fight, it's rear gunner leaking blood and intestines. The radios of the Stukas were very close to the frequency of the Spits and the RAF pilots heard a constant cry of, "*Achtung Spitfeur.*"

The pilots called it the grouse shoot over Lyme Bay. Six Stukas had been destroyed and five more were damaged beyond repair. Several crash landed in the Channel and many of the pilots and gunners, seriously wounded, barely made it home. It wasn't all tea and roses for the home side, however, the Coastal Command station at Detling was devastated by a Stuka raid. The mess hall took a direct hit, killing sixty-seven.

*

The chalk boards, set up by the bookies on London streets, scored it forty-five shot down by the homeside for a loss of thirteen Spitfires and Hurricanes. Soiled coin of the realm changed hands based on these tallies. Seven RAF pilots had lost their lives and again the Panthers were amongst that grim statistic. The body of Sergeant Pilot Charles Goodue was never found. Hardest hit that day was 238 Squadron who reported three of their pilots as killed in action. The success of 689 was due to their horrific sacrifice.

When the news of Goody's, "missing and presumed dead" came through to Stonecroft Burnsey, alone in his office, quoted a bit of poetry from a bard who's musings were written long ago and far away, stubbing out a half smoked Woodbine, Squadron Leader Robbie Barnes rasped, "The Channel it's said devours her dead, and the sea runs blood into water."

*

Adlertag had been a disappointment for the Germans and Goering would be furious. The head of Lufftwaffe intelligence, Colonel Josef "Beppo" Schmid had got it completely wrong as most of the bases attacked by the Stukas and Dorniers were Coastal Command airfields. The large sacrifice of men and machines by the Germans had, in fact, done very little damage to Fighter Command. At Bentley Priory WAAF Corporal Emily Smith-Barton, standing near a group of senior officers in the filter room, overheard Air Chief Marshall Hugh Dowding say,"Gentlemen, we have witnessed a miracle."

20
*

15 August, 1940

In the early morning light, of what looked to be a quiet morning, due to the low ceiling and light rain, Andy and Billy made their way to dispersal. Whitey who had mysterious sources in low places, namely the NCO grapevine, informed his two charges that the Wingco had found a replacement for Goody. They of course expected a wet-behind-the-ears nimrod fresh from an Operational Training Unit. Yawning openly and rubbing dry, blood shot eyes, from one too many at the bar the night before, Pilot Officers Andrew Duncan and William Allison entered the ready room. Everyone was there except Burnsey and the new guy.

*

"Any word on the bonnie wee sprog," Gus asked, before Andy sat down.

"Whitey had no details other than he's in for Charlie."

"Probably two bloody hours on Masters," Rex moaned softly.

"So who's to be his wet nurse?" Woody mused openly.

"I guess it'll have to be me, now that I'm almost an old sweat." Birdie piped up.

"The blind leading the blind so it t'is." Buzz playfully brushed Robin Alesworth's hair.

The idle chit-chat came to a grinding halt when Squadron Leader Robert Daniel Barnes, accompanied by another officer, walked through the door. "Gentlemen, and I use the term loosely," Burnsey paused for a moment until the laughter subsided. "I'd like you to meet Squadron Leader Ernie McNab of the Royal Canadian Air Force, our temporary replacement pilot."

For a brief moment everyone was speechless and frozen in place. Andy was the first one to regain his composure and stepped forward, "Andy Duncan sir, I think we're from the same country."

Ernest Arichibald McNab, a short, athletically built, steely eyed, thirty-four-year-old native of Regina Saskatchewan and the Commander of No. 1 Squadron RCAF shook the hand that was extended in his direction, "I guess that makes two Johnny Canucks in the Panthers, doesn't it Duncan."

"Yes sir,"Andy smiled broadly.

The rest of the pilots followed line astern and introduced themselves. Ernie McNab, who was called Pee Wee by his friends, had been assigned by Air Vice-Marshall Park to 689 in order to gain combat experience on Spits. No. 1 Canadian flew Québec built Hurricanes and McNab an exceptional pilot, who'd already flown operational sorties with a Hurri squadron, breezed through a short conversion course on Spitfires. The RCAF had earmarked McNab for command and wanted him to have hands-on battle time with both of the British front line fighters.

"We're currently on readiness chaps, so be alert for the scramble call." Robbie Barnes informed them.

"No chance of a card game then mate." Knobby joked.

"A lucky break for you Knobby. You already owe me eleven shillings six-pence." Woody dug into his wallet and held up an I.O.U.

The day started off slowly in France as well. Goering expecting the weather to be unflyable had summoned his air fleet commanders to a conference in Germany.
He wanted answers for the poor performance of the Luftwaffe on *Adlertag*. Shortly after 11 a.m. the winds became light and the skies cleared. *Oberst* Paul Deichmann, Chief of staff of II *Flierkorps*, whose 800 bombers and 1000 fighters were ready for a massive attack, took things into to his own hands and ordered all squadrons to proceed as planned. He'd put a call through to Luftwaffe headquarters but Goering had made it clear to everyone on his personal staff that interruptions would not be tolerated.

Initially, *Luftfotte* 5 launched seventy-two He 111s escorted by twenty-one Me 110s from Stavanger in Norway to bomb targets in Scotland.

This was followed by fifty-five Ju 88s from Aalborg in Denmark to hit the airfield at Drifield, a Bomber Command base in Yorkshire. Again Beppo Schmid had got it wrong. The Heinkels were intercepted by five squadrons from 13 Group, the northern most in Fighter Command. It was a slaughter as the *zerstoerers*, to save fuel, had left their rear gunners behind. Eight He 111s and seven Me 110s were shot down. The Junkers made it through to their target and clobbered ten Whitleys on the ground. Air-Vice Marshall Leigh-Mallory the commander of 12 Group, the squadrons that covered the Midlands, dispatched eighteen fighters who managed to destroy seven of the German bombers. From the Luftwaffe's point of view, it was a disastrous start to day three of *Adlerangriff*.

*

In the afternoon the forward bases at Manston, Hawkinge and Lympne were attacked along with radar installations at Rye, Dover and Foreness. The sector stations at Kenley and Biggin Hill were also on the Luftwaffe target list. The Panthers were scrambled to intercept the raid approaching Biggin Hill.

*

"Fox-trot Control, Panther leader now at angels five." Burnsey reported while climbing towards the sea.

"Panther Leader, Fox-trot Control, vector zero-nine-zero, fifty plus bandits at angels sixteen."

"Roger Fox-trot-Control." Burnsey and the Panthers continued their battle climb to nineteen thousand feet.

Ernie McNab flying as Red two was the first to spot the bombers, "Red Leader, Red two, Dorniers at one o'clock low. I count sixty plus."

"Got them Red two, Red and Green Tally Ho! Blue keep your eyes peeled for the escort."

Squadron Leader E.A. McNab flying as Burnsey's wingman picked out a Do 17 and dove to the attack. Pulling up underneath the lumbering flying pencil he blasted the enemy aircraft with a four second burst.

The diminutive RCAF commander steep turned to avoid return fire and watched as the doomed bomber, it's pilot dead at the controls, began at slow, flat spin towards the Thames estuary. Pee Wee McNab then pulled the knob for full emergency boost and gained quickly on a second Dornier. As soon as the enemy aircraft filled the glowing amber cross hairs of his reflector gunsight, he pressed the firing button on the control column. The Spit shuddered as the wing mounted Brownings sprayed the Do 17 with a red hot stream of incendiary rounds. Most of the high velocity lead hit home and the twin engined bomber burst into flame.

Several seconds later McNab counted as four bodies hurled themselves into space. Two of the parachute packs were on fire and the chutes failed to open. Like flying bricks the terrified German airmen screamed towards the hard ground of England. He watched for a moment, slightly nauseated by the terrible deaths he had caused, but it could have been him on that rocket sled to hell. Automatically he went back to scanning the skies. The momentum of the chase had taken him away from the battle and no aircraft could be seen. Squadron Leader Ernest Archibald McNab was the first RCAF pilot to shoot down a Luftwaffe bomber.

*

Andy, Billy, Knobby and Buzz had tackled the Me 110 escort. Wanting no part of a dogfight with the Spitfires the Messerschmitts had formed a defensive circle. Much like the covered wagons in a western movie this allowed the rear gunners to shoot outwards at the British fighters. Blue section had encountered this tactic before and dove below the *zerstoerers*. Attacking from underneath they were able to severely damage two of the Me's and caused the others to abandon their circle. The enemy aircraft scattered like a pack of harried foxes, skulking away to the safety of their French dens.

Even though 689 had destroyed several of the bombers and driven off the escort, fifty Dorniers managed to fight their way through.

A thick layer of cloud hung over southern England and the Do 17s had become lost. A break in the overcast revealed an airfield below and mistaking this for Biggin Hill they dropped their 110 pounders. The howling high explosives fell on the West Malling aerodrome near Maidstone. The Me 109s and Me 110s of Experimental Group 210 assigned to bomb Kenley hit Croydon instead. The two vital sector control stations had been spared, however, the airfields at Martlescham Heath, Odiham and Worthy Downs were hit hard and the Shorts factory at Rochester was badly damaged. The new four engined Sterling bombers were being built there.

At the end of the day when the bookies in London wiped their chalkboards, in preparation for putting up the daily scores, money again changed hands on the totals posted. Seventy-one Germans destroyed for a loss of thirty Hurricanes and Spitfires. The Germans called it, 'Black Thursday'. Churchill who'd visited Bentley Priory that afternoon said to his secretary on their drive back to Chequers, "It is one of the greatest days in history."

*

"Hey Knobby, howsh about anudder roun," Billy Allison hiccupped loudly, as he wobbled up from a crowded table at the White Horse.

"Too right mate, make mine bitter and the same for me cobbers."

Billy staggered towards the bar to order ten pints. Birdie and Paddy being lowly Sergeants were at the Red Lion.

It was a very relaxed atmosphere at the pub, and off duty everyone was on a first name basis. In keeping with RAF tradition an officer senior to another was usually addressed as sir upon their first encounter of the day, and after that things were much more casual. A Sergeant Pilot of course would never dream of calling an officer by his first name.

"So you snuck up underneath and gave him the old wrist shot eh?" Andy smiled crookedly at Ernie McNab.

"Yep, that's about it Dunc." McNab smiled right back.

"You know Pee Wee, you're all right."

Andrew James, deemed an officer and gentleman by the RAF and his Royal Majesty King George VI, emitted a world class belch before continuing, "You'll have to get out and visit us on the coast sometime."

"Love to Andy and I'd really like to meet your dad. He was one of the greats on the western front."

"I think now that this war's heating up Pop will get involved. Probably run an SFTS or something."

"Yeah, I've heard talk about the formation of a British Commonwealth Air Training Plan and your father would be perfect for that."

"If he were younger I know he'd rather fly fighters but even he admits that the G forces in the kites we go up in would be too much for him."

"I can understand that one," Ernie frowned, realizing that a man in his thirties, like himself, had to be in top physical shape in order to fly high performance fighters.

Andy seeing the look of concern on McNab's face, slapped his fellow countryman on the back and pontificated, "Jeez Pee Wee, no sweat eh? You'll be riding around in Spits till the cows come home."

"It's a great kite but I like the way the Hurri handles when you press the tit."

"The Hurricane's a wizard gun platform Ernie, but when it comes to taking on a snapper give me a Spit any time!"

The party grew louder and the latest fad of blackening your shoes with polish, then holding someone inverted so they could stamp their footprints on the ceiling of the public house, was kicked off by Rex Kingsford.

"Christ you're a heavy bugger," Billy Allison puffed as he helped Knobby lift the New Zealander past a supporting beam.

"It's the sheep," Rex belched loudly after regaining the floor."the lanolin causes you to beef up."

"Good on you mate, that's pretty clever for a Kiwi, but these Pommie bastards we've become so fond of might not appreciate your wit." Knobby winked at Burnsey.

"Quite the contrary old boy," Burnsey burped. "we beef eater's are quite fond of you chaps from the armpit of the Empire."

"Your turn now Alley," Andy shouted as he and Erine McNab joined in on the fun.

"On three then Dunc," Pee Wee grunted while helping to lift the American flyer towards the ceiling.

Before the publican called time, the ten officer pilots of 689 had left their mark on the white plaster. Just before departing the White Horse, Burnsey announced that Squadron Leader McNab would be leaving them the next morning and returning to No. 1 RCAF stationed at Northholt. Knobby Clark and Rex Kingsford immediately stepped forward, hoisted the popular Canadian on their shoulders and marched him around the room, with rest of the Panthers following and singing gleefully, "For he's a jolly good arsehole, for he's a jolly good arsehole, for he's a jolly good arsehole which nobody can deny."

Pee McNab knew that he'd been accepted.

21

*

At dawn the Panthers were sent aloft to intercept a pair of reconnaissance Dornier 215s but lost them in a large bank of cumulus cloud. After refueling they were scrambled again and fought a running battle with a horde of Stukas and their escort that had attacked Tangmere. The base was badly damaged by the raid but Buzz and Paddy each shot down a dive bomber. Shortly after lunch 689 took to the air again to protect the radar station at Ventnor. They arrived too late to prevent a swarm of Ju 87s from destroying the receiving room and several tall antennas. Ventnor was out of action for a week. In the air battle that followed, Burnsey damaged a 109 and Taffy nailed a 110. Again they pancaked at Stonecroft to be rearmed and refueled. In the late afternoon the Panthers tangled with thirty plus Ju 88s that had dropped high explosives on Manston. Being the closest RAF base to France 'Charlie 3' was attacked most often. Knobby and Woody had scored and two more Nazi bombers failed to make it home. After a hurried meal of mutton sandwiches and lukewarm tea the Panthers were again called upon to take to the skies. It was another attempt at bringing down a lone Dornier 215 that was assessing the days results. This time Rex got in a killing burst and a brief radio report was all that reached Luftwaffe Intelligence.

The pilots of 689 were dog tired when they landed after their fifth sortie. Andy had parked his Spit near Billy's aircraft. His gut clenched tight when he saw the young American slumped over the controls. He immediately raced towards Billy's Spitfire.

"Alley, are you okay?" Andy shouted before climbing onto the wingroot.

Billy hadn't moved a muscle and Andy was starting to panic. He worked frantically at the hood and finally got it to slide back. Andrew James breathed a thankful sigh of relief when he heard soft, snoring sounds resonating upwards from the sleeping beauty in the cockpit.

Andy shook Billy's shoulder, "Come on Alley, rise and shine, time for a pint at the mess bar."

Billy moaned loudly before opening one eye, "I'm so friggin' tired I could assume the horizontal for a week, but I'll take you up on that drink pardner."

*

Churchill was also out and about on 16 August, 1940 and paid a visit to Group 11 headquarters at Uxbridge. He spent the afternoon in the underground plotting room. There was a no smoking rule in the subterranean facility but Air-Vice Marshall Park waved the regulation for the day, so that the P.M. could enjoy one of his famous Cuban cigars.

Loudspeakers blared as squadrons were ordered to the attack, teleprinters chattered continuously as information was fed to them from Bentley Priory and chalkboards squeaked like frightened rats as losses and victories were entered. Churchill, his brow furrowed with concern, watched new waves of attackers being plotted on the map table.

Park, seeing clearly the various pieces of the three dimensional puzzle, ordered up a hundred plus fighters to meet the massive threat. The Prime Minister of Great Briton was deeply moved by the events of the day. The tallies recorded by RAF Intelligence showed a kill/loss ratio of exactly two to one in favour of the home side. Forty-four Luftwaffe bombers and fighters had been shot down. The Royal Air Force lost twenty-two Hurricanes and Spitfires.

*

The 17th brought light winds along with unlimited ceiling and visibily, but all remained quiet on the English front. The Germans, demoralized by their loses over the past two days, took a breather in order to again analyze the reasons for their failure to gain air superiority. Goering, however, made a major mistake when he decided to stop attacking British radar stations. They hadn't been knocked off the air and he concluded that further attempts to destroy them, aside from a raid scheduled on the 18th, would cost too many of his prized Stuka dive-bombers.

The Fat Man's logic went something like this: 'If the British know we're coming, then their ability to intercept could work to our advantage. Large numbers of enemy aircraft will be drawn into battle and provide the 109s and 110s with a golden opportunity to blast the English fighters from the skies.' He stressed that attacks should be concentrated on Fighter Command bases and the factories that produced Hurricanes and Spitfires. The last part of his strategy was a sound one and would eventually bring the RAF to the brink.

*

"Heard anything from Emily Dunc?" Billy Allison asked, as the two pilots sat on deck chairs under sunny, warm August skies.

"Good news Alley, the girls are going to be in London on the 20th," Andy looked over his shoulder to make sure they were still alone." if we can get leave it'll be a hot time in the old townhouse tonight."

"Dream on Romeo, the way Jerry's been pounding us, getting off base will be like breaking out of Alcatraz."

"Maybe so Billy, but if we run into some duff weather who knows."

"Always Mr. Optimistic. Hey, that reminds me!" Alley grinned while reaching into the front pocket of his tunic."What do ya think of this rock?"

Andy nearly fell out of his chair when he saw the ring with a large sparkling diamond attached to it, "Jeez Alley, who'd you have to kill for that one."

"Relax Dunc, got it from a plumber who's cousin knows someone who does a little business in the black market."

" Sounds like a typical Allison deal," Andy kidded. "You've got it pretty bad for Maggie eh?"

"Just about as bad as you have it for Emily."

"Well now that you mentioned it," Andy dug into the breast pocket of his Irvin jacket and pulled out a small velvet lined box containing an engagement ring. "Not as big as your's, but the question that goes along with it will be the same.'

"Hey, how can I be your best man at a double wedding?"

"Elementary my dear Allison. You get married first and I'll be the best man at your wedding and uh, do I have to draw diagrams?"

"Wizard Dunc! Is everyone as smart as you in Canuckland?"

The Panthers were stood down in the early afternoon and the weary pilots got caught up on some much needed rest. The evening brought the usual party at the pub and fortified by a barrel full of strong English ale the fighter boys of 689 slept like old Rip Van Winkle until the pre-dawn wake-up call.

The eighteenth day of August, another perfect summer's day, started out peacefully enough for 11 Group but that would soon change. Goering, desperately seeking a killing blow, had assembled one-thousand bombers and nine-hundred fighters in an attempt to batter the RAF into submission—Beppo Schmid had reported confidently that Fighter Command had only three-hundred Spitfires and Hurricanes left. Hopefully, by night fall, the corpulent *Reichsmarschall* would be able to inform Hitler that the skies over England were controlled by the Luftwaffe.

*

"Looks like Jerry's on strike." Pilot Officer Alexander Harrison a scrawny, rat faced, beady eyed, red headed son of a Scouser dock worker, squeaked nervously. The sprog from Liverpool was the replacement for Goody. Squadron Leader Ernest Archibald McNab was back with No. 1 Canadian.

"Fritz'll be here soon enough, so he will Sandy." Buzz predicted ominously.

"Hey, isn't it just about time for the chow call," Billy looked at his watch. "the little hand and big hand are both straight up."

"Good on you Yank and I'll bet you can read too." Knobby snorted.

"Just the funny papers Flight Lieutenant Clark, sir." Billy gave a mock salute.

The good natured banter ended abruptly when the Tannoy clicked on.

It was a announcement that lunch would be delayed. Everyone started to relax. Rex, however, feeling the hyper-stress of pre-combat got up quickly and disappeared behind the dispersal hut where he threw up.

"Jeez, that damned public address system's starting to make me nauseated too," Andy half-gagged. "it's training us just like that Russian shrink and his bloody dog."

"You mean Pavlov old sport," Burnsey interjected. Andy was about to reply when the scramble call came.

*

RAF Kenley, a vital sector station, had been hit hard by one-hundred plus bombers in a high-altitude raid. Six Hurricanes were destroyed on the ground along with ten hangers and the operations room. A low-level attack by nine Do 17s had managed to fly under radar detection and did damage to the aerodrome as well. The hedge hopping flying pencils, however, were tracked by the Royal Observer Corp and four of the Doriners were brought down by ground defences. Two of the bombers were plucked from the skies by the parachute and cable launchers installed at Kenley. A long cable attached to a rocket was fired into the air. When it reached six hundred feet a parachute was deployed. If an aeroplane struck the cable, a second parachute at the lower end of the cable would pop open. The combined drag of the two chutes could stop an aircraft dead in its tracks.

*

"Red one, Blue two, Heinkels twelve o'clock high," Andy's voice ruptured the silence on the R/T.

"Red one to all sections, battle climb." Burnsey ordered, keeping his eyes riveted on the spread out gaggle of bombers.

The He 111s were on their way home after attacking Kenley. Only Me 110s remained to protect them. The 109s with a battle endurance of less than twenty minutes over targets in the London area had set course for France, hoping to make it back safely on the fumes.

"Red and Blue Tally Ho! Green engage the escorts."

Andy picked out a 111 that had become separated from the pack and attacked from behind. His initial burst hit the rear gunner in the head killing him instantly. Applying right rudder Andy raked the starboard wing of the German bomber. A stream of incendiary rounds punctured the gas tanks and within seconds the Heinkel was transformed into an expanding reddish-black sphere of metal, plastic and flesh. At the last moment, Andy jammed his stick forward narrowly missing the blazing inferno he'd created. Recovering from the vertical dive, Andrew James worked his way back to the fight. Paddy and Gus sent a bomber to a shallow grave in Kentish farm field while Knobby and Buzz obliterated a straggler that had already been damaged by anti-aircraft fire. Rex and Birdie shot down a *zerstoerer* but in a dogfight with the Me 110s Glynn Morgan's Spit was hit and the likeable Welshman was forced to bail out.

*

"Any word on Taffy Burnsey?" Harry Woodston asked as the pilots gulped down a late lunch by the side of their Spitfires.

"Nothing yet old boy." Robbie Barnes mumbled, between bites of a spam and mustard sandwich.

"He's a tough bird, I think." Woody spoke softly in his lilting Afrikaner's accent.

"Don't worry sir, Taffy'll be right as rain." Birdie smiled reassuringly.

"Come on Woody, let's have a quick game of draughts?" Rex Kingsford, tapped Flight Lieutenant Harry Woodston on the shoulder. He knew that the rugged South African needed something to keep him occupied while they awaited word on Taffy.

*

Rex had set up the cardboard playing surface on the trailing edge of his port wing and was about to crown one of Woody's pieces when Billy Allison, who'd been watching the match, scratched his head before saying, "You know Birdie in the states we call this game checkers. Draught usually has something to do with horses or beer."

"I'd suspect sir, it's like me dear old dad would say, the Yanks and the English are two peoples separated by a common language."

"Holy Mackinaw Birdie, that doesn't make a lot of sense cuz we speak American."

Birdie, his mouth half open for a reply, never got a chance. A Corporal had charged out of the dispersal hut yelling like a man possessed,"All squadrons scramble!"

*

They were vectored to intercept a dive bomber raid on the Thorney Island Coastal Command airbase and Billy was the first to engage the enemy, "It's a turkey shoot," he whooped over the radio before peppering the underbelly of a Ju 87 with a four second burst. The Stuka jerked violently upwards, ran out of lift, then entered a full spin. Moments later it slammed into a salt marsh.

"Behind you Sandy," Gus shouted into his oxygen mask mic. Alexander Harrison, with nine hours total on Spits, was not watching in his rear view mirror and never saw the 109 that had sent a flurry of cannon shells into the Supermarine's cockpit.

"Get out," Paddy cried when he saw Sandy's Spitfire in a vertical dive. The Pilot Officer from Liverpool, now a blood soaked corpse, was well beyond radio range.

"Nail the one on the right Birdie," Rex screamed over the airwaves.

Robin Alesworth reacted quickly by sending a river of white phosphor rounds into a Stuka that had just dropped a five-hundred pounder on a hanger at Thorney Island.
Two squadrons of Hurricanes had joined the fight and in a running battle down the Thames Estuary nine more Junkers were shot down. Gosport and Ford were also attacked but neither was a Fighter Command station. Old Beppo had egg on his face again.

*

"The poor wee bugger never got out Burnsey," Gus rasped, the lump in his throat making it difficult to speak.

The pilots had reported to Holmes and were now grouped around the NAAFI van.

"I'll list him as missing and presumed dead then," Robbie Barnes croaked, absentmindedly reaching for a pack of cigarettes that wasn't there. In the dogfight he'd lost track of Sandy and had feared the worst.

"Any news about Taffy?" Rex asked, between mouthfuls of jam tart.

"Well, actually old chap I have," Burnsey grimaced. "the Home Guard found him hanging in a tree. He'd been machine gunned on his way down."

There was complete silence for a moment before Knobby erupted, "No bloody quarter then mate," he shouted. "the next Jerry bastard that bails out near me is dead meat."

The rest of pilots snarled in agreement and before anymore could be said the scramble call echoed from the Tannoy.

*

The last sorties of the day planned by the Luftwaffe were to be on the Panthers home base at Stonecroft. Cloud had covered most of eastern England by the late afternoon and the Dorniers, unable to find the busy sector control station, bombed targets of opportunity doing very little damage. Park had ordered 689 and several other squadrons to attack the retreating bombers. Again their 109 escorts, low on fuel, had reluctantly abandoned the Do 17s

"You nailed him boyo," Buzz screamed over the radio when he saw the Dornier that Andy had shot at go into a flat spin.

"G'day mate." Knobby piped up through the crackling static. He'd been watching the rapidly descending flying pencil and smiled to himself as two chutes appeared.

Closing in on the German flyers, who dangled puppet-like below a pair of silk canopies, he growled like a made dog over the airwaves, "Root you Nazi bastards." His Spitfire shuddered in the air as the wing mounted Brownings disgorged a flaming fountain of death. Knobby, a grim look of satisfaction on his face, watched as the lifeless bodies drifted slowly downwards.

When the scores were finally posted the chalkboards read: 69 aircraft shot down by the RAF for a loss of 31 Spitfires and Hurricanes. An additional 29 British aircraft were destroyed on the ground none of them fighters. Keith Park told his Group Captains that the 18th was the 'hardest day' of the battle so far. The tallies for enemy aircraft blasted from the skies should have brought joy to Stuffy Dowding, but he was well aware of another statistic that churned the blood in his veins to ice water. In the past nine days eighty-eight pilots had been killed and another forty severely wounded. To date, in the month of August, Training Command had sent him seventy replacements. The Beaver had fighter production rolling along at over four-hundred per month, but Air Chief Marshall Hugh Dowding feared that the pilots to fly his precious high performance, eight gun monoplanes would not be available. The Germans were beginning to win the battle of attrition, but Goering could not guarantee air superiority over England, and the following day Hitler postponed Sealion until the seventeenth of September.

22

*

20 August, 1940

It was the second day of duff weather, but the low cloud and rain were a welcome change because the down-on-the-deck conditions kept Jerry on his side of the fence. The Panthers had flown only one sortie on the19th. It was almost like a day off. That evening Burnsey had placed three pieces of paper in his flight cap, one for each section. Whoever was drawn would go on a 24 hour leave the next day. Basil Lewis, eyes shut, extracted one of the small squares and making a great show of cleaning his glasses in order to read the names on the lucky ticket. The amiable Adjutant finally announced, "The winner of the grand prize is..."

"Drum roll please." Woody interrupted, while tapping his index fingers rapidly on the bar top.

"Blue section!" Basil Lewis howled, before handing the paper to Burnsey.

Billy, Andy, Knobby and Buzz pounded each other on the back, celebrating like a bunch of prospectors who'd just discovered the mother load.

"I say Uncle, I thought we agreed you'd draw Red," Robbie Barnes winked, while lighting up a Woodbine.

"Should have bribed him with a few more pints Burnsey," Billy quipped.

"Aye laddie, that might have worked, but a wee dram of Johnny Walker Black Label would have been better." Gus smacked his lips.

*

Andy and Billy arrived at the townhouse shortly before noon. Emily had four passes, compliments of Lord Smith-Barton, to a matinee performance of George Black's revue "Apple Sauce" that was playing at the Holburn Empire. It proved to be a highly entertaining afternoon. They laughed till their sides hurt at Max Miller, the Cheeky Chappie.

The appreciative pair of couples were then mesmerized by the songs of Vera Lynn who was new to the London stage.

*

Before catching the tube back to Emily's "shack on Berkeley Square" as Billy called it, the foursome decided to have drinks at the Rose and Crown, a rustic little pub just around the corner from the theatre. After they were seated several RAF fighter pilots, top buttons of their tunics undone, rolled into the public house.

The last one through the door brought Andy to his feet with a joyous whoop, "Willie over here!"

Pilot Officer William Lidstone McKnight, his eyes slowly adjusting to the dim lighting of the pub, finally recognized Andy, "Dunc, boy what a surprise?"

After the bear hugging and hand shakes were over, Andy introduced Willie to Billy, Maggie and Emily, "Hey we should fly together," Alley piped up after everyone was seated—mugs of the house pale ale and several whiskies crowding the table. "the Billy and Willie show would really get the press going."

"Alley, you're my wingman and don't you forget it." Andy chuckled.

"That I am pardner." Billy snorted.

"So how're things with 242?" Andy inquired, before taking a sip of ale.

"Not as busy as you guys down in 11 Group. Our Squadron Leader, Douglas Bader, is really upset about being out of the action."

"What happened to Gobeil?" Andy frowned, fearing the worst.

"He got rotated back home," Willie smiled reassuringly. "and you won't belive this but our new CO has no legs."

"How can he work the rudders then?" Billy cocked his head in disbelief.

"Well, I should have told you, he has two artificial limbs and we all thought the same thing when Bader talked to us for the first time."

"Is he any good?" Andy looked doubtful.

"He's the best. Douglas knew we'd be skeptical, so he gathered us together on the flight line, and before we knew it the bugger had climbed into a Hurri and was in the air."

"Pranged the crate I'll bet." Billy predicted

"Nope, Bader did an aerobatic show that would have turned your hair white. He finished with a series of worm rolls ten feet off the ground then landed."

"Holy smoke, I'll bet the mob at Coltishall was surprized." Andy gasped.

"We've followed him like a bunch of puppies ever since." Willie grinned.

Emily had been listening quietly but there was one thing she was curious about, "We hear a lot about this Big Wing idea at the Priory Willie. What's your opinion?"

"It's too slow. Trying to assemble three or more squadrons above the base, then follow the vectors given by sector control has, so far, put us on the short end of intercepting a raid."

"Stuffy's dead against them and I'm astonished he lets Leigh-Mallory work on getting his Big Wing into action." Emily said.

"Dowding, from what I hear, likes to give his Group commanders a free hand. He's famous for delegating." Andy offered.

"You're right Dunc and I can see your point Willie. It's hard enough for the Panthers to scramble and get above the bombers let alone the snappers without waiting for another squadron to form up." Billy added to the conversation.

"I've heard that Keith Park and Trafford Leigh-Mallory are not very fond of one another." Margot Cooper joined in.

"You've got that right Margot," Willie nodded in agreement. "Trafford wanted to be the boss of 11 Group because he figures this is where the glory and promotions will come from."

"Hey, he can boogie woogie down here and fly my Spit any day," Billy smirked.

"Speaking of flying, does Leigh-Mallory pilot his own Hurri like Park?" Andy asked.

"No way, strictly a Penguin." Willie replied, while placing his fingers under his armpits and flapping his elbows.

This broke everyone up and when the laughter subsided, Andy was the first to speak,"So what's going to come of all this Big Wing stuff anyway?"

"I think that Dowding had better watch his back. Leigh-Mallory hates Stuffy too. He was denied 11 Group and wants to get even." Willie stated firmly.

"How on earth does he expect to do that?" Emily arched her eyebrows.

"Our Adjutant's an M.P. and he supports Douglas and Leigh-Mallory on the Big Wing concept."

"Why would someone who's a Military Policeman be a problem," Billy smiled innocently.

"Oh come now darling," Margot interjected. "surely Willie means a Member of Parliament."

"Gosh babe, are you ever smart." Billy gave Maggie a playful peck on the cheek.

"Cut out the clowning Alley and let Willie finish." Andy rolled his eyes.

"Our beloved Uncle," Willie paused waiting for Billy to say something. "has a pipeline into the Air Ministry. Apparently Dowding isn't very well liked there either."

"Pretty heavy odds against everyone's favorite Air Chief Marshall then." Andy shrugged.

"You can say that again ace." Willie nodded his head slowly.

"And from what I've been told he and the Prime Minister have crossed swords in the past." Emily added.

"Jeez, it kinda makes you feel sorry for Stuffy." Billy sighed.

"Enough politics folks," Willie half-pleaded. "I rubbed shoulders with a friend of yours Dunc the other day, when I dropped in at Northholt to refuel."

"Ernie McNab?" Andy predicted confidently.

"Nope, Johnny Kent. John's a Flight Lieutenant now and he's been helping to train 303 Polish since early August."

John Alexander Kent was a twenty-six-year-old from Winnipeg Manitoba. He'd joined the RAF in 1935 and was being groomed by the Air Force for Squadron Leader duties.

"Hey good for Johnny!" Andy brightened. He'd met the popular Canadian in a London Pub shortly after coming overseas and they'd gotten along famously. Kent was a gifted pilot as well as being one hell of a good guy.

"He says the Polish pilots are first rate and really hate the Nazi for what they did to their country." Willie continued.

"Yeah, I've heard they're itching to kill Jerries." Billy added.

"You'll love this Dunc," Willie said, while nodding agreement in Alley's direction. "the Poles like Johnny so much they call him Kentowski."

"Johnny would get a kick out of that, he's got a great sense of humour." Andy chuckled.

"From what Johnny told me, 303 and No. 1 RCAF should be operational any day now." Willie suddenly twisted his head in response to a booming voice from behind.

"Hey McKnight lets blow this joint. It's too dull." one of the 242 pilots bellowed from across the room.

"Sorry, duty calls." Willie grinned, getting to his feet."Nice meeting you folks."

"Take care Willie, no bad landings eh?" Andy spoke softly while shaking his friends hand.

"Yeah, anyone you can walk away from is a good one Dunc. Be seeing you." Pilot Officer William McKnight then left their table and joined his squadron mates. Seconds later the raucous gang of Canadian fighter pilots disappeared into the London night.

23
*

Their love making had been sweet and unhurried. It seemed like time had stopped and their world was an enchanted place of gentleness, caring and pleasure. Andy had gotten out of bed on the pretence of using the bathroom. On the way back he lifted his tunic and extracted the tiny box covered in blue velvet. Emily had her eyes shut, lost in a pleasant reverie. She was satisfied and felt like a woman complete in all things.

"Open your eyes sleeping beauty." Andy whispered, as he lay down beside her.

"That was quick darling." she murmured softly.

He plumped the pillow behind him and sat up. Emily remained where she was and cooed seductively, "So what's on your mind cowboy, something new we haven't tried?"

"Well sorta,"Andy began slowly. "I was just wondering if we could try this sex bit as an old married couple."

Emily rolled quickly on to her side and looked him in the eye,"Okay Drew you have my undivided attention."

Andrew James Duncan reached behind him and grabbed the small square box. He then handed it to Lady Smith-Barton. She was speechless for a moment when he opened it and realized what he was asking. Tears flooded down her cheeks as she lifted the ring form its velvet cushion. Andy didn't know what to think, listening to her quiet sobs he blurted, "I've upset you and the answer of course is no. I should've known better."

Emily quickly placed the ring on the second finger of her left hand and gasped tearfully, "Drew you've a lot to learn, these are tears of joy. Of course I will. I love you far more than you'll ever know. That's not very original darling but it's the best I can do."

Before Andy could reply, she wrapped her hands around the back of his neck and kissed him full on the mouth. Moments later they sealed their engagement with an act of tenderness and bliss as ancient as all mankind.

Margot and Billy were in the kitchen when Andy and Emily came down for breakfast. Alley, who loved to cook, was piling two plates full of bangers, scrambled eggs and fried potatoes. The toast and tea were already on the table.

*

"Hey that looks good. Got any extra?" Andy sniffed the air hungrily

"Sure have ace, hope you've worked up an appetite."

Margot couldn't contain herself any longer and held up the ring that Billy had given her, "We're getting married. I'm the happiest woman in the world."

"Well then, I must be the second happiest." Emily burbled as she showed Margot her ring. The two young women hugged each other and Billy came over to shake Andy's hand, "A double wedding, right pardner?" Alley said, smiling like a butcher's dog.

"Yep, get me to the church on time." Andy grinned coast to coast.

"Oh, this is going to be so marvelous darling," Margot sighed.

"Stunning, smashing wizard, wouldn't you say Maggie old girl?" Billy clowned.

While eating the feast that Billy had prepared they discussed their plans. Andy all of a sudden stopped what he was saying and turned towards Emily, "My God, I forgot something really important. I should have visited his Lordship and asked for your hand."

"He'd probably throw in an arm and leg too if you talked to him real polite like." Billy, gently elbowed Maggie in the ribs.

"You and Max Miller would get along well together." Emily chuckled. "Actually Drew, I did speak to Daddy about my feelings for you and we have his blessing."

"You were pretty confident then Corporal Emily."

"Sure as shootin' cowboy." she purred.

The breakfast over, the newly engaged couples left reluctantly for the underground and were back at their posts before noon.

Billy and Andy arrived in time for lunch but after their huge engagement breakfast, as Maggie called it, they ate sparingly. Everyone was at the mess table except for Woody, Rex and Birdie. The three surviving members of Green section had been drawn second and were now on leave. Seated across from Andy were two replacement pilots from 6 OTU.

"I say, it's great to finally be on ops," Pilot Officer Samuel Rosewood, a flop haired, beak nosed, pimple faced graduate of Eton simpered.

"Yeah, it's a piece of cake up there." Billy stated brightly.

"It must be frightfully exciting," Pilot Officer, Turner Upshaw, another Etonian sniffed noticeably when he spoke. His red hair, splotchy freckles and doe like brown eyes made him look younger than his eighteen years.

"It does get your blood flowing," Andy bit his lower lip to keep from laughing.

"Jolly good outfit the Panthers." Samuel Rosewood frowned when he saw the desert that was being delivered to the tables.

"Yes, rather Rosey, 689 is tops from what the old sweats say. I think they're serving us Spotted Dick." Turner Upshaw wrinkled his nose slightly when he identified the dish.

"Sounds like something from one of those VD movies." Billy quipped.

"That's a good one old boy, hey what Turnip." Rosey snickered.

Andy looked at the two sprogs and trying to be friendly said. "Rosey and Turnip, you guys will fit right in. Isn't that so Alley?"

"Yup, cuz they've already got nicknames."

Andy, followed by Billy, formally introduced themselves and tried their best to make Rosey and Turnip feel welcome.

Just before the pilots were about to leave the mess. Basil Lewis rose to his feet and asked for everyone's attention.

"Make it short Uncle I have to catch up on me beauty sleep, so I do," Sean Riley stretched and yawned.

"Two minutes of your time Buzz is all I need," the Adjutant then drew a newspaper clipping from the front pocket of his battle dress tunic. "Here's part of a speech the P.M. gave in the House of Commons yesterday.

Buzz groaned loudly, but was soon silenced by the powerful words of Winston Churchill.

"And I quote gentleman," Basil Lewis began. "The enemy is of course far more numerous than we are. But, our fighter strengths now, after all the fighting , are larger than they have ever been. We believe we should be able to continue the struggle indefinitely and the longer it continues the more rapid will be our approach into that superiority in the air upon which in a large measure the decision of the war depends. The Adjutant cleared his throat before continuing. "The gratitude of every home in our Island, in our Empire, and indeed throughout the world, except in the abodes of the guilty, goes out to the British airmen who, undaunted by the odds, unwearied in their constant challenge and mortal danger are turning the tide of war by their prowess and devotion." Basil Lewis paused briefly so that the final words of the speech would hopefully sink in. "Never in the field of human conflict was so much owed by so many to so few."

Andy was greatly moved by the words. He suddenly realized that they were taking part in a event of monumental importance. His most fervent hope, however, was that he'd live through it and be able tell tall tales to the children that he and Emily planned to have.

Bunrsey, displaying his renowned, dry sense of humour, had the last word. "I say Uncle, the P.M. must have been talking about the Panther's mess bill. Never was so much owed to by so few to so many."

The laughter was cut short when the Tannoy clinked on. Everyone relaxed when the orderly on the other end of the of the public address system announced calmly that the squadron was being stood down for the afternoon. Rex, his conditioned stomach on the verge of emptying its contents, excused himself and made a mad dash for the closest toilet.

24
*

24 August, 1940

On this clear Saturday morning all looked quiet until the coastal radar screens came alive at 8:30 am. Forty Do 17s and Ju 88s escorted by sixty-six 109s had set a course for Manston. The four day bad weather break was over. Six-eighty-nine along with several other squadrons were ordered aloft to respond to the threat.

"Red Leader, Green two," Rex's voice pierced the static on the R/T. "Bandits at twelve o'clock high."

"Roger Green two, that's the escort, battle climb." Burnsey rasped, while pulling the plug for full emergency boost.

The Spitfires would take on the snappers and leave the bombers to the Hurricane squadrons. This was common RAF practice as the Spits stood a much better chance against the world class German fighters.

*

The Me 109s, having the advantage of height and sun, dove on the climbing Spitfires. The Panthers accompanied by a supporting squadron of Spits were outnumbered three to one. The chaotic dogfight that followed proved to be an exercise in survival for the defenders.

"Break right Birdie."Woody screamed over the airwaves.

Robin Alesworth slammed his Spit into a vertical bank, then spun the aircraft. A determined pair of 109s continued firing until he reached the undercast but nothing vital was hit.

"Behind you Upshaw," Burnsey warned the moment he saw the sprog pilot in danger. Before the frightened Public School graduate could reply his Spitfire was riddled with a barrage of 20 mm cannon fire. A heart beat later the Supermarine blew apart like a giant firecracker on Queen Victoria's birthday.

Andy had managed to out turn one of the snappers and finally got the 109 to fill his reflector gunsight. A long six second burst tore the tail off the Messerschmitt.

The broken fighter flip-flopped like a beached fish and the wounded pilot was hurtled into space. His chute never opened.

"Dive Green three," Rex yelled, into his mic, while trying desperately to get behind the Me that was closing on Rosey's Spit.

Samuel Rosewood, fresh out of 6 OTU with eight hours on Spitfires, was hit in the head by a high velocity machine gun round. It made a hole the size of thin pencil at the base of his skull but formed a fist sized hole when it exited through what was left of his face. The British fighter flew on for several seconds before nosing over into a howling death dive.

By now the Supermarines were scattered across the sky and the gasoline starved 109s had fled for home. The Hurricanes that attacked the bombers were unable to turn back the raid and RAF Manston was severely damaged. It would be out of action as a forward refueling base for the rest of the battle.

*

"Turnip you say Andy, must be slipping old boy. I never knew that." Robbie Barnes looked pale and drawn after the morning's combat

"That's what Rosey told us," Andy coughed, his mouth dry and throat raw from inhaling bottled oxygen.

"They were just kids Burnsey." Billy lamented. "Jeez, they'll be wearing diapers next."

The pilots were at dispersal. They'd pancaked, refueled and rearmed. There was hot tea and bully beef sandwiches available on a table at the end of the ready room and everyone had eaten.

"Better draft two letters for me Uncle," Burnsey sniffed, while brushing his nose with the back of his hand.

"Not to worry Robbie, I'll have them on your desk in an hour or so."

"We'll be short again, so we will," Buzz looked worried.

"Not your section Buzz. Blue seems to be the lucky one." Woody said, before finishing a mug of strong orange pekoe.

"Comes from clean living and devotion to duty mate." Knobby grinned, a toothpick waggling in his mouth as he talked

"Aye, and lots of fine whiskey and wild wee women I'd suspect," Gus winked at Paddy.

"Rosey told me that he and Turnip had bought a car together, an old Austin two door." Rex added to the conversation.

"Right you are Rex," Basil Lewis nodded. "It's parked behind the officers quarters and..."

"Excuse me sir," Birdie interrupted. "but you may also want to know they told Paddy and me, that if anything happened, the squadron was welcome to use it."

"Birdie's right sir, nobody in their family knows how to drive, so it would be useless to them." Paddy confirmed.

"Hey, that's great Paddy," Billy thundered. "we'd better start a gas fund."

"After a good thrash at the pub sir, you could fuel it on the contents of Paddy's arse," Birdie chuckled, while nudging his fellow Sergeant Pilot in the ribs.

The phone rang, everyone stopped breathing, a Corporal bellowed, and ten battle weary pilots sprinted for their fighters.

*

"Panther leader, fox-trot control."

"Fox-trot control, Panther leader, go ahead," Burnsey replied laconically, as they climbed through five thousand feet.

"Panther Leader, fox-trot control, I have trade for you, vector one-zero-zero, fifty plus bandit at angels fifteen."

"Roger, Fox-trot control," Burnsey transmitted confidently as 689 began its battle climb.

The swarm of Heinkel 111s flying in tight formation were first spotted by Billy.

A second Spitfire squadron had been scrambled from Biggin Hill and were engaging the Me 110 escort. This allowed the Panthers to take on the He111s.

Knobby had told them that the next time Blue section had a crack at the bombers, he wanted to try a head-on attack.

"Line abreast," the big Australian called over the radio as four Spits rocketed towards the enemy formation.

"Blue two and three starboard, Blue one stick with me," Knobby ordered calmly.

While Buzz and his flight commander accelerated towards the port side of the bomber stream, Andy and Billy selected the lead Heinkel on the right. The opposing aircraft approached each other at over five-hundred miles per hour. Timing was everything in this real life game of chicken. If you misjudged then a midair was your reward. The spearhead pilots of the 111s panicked at the sight of four Spitfires flying a collision course towards them and they veered away. Just as the bombers started to turn Andy and Billy triggered a lethal spray of armor piercing, incendiary, and tracer rounds that tore apart the greenhouse-like nose of the lead twin engine bomber. The pilot and navigator were cut to shreds. The He 111 banked sharply, and now out of control, smashed into the bomber next to it. Andy got close enough to make out the blood spattered goggles of the German pilot before shoving the stick full forward. The Spitfire dove like a kingfisher, missing the big Heinkel by five feet. It was close but he'd gotten away with it.

"Two for the price of one!" Billy whooped over the radio as they climbed hard to rejoin the air battle.

The broken formation was now easy pickings for a flight of Hurricanes that had just joined the skirmish. Not all the bombers were engaged, however, and a second wave fought its way through to drop high explosives on their targets.

*

It was waking nightmare, hangers had been blown apart, the runways were pock marked with moon-like craters, orange black smoke boiled upward from a flaming bowser, the WAAF's quarters had disappeared, dozens of bright blue flags marked the resting place of unexploded bombs, and the skeletal remains of two Spitfires lay abandoned on the grass.

Andy, on final approach, shook his head several times and briefly closed his eyes, but the horrific scene would not go away. Stonecroft along with North Weald were on the target list for the day and the Luftwaffe had been frightfully successful. A landing path had been hastily laid out between the saucer-like depressions that littered the base. The Panthers managed to put their Spits down safely and were guided to the make shift flight line. A short thirty minutes later, refueled and rearmed they were ordered to stay beside their aircraft in case another raid appeared.

"The WAAF's trench took a direct hit sir," a weary Flight Sergeant informed Andy. He and Billy were sitting on the grass between the two Spits.

"All dead," Billy gulped reflexively.

"Not sure sir, they're still digging."

*

Several hours had elapsed before 689 was stood down. It was too dark for daylight interceptions. A Corporal told Andy, he'd heard through the NCO grapevine, that Keith Park had requested Leigh-Mallory to protect 11 Group bases. An attempt was made to assemble a Big Wing over Duxford, it took too long, and the 12 Group fighters arrived late. Park was furious but Dowding failed to reprimand Leigh-Mallory.

The entire squadron had volunteered to help with the search for anyone still alive in the pile of rubble and earth that had been the women's trench.

"Here's someone," Andy shouted, cupping his fingers into tiny rakes in order to clear away a mound of dried soil. A hand, then an arm appeared from beneath the dirt. Billy had come over to help and gently grasped the hand that was now fully exposed. He slowly pulled upwards but was thrown off balance when the arm came away on its own with no body attached. Pilot Officer William Allison fell to his knees and began to retch.

Digging continued throughout the night and towards morning the Air Ministry brought in a gang of miners to help with the excavations.

Detached heads, legs and torsos were ghastly reminders of the destruction that had rained from the skies. Three of the miners were unable to continue because of the horror they'd witnessed. Thirty seven bodies were removed from the soil. Miraculously, a large pocket was discovered where a group of WAAF's were injured but still alive. The rescue efforts continued for forty-eight hours but no one else was found. The bulldozers arrived on the third day and covered in the area. Everyone serving at an RAF base was now on the front lines.

*

Goering, wanting to keep the pressure on Fighter Command, had ordered a series of raids to be carried out in the inky darkness of a moonless night. Twelve Dorniers sent to attack the oil refineries at Thames Haven became lost. Unable to find their target due to cloud, and thinking they were twenty miles south of the Capital, the Do 17s jettisoned their bomb load. The high explosives were scattered over the City of London and several London Districts. Nine people were killed in the raid. The corpulent *Reichsmarshal* was furious and demanded to know the names of the pilots who had ignored the Fuehrer's explicit order not to drop bombs on central London. When Goering found out who the crews were, he immediately transferred them to the infantry.

The following night, 25 August, Churchill instructed Bomber Command to attack Berlin. A fleet of eighty plus Hampdens, Whitleys and Wellingtons made the hazardous nine hour round trip to the Capital of the Third Reich and were successful in bombing the city. Very little damage was done and no one was killed but Hitler and Goering were outraged. The Fat Man had promised the German people that if ever a bomb were to fall on Berlin then they could called him Meier, a common Jewish name. The Fuehrer was able to reign in his temper that night but when the raids continued and several Berliners were killed he was gripped by a frothing madness and promised all who were within hearing that the British criminals would pay.

25
*

4 September, 1940

It had been twelve days of crisis for Fighter Command. Biggin Hill was struggling to remain operational, Kenley, North Weald, Rochford, Eastchurch and Stonecroft were reeling under the onslaught. Damaged operations rooms at the sector stations made it difficult to control fighters in the air. The refueling and rearming of the Spitfires and Hurricanes was a constant problem due to the continuous raids. In addition to the airbases, Goering had also stepped up his assault on aircraft factories, but faulty intelligence resulted in attacks on the Vickers and Shorts facilities instead of the Hawker and Supermarine works. RAF losses compared to those of the Luftwaffe were now a one to one ratio and one-quarter of Dowding's pilots had been killed or seriously wounded during this period. Fighter Command was like a boxer on the ropes who'd been hammered without mercy and was about to receive a knockout blow. Dowding and Park had done the math and knew full well that the German Air Force was winning the battle of attrition.

*

"Anything new from Emily?" Billy asked, as they waited by their Spitfires.

"No, just the usual stuff but I'm glad she's able to write me every other day."

"Boy, I sure miss Maggie" Billy sighed plaintively. "her letters are the best."

"God, I wish we could get some leave." Andy groused.

"A thing of the past pardner, but you never know if old Stuffy will........" The scramble call came before Pilot Officer William Allison could finish his sentence.

*

For once the Panthers had been given enough warning and they were above the twenty plus Me 110s that had been dispatched to attack the Hawker factory at Brooklands.

Burnsey managed to position his squadron up sun and moments later ten Spitfires, intent on destroying the enemy, arrowed towards the twin-engined fighters. It turned out to be a shooting gallery and 689 was able to blast three of the *zerstoerers* from the skies.

One of the first things that Andy had learned from his dogfighting experience was not to fly straight and level in the combat zone for more than twenty seconds. In order to accomplish this he'd set his rudder trim so that instead of flying straight ahead, he was always wobbling from side to side. A 110 had come out of nowhere and tried to pummel Andy's Spit with cannon fire. The pilot, confused by the erratic movements of the British fighter, missed his target. All Andy needed was this split second of inaccurate shooting to escape the Me that was on his tail. Instinctively he dove the Spitfire and moments later entered a large cloud bank.

*

When Andy emerged from the mists of protection, he was unable to locate Alley or anyone else in the squadron. He decided to fly east. Ten minutes had elapsed when Andy, peering into the smoky late summer haze, spotted a single Dornier that was heading back to France. He pulled the plug for emergency boost and climbed above and ahead of the Do 17. He'd positioned himself for a head-on attack and closed rapidly on the flying pencil.

Eight Browning machine guns produced a dense cone of lead that converged on the cockpit of the enemy aircraft. The pilot and navigator were killed instantly. Andy dove below the bomber and cringed when he saw, wings and black crosses streaking by his canopy. Now at an airspeed of four-hundred miles per hour, Andy yanked back on the stick and blacked out momentarily as he executed a gigantic loop. When his sight returned he rolled out of inverted flight and found himself ahead of the Dornier. This time he focused his fire on the engines and seconds later the static propellers of the Do 17 ceased to give it lift. The ventral gunner had bailed out and Andy decided to pull along side the bomber.

The pilot was sitting up staring forward, but it was a corpse—hands frozen on the controls—flying the airplane. The Do 17 had been losing height continuously and was now below Angels six. Andy dropped back behind the crippled aircraft and was about to finish it off when he noticed a pair of legs dangling from the cockpit hatch. Someone was trying to bail out, but had become stuck in the narrow opening. Whoever was attached to the legs was kicking frantically and his shoes and socks had come off. It looked like the trapped airman was running barefoot underneath the fuselage.

The bomber was now below two-thousand feet and Andy realized that the German flyer would be sliced in two, like a log cut by a chain saw, when the Dornier hit the ground. As much as he hated the enemy—the image of a decapitated WAAF flashed across his mind—he decided to put the Nazi aviator out of his misery. Andy positioned the nose of the Spit so his guns would fire where the man's body would be above the thrashing legs. He pressed the firing button and a second later the legs went still. The bomber plodded on then bellied into a hop field, before breaking up into a pile of scrap metal. Andy found no satisfaction in the victory.

*

"The Home Guard reported a Dornier crashing exactly where you've described it Andy." Basil Lewis smiled.

"Well Uncle, that sure is one hell of lot better than the claim on that snapper."

"As a matter of fact dear boy, I reviewed the incident where you forced the 109 to crash-land, and the Army confirmed that a Messerschmitt had been found in a wheat field that day. The location was consistent with what you told me and you've been credited with one destroyed."

"Jeez Uncle, there is a good fairy after all."

"So did anyone see my 110?" Billy Allison asked, biting his nails. He was behind Andy and ready to report

"Indeed they did Alley old bean. Paddy saw the kite explode."

"Hot dog," Billy whooped "that makes me an ace!"

"Way to go Billy," Andy reached out to shake his wingman's hand.

"The drinks at the White Horse are on me tonight pardner."

Andy suddenly turned around and spotted Knobby walking towards them, head down. He'd just landed. A cold chill ran up the spine of Pilot Officer Andrew James Duncan.

"The poor bugger," Knobby croaked, in a sandpaper voice, when he reached Billy and Andy.

"Buzz?" Billy chocked on the name.

"He got out mate, but his chute never opened." Knobby replied in a hoarse whisper.

"Those lousy Jerrys," Andy growled. "we'll get a couple for Buzz on the next one."

"Too right Dunc, are you ready then Uncle?" Knobby turned his attention towards Basil Lewis.

"Yes I am dear boy, it's hard but we must carry on. Stiff-upper-lip and all that." the squadron Adjutant rasped, his eyes misting with slow salty tears.

There was little time to mourn the missing faces at the mess. In order to ease the pain the pilots spent a fortune at the local pub. Death had become such a common thing that in public, they had to put on a front or go mad from grief and hopelessness. Underneath, the strain and anxiety was bubbling like an over heated cauldron of oil about to boil over.

*

That evening in Berlin Hitler addressed an audience of nurses and female social workers. His speech soon had the Nazi matrons leaping to their feet, presenting the party salute and wildly cheering their God-like hero.

"Mr. Churchill is demonstrating his new brainchild, the night air raid. Mr. Churchill is carrying out these raids not because they promise to be highly effective, but because his air force cannot fly over German soil in daylight. For three months, I did not answer because I believed that this madness would be stopped. Mr. Churchill took this as a sign of weakness. We are now answering night for night.

When the British air force drops 3000 or 4000 kilograms of bombs, we will in one night drop 200,000, 300,000, or 400,000 kilograms. When they declare they will increase their attacks on our cities, then we will raze their cities to the ground. We will stop the handiwork of these night pirates, so help us God...The hour will come when one us will blink, and it will not be National Socialist Germany!"

Hitler paused to return the salutes of the frenzied female audience, then held his hand up for silence before continuing. His next words gave promise to the invasion that everyone was expecting. "In England they're filled with curiosity and keep asking, 'Why doesn't he come. Be calm. Be calm. He's coming! He's coming!" The enraptured women once more erupted into a cacophonous chorus of applause, foot stamping and continuous volley of, "Sieg heil!"

Aldoph Hitler had already ordered Goering to stop his attacks on British airfields and aircraft factories. He had given the blimp sized *Reichmarschall* the go ahead for reprisal attacks on London. This decision would ultimately cost the Fuehrer his life, ensure an Allied victory and the destruction of every major centre in the Third Reich.

*

7 September, 1940

"Just feels those rays," Billy yawned openly. He and the rest of the Panthers were sitting on deck chairs that had been placed in front of the dispersal hut.

"Yeah, back home this would be the first day of the weekend and not too far from the opening of the deer season." Andy reminisced.

"You're a hunter then, are you sir?" Sergeant Pilot Oliver Wendel Miller, a replacement from 6 OTU, looked surprised.

"Sure am Twist." Andy smiled.

The sprog pilot, a handsome, blonde haired, blue eyed six footer from Birmingham looked concerned, "But sir, you're killing innocent, defenceless animals."

"Do you like roast beef and Yorkshire pudding Twist old sport?" Burnsey asked. He'd been sitting quietly listening to the conversation, but couldn't resist butting in.

"Why yes sir, as matter of fact I do." Oliver nodded his head.

"Wouldn't you say dear boy, that cattle are innocent, defenceless animals." Burnsey grinned, trying to get the smugness out of his voice.

"Y-Yes sir." Oliver "Twist" Miller turned beet red, realizing he'd been painted into a corner by his squadron leader.

"Watch out for Burnsey mate, he was on the debating team at Cambridge, couldn't row a stroke." Knobby winked at Robbie.

"Sure hope Jerry isn't on the hunt today," Woody frowned, while looking up at the clear blue skies.

"It's late afternoon and maybe he's lost interest in smashing our airbases." Rex added hopefully.

"Aye, it's a bonnie day, but I doubt if the Nazis are taking a wee nap." Gus sighed.

"They've sure hit us hard over the past two," Paddy lamented.

"Cheer up Paddy, it's fish and chip night at the Red Lion and I'm buying." Birdie smacked his lips noisily.

The Tannoy suddenly came alive and the scramble call was given, "Stick to me like glue mate," Knobby puffed behind Oliver Miller, as they sprinted towards the flight line.

"T-Thank you sir," Twist gulped nervously, his heart firing like a trip hammer. The Hun was up there waiting and the vicious rat of terror gnawed at his guts.

On this beautiful September Saturday, Goering stood on the cliffs at *Cap Blanc Nez* marvelling at the airpower under his control. One thousand aircraft, a third of them bombers, thundered overhead. The formations above were stepped up in layers a mile and a half high, and covered eight-hundred square miles of sky. That morning the portly *Reichmarschall* had proudly told the German people over the radio that; "I myself have taken command of the Luftwaffe's battle for Britain."

Park was at Bentley Priory attending a meeting called by Dowding. Shortly after four p.m. the plotting tables began to display the mammoth German raid that was inbound from France. Park and Dowding at first assumed that the attack would be on the battered sector airfields and ordered twenty-one squadrons aloft to protect the airbases. Park knew that he couldn't trust Leigh-Mallory to do the job. The Nazi armada, however, flew an arrow-like course up the Thames Estuary. Twenty minutes later, a series of frantic orders were passed along to the sector controllers. It had become obvious that the target was to be London. The British fighters were hurriedly diverted from their guarding role and vectored to intercept the enemy onslaught. The 109s and 110s protected the bombers on their run in and the capital of the Empire was dealt a massive blow. Hitler would now have his revenge.

*

"Red Leader, Red one Heinkels nine o'clock low." Andy's voice cracked, when he saw the size of the formation retreating to the east.

"I see them Red one, Blue take the escorts, Green stick with me," Burnsey roared over the airwaves, as he jammed his stick forward.

Six Spitfires, spread out line-abreast, initiated a head-on attack. The lead bomber pilots, terrified at the sight of the enemy racing towards them with forty-eight Browning machine guns spraying a lethal stream of deadly metal, took violent evasive action and the formation scattered across the skies.

"Take the one on right Birdie," Rex called over the R/T as he focused on another He 111 that was off his port wing.

"Got the bugger," Gus shouted in triumph when he saw the Heinkel he'd been shooting at start to trail smoke from its starboard engine.

"Three o'clock low Paddy, he's trying for the cloud." Burnsey directed from above and behind red two. Red and Green sections continued to hack at the bombers. It was an effective attack and two of the 111 crews would not be having dinner that evening in their French mess.

"Behind you Twist," Knobby yelled into his mic.

The sprog pilot reacted quickly, throwing the Spit into a tight right turn. The 110 overshot and moments later the tables were reversed. Oliver Miller was a natural pilot with the ability to think quickly in the three dimensional arena. He pulled the plug for emergency boost and rapidly closed on the *zerstoerer*. The chattering machine guns shook his Spitfire and the raw smell of cordite filled the cockpit. Twist cheered out loud when he saw the Me nose up sharply, stall and spin. Oliver watched until the twin engined fighter lit up a farm field in Kent.

Andy and Billy tangled with a pair of Me 110s. The Germans had no stomach for a fight and dove towards the east. Knobby, however, shot the tail off a 110 that had fired at him seconds before. The big Aussie, seeing the damage he'd done, whooped over the radio, "Rot you Nazi bastards!"

After the escort departed, Andy and Billy chased a He 111 in and out of clouds in a running battle.

First one engine of the bomber caught on fire then the other.The crew of the crippled Heinkel bailed out—frightened rats abandoning a sinking ship. Four German airmen, fearing for their lives, waited until they were safely inside a cloud bank before pulling their ripcords. It had become common practice on both sides to go after parachutes.

The Panthers had destroyed four enemy planes and counted two more as probables. Overall on the day the RAF claimed forty enemy shot down for a loss of twenty-one fighters and seventeen pilots killed. Twist had scored his first victory and proven himself to be a valuable addition to 689. These Squadron achievements, however, brought little joy when they learned of the horrific pasting that London had taken.

*

London was burning.The East End and the docks had been blasted by tons of high explosives. Warehouses containing, rubber, rum, ammunition, pepper and food stuffs were set ablaze. After the daylight raids, three-hundred bombers attacked in pairs or small groups over the course of the night. The bombers were guided to their targets by the raging conflagrations below. The Blitz had begun and would continue without a break for the next seventy-six nights.

The burning material around the Québec and Surrey docks spread, like a wildfire on a dry windy day, eventually developing into the fiercest fire in British history. Smoke chocked the air and the light from the fires turned night into day. Viewed from a distance the red glow resembled a continuous sunrise. Firemen from as far away as Coventry fought long and hard to contain the nine conflagrations that were devastating the warehouse district. The all clear was finely sounded at four-thirty in the morning. Causalities were staggering: 448 civilians had been killed and 1600 were seriously injured. Ironically, more people were found dead following this single raid than all the fighter pilots that had lost their lives in the Battle of Britain so far.

"My God, it's a bloody great inferno," Rex croaked.

"Must be hot enough to roast a pig at the docks." Andy spoke in hushed tones.

"It's beyond me old sport why Jerry keeps on dropping those chandelier flares," Burnsey said to Knobby."

"They think it's a fireworks display mate. Look at those colours." Knobby marvelled at the sparkling, greens, reds and blues that were drifting slowly downwards on tiny canopies of silk.

"The Hun's can't miss, all they have do is aim for the big red bulls eye." Billy looked bewildered by the blazing, fiery glow, smeared across the sky.

"Your wee lassies a place in town Andy?"

"Yeah, that's right Gus but Emily and Billy's finance are at the Priory."

"They'll be safe there dear boy," Burnsey said."that underground ops room is the best air raid shelter in the Kingdom."

"If you were in the city right now you wouldn't need a light of to read a book, I think." Woody frowned.

"One good thing may come out of this though." Basil Lewis stated cautiously.

"And what's that Uncle?" Rex looked over his shoulder at the Squadron's Adjutant who was standing behind him.

"The sector airfields old chap. If Jerry's intent on attacking London then we'll be able to get all stations fully operational again."

"Hitler's mad as hell at the raids on Berlin," Andy offered. "so I think you might be right Uncle.

"I sure hope that the poor old darlin' can take it mate." Knobby sighed. A night raider had just dropped a load of incendiaries and the Panthers watched in horrified silence as jagged, bright, orange flames shot towards the heavens.

As the pilots of 689, standing on an observation platform above the control tower, continued to stare in disbelief at the terrifying light show that was London, a steamroller was smoothing out a bomb crater that had just been filled in.

A bulldozer was pushing earth into a large depression, Riggers, fitters and armorers were attending to their Spitfires and Hurricanes, and Post Office engineers were repairing shredded telephone lines. Radar stations that hadn't been attacked for nearly three weeks were all up and running. The bomb disposal squad was busy defusing deadly packages of high explosives and the beleaguered erks would get a good nights sleep for a change. If London could take it, the battle might just turn in favour of the defenders.

27
*

11 September, 1940

Two days previous the bombers came in the afternoon, wave upon wave. The Panthers and five supporting squadrons managed to break up one of the attacks but many of the day raiders slipped through to London causing substantial damage. The Blitz continued into the night and when the all clear sounded three-hundred and twenty civilians were added to the death toll. Leigh-Mallory once again failed to protect 11 Group airfields, instead Bader's Duxford Wing flew south to join the battle. The Big Wing fighters claimed nineteen destroyed but none of these were ever confirmed by German records.

*

This 11th day of September was a busy one as well and the Panthers were scrambled shortly after lunch. A large formation of Heinkels was intercepted without escort. The 109s had stayed with the bombers until they reached London, but when their red, low-fuel warning lights started to blink the German fighters were forced to withdraw.

"Where are the bloody snappers?" Knobby called over the radio.

"Gone back to frogland for gas." Billy replied over the R/T

"Bandits at twelve o'clock low." Twist shouted into his oxygen mask mic.

"I see them," Burnsey affirmed. "emergency boost now."

The Spits jumped forward like a coal car bunted by a locomotive. Several minutes later they were in front of the Heinkels. Robbie Burns ordered a line-abreast, head-on attack and the tightly grouped 111s were soon scattered across the sky. It would now be easier for the Panthers, and a Hurricane squadron that had just arrived on the scene, to go after the bombers without encountering the withering crossfire from a compact formation.

"Underneath him Billy." Andy transmitted to his wingman.

"Roger Dunc." Alley replied, pulling his stick back to climb towards the 111 above them.

Andy opened up first. His eight Brownings pushed a flood of de Wilde incendiary rounds into the gas tanks mounted in the wings of the Heinkel. Billy right behind his leader followed suit with a barrage of his own. Andy rolled off to the right and Billy to the left. Looking back at the twin engined bomber they could see their handy work had started a roaring blaze that was fast consuming the enemy aircraft. The pilot and navigator managed to escape from the flying crematorium but their chutes, smoking like a skywriter, never opened. Andy and Billy harassed another He 111 until it disappeared into a large cloud bank. It was steaming oil from the port engine but would probably make it back to France. Their gun boxes now empty the two pilots from across the pond were forced to pancake at Stonecroft.

*

Andy taxied his Spit to the flight line, then pulled the mixture to full lean and waited until the three bladed prop clattered to a halt. He quickly unbuckled, opened the side folding door and climbed out on to the wingroot. He was surprised to see a Hurricane parked next to him and went over to talk to the pilot. The Hurri driver had his back turned to Andy. When the mystery airman looked over his shoulder and realized who was behind him his seemingly jovial greeting carried a flat edge, "Hi there Ace, how are things on the big Island?"

Andy did a double take when he recognized the pint sized figure who was leaning against the fuselage of the Hawker aircraft. "A hell of a lot better than it would be in Regina Pee Wee."

"Good to see you Dunc." Ernie McNab rasped, in a tone that betrayed strain and fatigue.

"You okay Ernie?" Andy asked.

"Bad one today, we lost five kites and three of our guys didn't get out."

"Jeez, that is tough." Andy frowned.

"Got called in low by sector control, and the Jerrys hit us hard with a swarm of 109s. It was a field day for the bad guys."

"We lost two sprogs a while back in one sortie and it sure was hard to take." Andy commiserated.

"We've had a real rough start Dunc. On our very first op we mistook a Blenheim for an 88 and shot if up pretty bad. Thank God the crew got out okay."

"That's happened to a lot of other squadrons Pee Wee, so don't feel guilty. I almost did that myself back in July."

"Our next time up Andy, we lost three kites and one of them was mine. I bailed out and was lucky to come down on land."

"Yeah, I went for a swim in the Channel once and believe me once was enough."

"We've managed to ring up several destroyed and we're getting better, so there's hope for us yet."

"Don't sweat it Pee Wee, the Brits didn't do all that well against the Jerrys at first either."

"Thanks for the pep talk coach." McNab forced a grin.

"Got time to come over to the mess Ernie?" Andy asked, hoping to get away from the war for a minute or two.

"Sorry Dunc as soon as I'm topped up here, it's off to Northholt for me, I'll have some very sad letters to write this evening." The two Canadian pilots shook hands before Squadron Leader Ernest Archibald McNab climbed into his Hurricane and set a course for Norhtholt.

Churchill and his commanders were concerned about the attacks on London but they were also aware of the build up across the Channel that suggested an invasion was imminent. That evening the British Prime Minister once again sat behind a British Broadcasting Corporation microphone, "We cannot tell when they will try to come; we cannot in fact be sure that they will try at all; but no one should blind himself to the fact that a heavy, full-scale invasion of this Island is being prepared with all the usual German thoroughness and method and that it may be launched any time now."

Churchill paused for a moment to let his words sink in then continued. "We must regard the next week or so as a very important week in our history. It ranks with the days when the Spanish Armada was approaching the Channel and Drake was finishing his game of bowls; or when Nelson stood between us and Napoleon's Grand Army at Boulogne. Every man and every woman will prepare himself to do his duty, whatever it may be, with special pride and care." Churchill then changed directions and spoke directly to the people of the nations capital about the Blitz. "These cruel, wanton, indiscriminate bombings of London, are of course, part of Hitler's invasion plans. He hopes by killing large numbers of civilians, women and children, that he will terrorize and cow the people of this mighty imperial city, and make them a burden and anxiety to the Government. Little does he know the spirit of the British nation, or the tough fibre of Londoners, whose forebears played a leading part in the establishment of Parliamentary institutions."

*

In Berlin Aldoph Hitler had chosen September the 24th as the date for the commencement of Operation Sealion. He only required Goering's assurance that the Luftwaffe had control of the skies over Britain. The *Reichmarschall* was busily planning a gigantic knock out blow for the 15th. Beppo Schmid had reported confidently that the British were down to their last one-hundred fighters. If all went well the Fat Man would soon be able to tell his Fuehrer that the airspace over England belonged to the Fatherland.

28
*

13 September, 1940

It was the second day of duff weather and the ceiling was less than three-hundred feet. The Panthers had been stood down at noon and Andy was heading for the mess when a WAAF called to him. She walked quickly to where he was standing and handed him a piece of paper. He thanked her and carefully unfolded the yellow lined sheet. It was a message from Emily. She had come up to London on her own and would be at the townhouse until late in the evening. Could he join her?
Andy double timed it over to Burnsey's office and pleaded his case. Robbie Barnes was reluctant, but when Andrew James promised to be back on base by midnight, he relented and signed a twelve hour pass.

The phone lines were still up and he was lucky enough to reach Emily. She had just arrived and was pleased that he would be able to visit. Billy was disappointed that Maggie wasn't along but he knew that his best friend was about to be well taken care of and jokingly said, "Don't do anything I wouldn't do Dunc, but if you do, name it after me."

*

Andy hurried to the bus stop and was just in time to climb aboard a double double-decker that would take him to the Underground. He flew down the steps to the tube and was on his way in record time. All the rushing around didn't help because the subway trains were being re-routed due to bomb damage, and it took over an hour to get to a station that was within walking distance of Emilys'.

When he emerged from the bowels of the earth Andy had a hard time getting his bearings. Several of the buildings that should have been there were just piles of rubble. The air was thick with brick dust and water from broken mains flooded the street. He had to walk carefully as shards of broken masonry and glass were everywhere.

His nose wrinkled when he smelled the nauseating stink of raw sewage from a ruptured sewer pipe. Live electrical cables were snaked about the pavement and the acrid odour of ozone assaulted the late summer breezes.

Turning a corner Andy was startled to hear hissing and screaming coming from a large crowd that had gathered in a small park across the road. A dozen London Bobbies were trying to break through to the centre of the throng. Andy immediately ran over to see if he could help. The people on the outside of the circle moved back to allow him to pass once they recognized that he was RAF.

Andy finally got to the middle of the disturbance and was horrified at what he saw. A crazed mob of young women had a German airman pinned to the ground. One of the girls was jabbing at the helpless victims chest with a hat pin while another solidly built matron was kicking the man in the head. A number of the ladies had their high heel shoes off were beating the enemy pilot on the arms and legs. The police were trying to pull the women off, but as soon as they removed one of them another would take her place.

One of the women, spittle running down her chin, yelled at the enemy airman, "You murdering bastard, my baby's dead because of you."

Another woman kept on screaming, "You're a lump of shit, a Nazi lump of shit."

The policemen were finally winning the battle and had just forcefully removed a small, compact girl, but not before she'd booted the battered man in the crotch.

Andy helped the Bobbies to pick up the unconscious German and carry him to a waiting police car.

"He's not breathing constable," Andy shouted, when they were clear of the mob.

"Let's check his pulse then lad." the rotund policeman quickly applied two fingers to the German's upturned wrist. "I'm afraid he's gone, too many kicks in the head."

"Poor chap," a second officer spoke softly.

"Screw the bastard," a third cursed. "Look at all he's done."

The disgruntled copper pointed his finger to a house that had taken a direct hit. A smoldering heap of charred lumber was all that was left of a home where four of its occupants had been incinerated like a pile a garbage.

Andy could no longer be of assistance, so he shook hands with the constable in charge and resumed his trek to Emily's townhouse. He had a block to go when he saw a young woman sitting on the steps of the Community Hall. She was bent over holding her knees and rocking back and forth. Her agonizing sobs could be heard from across the street where Andy had stopped. He desperately wanted to get on his way, but his compassionate soul won out and he crossed over.

"Is there anything I can do to help miss?"

"Not unless you're all the King's men," she snuffled.

"Sorry I don't get it." Andy replied.

She looked up and saw that Andy was in uniform, "RAF?" she questioned.

"I'm on Spits at Stonecroft."

"I apologize love," she chocked back a sob. "that was a dumb thing to say about the King's men, but I was thinking about Humpty Dumpty."

"You'll have to explain miss, I'm not very good a nursery rhymes."

A half-hearted smile formed on the face of the young woman. "From the beginning then." she now spoke in a slow steady voice. "Inside," she chucked a raw, red thumb over her shoulder to indicate the community hall, "is a temporary morgue. I'm a nurse and it's my job to inspect, then identify body parts and hopefully get enough of one person back together again so there'll be something to put in a coffin."

Andy recoiled slightly, in horror, but he finally understood. "That really is a tough one miss and I can see why you're so upset."

"A German bomb can literally blow someone to bits. I don't like it, but I volunteered to help and here I am. Sometimes I just can't take it, the stench is enough to rot your socks, so I come out here and let off steam."

"You may not think so, but you're doing an important job miss," Andy encouraged.

"Thank you love, nobody's ever told me that before, and coming from a fighter pilot it really means something."

"Good-bye then miss," Andy backed away slowly.

"Get one of those Jerry bombers for me, will you love?" she called after him.

*

A brisk, five minute walk brought Andy to Emily's front door. She was overjoyed to see him and listened closely as he filled her in on his journey through, what he called, a frightening look at a living hell. Emily had tears in her eyes when Andy finished but he kissed them away. They ascended the stairs hand-in-hand and entered the large master bedroom.

Naked now, the young lovers cuddled under the covers like pair of well worn spoons. In time the soothing salve of their intimacy washed away the waking nightmare of the London streets.

*

It seemed like he'd just arrived, but if Andy was to make it back to Stonecroft by mid-night it was time to go. Emily turned on the shortwave set by the bed as Andrew James dressed quickly. Through the howls, squeals and static they listened to Edward R. Murrow's CBS radio news broadcast.

"We are told today that the Germans believe Londoners, after a while, will rise up and demand a new government, one that will make pease with Germany. It's more probable that they'll rise up and murder a few German pilots who come down by parachute. The life of a parachutist would not be worth much in the East End of London tonight." Murrow paused for a brief moment.

"Not worth a whole hell a lot in the West End either." Andy mused out loud. They could here the American broadcaster take a short breath and the soft flutter of typed pages.

"The politicians who called this a "people's war" were right, probably more right than they knew at the time."

Murrow covered the microphone to hide a hacking smokers cough, then continued. "I've seen some horrible sights in this city during these days and nights, and not once have I heard man, woman, or child suggest that Britain should throw in her hand. These people are angry. How much they can stand, I don't know. The strain is great." Edward R. Murrow then signed off, thanking all those in the United States for tuning in to CBS.

"I hope Roosevelt was listening to that Drew." Emily sighed.

"Yeah, it might just make the Yanks realize we're not caving in, and maybe they'll send us some help."

"That would be marvelous darling but we're not really alone in this. The Commonwealth's making a big difference."

"Yes, but will it be enough?" Andy shrugged.

"Do you really have to go so soon?" Emily frowned, abruptly changing the subject to something that was of an immediate concern to her.

"Sorry Em but I did promise Burnsey."

She saw Andy to the door, then kissed him good night. Several minutes later, in the dull light of her bedroom, Emily offered up a silent prayer for her very special flyboy.

29
*

15 September, 1940

Four daylight raids had been hurled against London so far. On September the 7th the RAF was caught off guard thinking that the sector stations instead of the Capital would be hit. During the next three attacks cloud cover had hindered the Royal Observer Corp from providing Fighter Command with accurate information as to the size and progress of the raiders. This lack of solid data had made it difficult for Dowding and Park to place their fighter strengths. The result: fewer war planes were in the right place at the right time to greet the enemy. This apparent lack of numbers observed by the Luftwaffe pilots, and the decreased intensity of attacks on the He 111s, Do 17s and Ju 88s by the defenders, led Beppo Schimid and the Nazi hierarchy to assume that the Royal Air Force was indeed reduced to less than one-hundred Spitfires and Hurricanes. Goering's answer was to launch a massive strike against the British homeland in order to punish the city on the Thames, and to draw into the skies the remainder of the English fighters.

It was a sunny Sunday morning. A perfect day for cricket or football. Churchill arose that morning with a sense of impeding history and asked his wife Clemmintine if she'd like to accompany him to 11 Group Headquarters. Lady Churchill accepted her husband's invitation and shortly after finishing a hearty breakfast of scrambled eggs, fired tomatoes, kippers, and toast they departed for Uxbridge in their four ton armored car—a tank quality vehicle, equipped with one inch bullet-proof windows.

*

"Not much happening Mr. Prime Minister," Park, a hawk faced New Zealander, announced after the Churchills were seated in the upper gallery.

"Thank you so much for allowing us to be here." Mrs. Churchill smiled graciously.

"Yes, indeed," Winston S. Churchill blustered. "you know Park, I have a feeling that this will be momentous day."

No sooner had the P.M. spoken when a Group Captain urgently approached Park, "I beg your pardon sir, but Pevensey radar has reported two-hundred and fifty plus forming over Calais."

"If you'll excuse me Mr. Prime Minister and Lady Churchill, I'll see what this is all about."

The smoking lamp had once again been lit for Park's special guest. Churchill gratefully extracted a fresh *La Aroma de Cuba* cigar from a vest pocket and clamped it firmly between his teeth. An attentive Wing Commander standing nearby offered the senior statesman a light. The tension in the control centre mounted steadily as the beauty chorus, using their croupier rakes, pushed coloured blocks across the huge map table below. Jerry was coming over for a visit but tea and crumpets were not on the trolley.

*

Goering stood, half-stooped, on the viewing platform overlooking the cliffs at *Cap Griz Nez*. He peered through a set of pedestal mounted binoculars and was amazed at how close the English coastline appeared to be. Kesselring standing by the *Reichmarschall's* side looked to the east and was pleased to see his airfleet assembling. One-hundred and fifty bombers escorted by four-hundred and fifty fighters, poised for the kill, caused the *Generalfeldmarschall* to smile. This was the first of two raids that he'd planned for the 15th. Goering hearing the thunderous roar of massed formations looked up. As the armada drew closer, he covered his ears with the palms of his hands. The Fat man was confident that, by days end, his dream of air superiority would finally be realized.

*

"If all were right and proper old boy, we'd be at Brighton enjoying a day at the pier," Robbie Barnes sighed. The Panthers were outside in the morning sun slouched in deck chairs.

"Quite right, Burnsey." Basil Lewis agreed. He'd just arrived and handed his squadron leader a signal form.

"Two more lambs, I think." Woody predicted, watching attentively as Burnsey read the message.

"Likely from the King mate, we've finally been recognized as the best. Sherry and fruit cake at the palace." Knobby yawned openly.

"Probably a gong for Birdie," Paddy chuckled. "He's become a legend in his own mind."

"Sod off you great flit." Birdie countered, giving Paddy a playful jab on the shoulder.

"We're going up to the bonnie highlands for a wee rest." Gus brightened at the thought.

"Yeah, Scotch and scones with 13 Group would be gangbusters." Billy added.

"Betcha it's a weeks leave." Andy said, crossing his fingers.

"Well chaps, you'll have to give Woody the prize for reading the tea leaves. Two sprogs are being parachuted in on Tuesday."

"Jolly good sir, then I won't be the junior man." Twist looked pleased.

"Yes, and I'll lend you my razor for your first shave." Rex kidded the Sergeant Pilot.

George Kingsford had barely got the words out of his mouth when a Corporal charged out of the dispersal hut door and bellowed, "689, SCRAMBLE!!"

*

Five minutes later, while climbing through three-thousand, the Panthers were directed by sector control to hold station over London at Angels twenty. Park had assembled two-hundred 11 Group fighters to meet the German attack. The Air-Vice Marshall from New Zealand had also requested help from Leigh-Mallory in 12 Group. Douglas Bader's Big Wing responded and sixty Spitfires and Hurricanes departed Duxford to help defend the capital. The initial interceptions, however, were made along the coast as the massive air armada, fought a running battle inbound to their target.

The Messerschmitt 109s were at the limit of their range when the objective was reached. Dangerously low on fuel they were forced to abandon the bombers. Several of the Do 17s and He 111s, having been harassed by the British fighters as soon as they were over English soil, unloaded their bombs on small towns and villages. Those who made it through to the city on the Thames were unable to hit their assigned military targets and bombed indiscriminately. On the way back to France, without escort, the German bombers were extremely vulnerable to attack.

*

"Line abreast," Burnsey ordered as the ten Spitfires of Panther Squadron raced towards a formation of Heinkels.

"The one on the left Alley," Andy shouted over the R/T. Each pair of Spits had now picked out their individual targets and were about to open fire.

"Aye, Aye sir." Billy chortled.

An He 111 was right in the middle of Andy's reflector gunsight when he pressed the firing button. The Spit shuddered from the recoil and slowed slightly. Andy frantically rammed the stick forward and ducked instinctively as the greenhouse-like nose of the Heinkel streaked by, five feet above his canopy. He quickly took a quick peek at the rear view mirror and saw smoke coming from the port engine of the 111.

*

Recovering from the dive Andy found himself in different part of the sky. He searched the horizon and spotted three Ju 88s setting up for their bombing run. Andy pulled the plug for emergency boost and flew straight at the lead Junker. He waited until he was within two hundred yards of the enemy aircraft before squeezing the tit. He'd hit something vital because a stream of oil shot out of the 88s starboard engine. Andy again dove below the crippled bomber. His dive was a shallow one and he quickly located the second of the trio. This time he launched a beam attack and was successful in hitting the wing tanks of the Junkers.

Flames soon engulfed the bomber and it began a death dive towards London Bridge. The pilot of the Ju 88 escaped through the hatch under the cockpit and immediately opened his chute. Andy tried to avoid hitting the falling German but the parachute had wound itself around the starboard wing of the Spitfire. Andy violently banked the Spit left, then right, to get rid of the unwanted drag and was gratefully relieved when the chute, with the German attached, slid off his wingtip. By some miracle the parachute opened and the stunned pilot began his descent towards the centre of the city. Andy wondered what kind of reception the enemy airman would get.

*

Several minutes later Andy, positioned in front of the remaining Junker, had lined up the 88 for a head-on attack. When he pressed the firing button nothing happened, his ammunition boxes were empty. Andy, his fighting blood at fever pitch and scenes from the walk through the streets of London playing like a horror movie on the silver screen of his minds eye, hungered for revenge. Deliberately and with purpose he angled his port wing toward the tail fin of the bomber. The impact was catastrophic. In less than a second the tail section of the Junkers was sheared off and the bomber was transformed into a flying sledgehammer. The stress on the wings was tremendous and the tips crumpled as if they were made of twigs and paper. Andy fought for control of his Spitfire but the wounded Supermarine slammed into an inverted dive. Fighting the wicked G forces that held him in place he managed to smash open the canopy and get his upper body into the slipstream. Andrew James was sucked out of the cockpit like a speck of dust drawn up by a vacuum hose. His free fall took him well below the air battle and finally clear of the action he pulled the ripcord. The chute was twisting and turning but Andy managed to shake the guy ropes hard enough to stop the spinning. Victoria Station was directly below and he marvelled at the pile of junk in the forecourt that moments before had been a Ju 88.

Andy was coming down rapidly over a series of row houses in Pimlico. He attempted to land in the street, but a gust of wind forced him onto the slate roof of a three story building. He tried desperately to gain a foot hold on the slippery surface but tumbled forward over the gutters. Andrew James figured he'd be a mass of broken bones, if his neck didn't snap, when he collided with the sidewalk below. Andy braced himself for shattered ankles and legs, but at the last moment the harness tightened noose-like around his shoulders and upper thighs. The chute had caught on an up-pipe and his fall was stopped. Andy quickly hit the release mechanism and thankfully walked away.

Two very pretty young ladies had been watching his progress from across the street. Once they saw that Andy was unhurt and safe, the pair of English beauties ran towards him, "You're one of those fighter boys, aren't you love?" a raven haired, full figured nineteen-year-old gushed breathlessly.

"Yes miss," Andy blushed.

"Such a brave lad," a flaxen haired, blue eyed lovely swooned.

Before he could stop her, the brunette had thrown her arms around him and was kissing him full on the mouth. "A hero is what you are love," she gasped, reluctantly releasing Andy from the embrace.

The blond wanted her turn and didn't hesitate in duplicating her friends greeting."A regular knight in shinning armor." she cooed.

Several other women and men had arrived on the scene. The girls showered Andy with kisses and hugs and the men gratefully shook his hand. A police car screeched to halt in front of the crowd that had gathered and two Bobbies pushed their way through, "Are you the one who brought down the Jerry?" a burly constable asked.

"Y-yes sir, Andy stammered.

"Bloody great show!" the second of the two coppers enthused.

"Is there anyway you can help me get back to Stonecroft?" Andy pleaded.

"Hop in lad," the stocky constable smiled. "we'll have you there in half-a-mo."

The police officer, who drove the car, knew his way around the bomb damaged streets and with the siren blaring they set a land speed record across the top of the Capital. Andy was back at his home base and reporting to Holmes in less than an hour.

"The collision was accidental you say?" Holmes looked unconvinced.

"Yeah, I misjudged my dive and clipped his tail." Andy flashed a winning, choir boy smile.

"And the other two crashed somewhere on outskirts of the city?"

"I suspect so Holmes, but I didn't see them hit the ground."

"With all the ack-ack crews around, we should have a confirmation for you soon old chap." Holmes beamed at the possibility of another three chalked up to the Panthers.

*

Andy hurried over to the flight line and found his ground crew working feverishly on a factory new Spitfire. He chatted for a minute or two and they assured him that the kite was ready to go. Andrew James then entered the dispersal hut. He counted heads immediately and was relieved to find everyone there. He grabbed a sandwich and wolfed down the greasy bully beef as it were a feed of tender sirloin steak. Between mouthfuls he told his squadron mates what had happened. The 689 pilots were glad to hear about the three Junkers he'd brought down but the thing that impressed them the most was his reception at Pimlico.

"Should've dragged some of those Sheilas over here mate." Knobby leered.

"Shame on you Dunc, a guy who's engaged needs to be more careful." Billy kidded.

"Must've been wizard old boy to have all those popsies after you, and not a word to Emily chaps." Burnsey winked.

"Come on fellas, give me a break, I didn't have my hockey stick to fend them off." Andy led them on.

"Aye laddie, I usually carry a cricket bat when the lassies get too friendly." Gus added to the good humour.

Once again the light banter was brought to standstill by the ring of the telephone and the urgent scramble call. The British newspapers were calling this phase of the war the 'Battle of London'.

It was now late afternoon and the Luftwaffe had sent over three-hundred bombers escorted by six-hundred Me 109s. A running battle was fought up the Thames Estuary and many of the 111s, 17s and 88s were forced away from their targets. A massive dogfight, fighter against fighter, broke out over the approaches to London and the RAF traded blows, one on one, with the nimble Messerschmitts. The 109s, again low on fuel, were forced to leave the scrap early—red warning lights winking incessantly on their instrument panels. Those bombers, who did reach a target area had to run the fighter gauntlet, unescorted, on their return to the continent. One group of Heinkels lost eleven out of the eighteen that had taken off from French soil two hours before.

At the underground operations centre at Uxbridge, Churchill watched the tote boards that showed the status of all the squadrons in action. He looked concerned and questioned Air-Vice Marshall Park who was standing next to the Prime Minister's chair, "Tell me Park, what other reserves have we?"

"There are none." Keith Park replied tersely, his craggy face, drawn and pale.

Churchill puffed nervously on his cigar while Park contemplated the disaster that lay ahead if further fifty plus raids were to attack his airfields. The Hurricanes and Spitfires would be caught on the ground, easy prey for marauding bombers and *zerstoerers.* The Air-Vice Marshall remained taut as a guitar string until, thirty minutes later, the tote board showed that No. 213 at Tangmere had pancaked, refuelled and rearmed.

Slowly but surely other Squadrons came to readiness and the crisis was over. The gamble of throwing everything at the Luftwaffe had paid off.

The air battle of September 15th was a stunning victory for the RAF. The headline in the *Daily Express* the next day boasted to the world: **175 SHOT DOWN.** In the heat of a dogfight it wasn't unusual for two or more pilots to claim the same aircraft destroyed. One setting an engine on fire, another clobbering the second engine and still another seeing the crew bail out after his attack. When the charred carcasses of German fighters and bombers, that had actually crashed on English soil, were tallied up the figures read; fifty-eight destroyed for the loss of twenty-nine Spitfires and Hurricanes. The Panthers had accounted for six of these victories and No. Canadian had its best day so far with three shot down. Leigh-Mallory's Big Wing, still having problems assembling in time, arrived late and below the raiders for its second engagement of the day and were bested by the snappers.

The next day Goering tried to make light of the situation and proclaimed to the Fuehrer that he could still rule the skies over Britain in four or five days. The *Reichmarschall ordered* Kesselring to launch another daylight raid on the 18th. It achieved little success and a large group of unescorted Ju 88s, attacking in the late afternoon, were mauled by one-hundred Spitfires and Hurricanes.The Duxford Wing arrived on time and claimed thirty destroyed but German records later proved they had shot down only four. That night Bomber Command put the finishing touches on the Fat Man's pipe dream. A fleet of twin-engined Wellington, Whitley and Hampden bombers raided the invasion ports; sinking 150 landing barges and blowing up a major ammunition dump.

Hitler and the OKW, disappointed by the poor performance of the Luftwaffe and fearing the Channel's late September storms, in addition to the threat posed by the Royal Navy, went into a huddle regarding 'Sealion'.

The Nazi quarterback emerged on the 19th and issued a secret directive stating that the English Invasion would be postponed until the spring. Somewhere in the deep recesses of his bent, megalomaniacal mind, Hitler knew he would never again assemble a fleet of barges and battle hardened divisions of infantry to assault the shores of Great Britain. He now looked to the planning of Operation 'Barbarossa' the conquest of the Soviet Union. The two front war his Generals dreaded would eventually become a reality.

30
*

21 September, 1940

It was the first day of fall. The autumnal equinnox slithered in, accompanied by a chilling drizzle and light winds. The only activity of the day had been the usual reconnaissance flights by several Do. 215s. The Panthers, at dispersal since first light, were becoming restless.

"Either scramble us, or call for a stand down."Rex groused.

"Perhaps it'll clear sir," Brian Barker, a straw haired, blue eyed, pasty faced Sergeant Pilot fresh from 6 OTU, smiled brightly.

"Bad weather's good Pup," Birdie shifted in his chair. "it makes Jerry sleepy." After Birdie had been introduced to Sergeant Pilot Brian Anderson Barker at the Sergeants mess, he thought for a moment and came up with Pup for a nickname. Sergeant Barker protested loudly but the label stuck like a wasp to flypaper.

"We'll get a chance soon though won't we sir?" Peter Winslow, a tall, slender eighteen-year-old whose curly, black hair needed brushing, squeaked nervously to his Squadron Leader.

"Not to fret Pooh old chap, Fritz will be over soon enough." Burnsey smiled reassuringly.

"Holy mackerel, Pooh Winslow and Pup Barker," Billy shook his head, "we sure get some good ones around here don't we Twist?"

"Not very creative though sir." Oliver Wendel Miller lamented, while staring out the window at the gathering scotch mist.

Brian Barker had been assigned to Green section and Peter Winslow to Red. They'd just converted to Spits with barely thirty hours between them. Two days of duff weather, however, had allowed Burnsey and Woody to take the newly arrived sprogs up, in the clearer skies to to the west, for some much needed airwork.

Squadron Leader Barnes and Flight Lieutenant Woodston were impressed by the flying abilities of the rookie pilots. The Panthers, now at full strength, hadn't been in action since the 18th, and there were no complaints from the war weary aviators.

"Look at this chaps," Basil Lewis shouted, as he charged through the dispersal hut door. "it's the King, he'll be here in two days!"

"I say Uncle, settle down, what's the gen?" Burnsey chided the exuberant Adjutant.

"S-Sorry Robbie. Gongs, three bloody gongs!"

"That's great mate but who gets the brass pot?" Knobby jumped to his feet.

"Burnsey's to be awarded the Distinguished Service Order, Dunc and Knobby will get the Distinguished Flying Cross!"

The pilots, now standing in line a stern formation, back slapped, bear hugged or shook the hands of the proud recipients. When the pandemonium had ended Gus frowned before saying, "It's not the bonnie wee Palace then Uncle."

"Jerry's hit the Royal Residence twice now Gus. London's a mess as you well know, besides, his Majesty feels more a part of things if he visits the dromes."

When Buckingham Palace was bombed by the Luftwaffe on the 7th the bombs failed to explode but on the 13th the Royal couple narrowly missed being killed. Queen Elizabeth remarked to her husband, "Thank God Bertie, I can at last look the people of the East End in the eye knowing that we've had a close call too."

The King and Queen had been booed when they first visited the ravaged East End. There had been civil unrest bordering on a workers uprising when the housing area around the docks was badly damaged by the Blitz. Communist agitators had stirred up the Eastenders and petitions were drawn up demanding that Churchill sue for pease. Now that the West End of the capital as well as the Palace were under attack the momentum of the mini-revolution had slowed to a snails pace.

The poorer sections of London were now squarely behind the government and the monarchy.

"I was thinking brandy and shortbreads at Buckingham mate." Knobby looked disappointed.

"Not to worry old chap," Burnsey patted the towering Aussie on the shoulder. "we can have bully beef on crackers when the King visits the mess."

*

The entire base was on parade the day the forty-five-year-old King of England paid a visit to Stonecroft. George VI was a military man in his own right having served in the Royal Navy at the Battle of Jutland during the Great War and with the Royal Air Force after World War One. Burnsey was presented first. The King, wearing an RAF uniform, took time to chat with the popular Squadron Leader. Knobby was next and the King was delighted by the easy manner of the Flight Lieutenant from down under. Andy being the junior most in rank was presented last. He marched smartly across the tarmac and came to a halt three feet from the King. George VI stepped forward and pinned the DFC medal underneath the wings sown onto Andy's tunic. The King stepped back a pace and Andy saluted smartly. The King then reached out and shook hands with Andrew James. Much to Andy's surprise the British Monarch asked him several questions, "I-I see f-from your record Pilot Officer Duncan that you c-come from British Columbia." the King had a stammer which caused him embarrassment when he spoke in public, but it would usually disappear if he was speaking one on one.

"Yes sir, Campbell River on Vancouver Island."

"You know, my father, after the war, talked to me about an RFC pilot Major James Duncan. He'd presented him with a DSO and MC at the Palace."

"That's my dad sir!"

"Remarkable, we have father and son serving in two different wars. I believe our Commonwealth will, in the long run, be our greatest strength in helping to defeat Hiltler."

"I think you're right sir, the Panthers have an Aussie, a Kiwi, a Canuck and a Flight Lieutenant from South Africa on the roster, so the Commonwealth's well represented here."

"That's splendid Duncan and I hope to speak to you again at the reception in the officers mess."

"Yes sir," Andy smiled, before about facing and marching briskly back to the ranks.

*

Burnsey had assigned Andy the task of being the first to offer His Majesty a drink at the mess. When the Royal Monarch, accompanied by Wing Commander Stevens, came through the door Andrew James stepped forward and spoke to the King, "Sir it's my houour to welcome you to the Panther's mess." Andy was very nervous and blurted. "How about a pint of bitter sir?"

George VI, a whiskey drinker, smiled politely before saying, "That's most generous of you Duncan, a pint would be perfect." The King had been taught, an early age, to be receptive to whatever his host or hostess had to offer.

"Coming right up, and you sir?" Andy turned to the Wingco.

"Bitter please Andy." Stevens nodded politely.

Robbie Barnes was standing next to Andy when he placed his order and spoke softly,"Are you daft old boy, the King prefers Scotch."

"He said he wanted a beer Burnsey, so that's what he's getting." Andy whispered back.

*

Andy returned with three pints of fine English Ale and handed one to the King and one to the Wingco. George VI took a sip of the dark brew and smiled appreciatively, "Tell me Andrew," the King said trying to put the young Canadian at ease. "does your father ever talk about the Great War."

"No sir, he's as close mouthed as a clam when it comes to his days in the Royal Flying Corp."

The King seemed pleased by Andy's answer and said, "Yes, I find that too with many veterans I visit at hospitals. It's a time they prefer to forget."

"Are your daughters staying in London sir?" Andy abruptly changed the subject, wanting to steer the conversation away from the Great War and the suffering it had caused.

"No, we think it's safer if they remain at Windsor Castle," the King brightened now that he was talking about his children. "Lilibet is planning to make a short speech on the BBC's children's hour and Margaret keeps the Queen busy answering a multitude of questions about the war. "

Andy could see the King was beginning to look around the room and knew he'd want to meet, and talk with other members of the Squadron, "If you'll excuse me sir," Andy improvised. "I have something to discuss with my wingman."

"Of course Duncan, good luck and good hunting." The King shook Andy's hand before he and Wing Commander Stevens joined Burnsey, Knobby and Woody who were standing at the bar. George VI gratefully accepted a glass of single malt from S/L Robert Daniel Barnes after dutifully finishing his pint of bitter.

31

*

Later that day Andy was granted permission to leave the base in order to attend a reception, held in his honour, at Emily's townhouse. The gathering had been arranged by Lord Anthony Smith-Barton. Emily was on duty at Bentley Priory during the medals presentation at Stonecroft and was anxious to congratulate her finance in person.
It also provided Tony Smith-Barton with an opportunity to meet his future son-in-law.

After knocking on the door of the fine residence at Berkeley square, Andy was astonished when a butler greeted him and took his great coat. The elderly servant, who'd been in the employ of the Smith-Barton family for thirty years, ushered Andy into the crowded living room. Emily's father, a handsome, stately man, whose dark hair was greying at the temples, was in conversation with Lord Beaverbrook, but jumped to his feet when he saw Andy enter the room and asked for everyone's attention.

"Ladies and Gentlemen," his Lordship resonated, while striding towards Andy then shaking his hand. "it gives me great pleasure to introduce you to my future son-in-law Pilot Officer Andrew James Duncan DFC."

A round of spontaneous applause erupted from the upper crust crowd. "T-Thank you sir," Andy stammered. "it sure is swell to meet you and your friends."

Emily was half-way down the stairs when her father had spoken. Abandoning any pretence at lady-like behavior she took the runners two at a time and launched herself into Andy's arms just as he said friends.

After a breathless kiss she turned to the small but appreciative audience, who were now on their feet smiling warmly at the young couple, and burbled. "Daddy has presented Drew as his future son-in-law but I'd like you to meet the man I love."

Andy was escorted around the room and introduced to some of the most influential people in England.

The last person to acknowledge Andy was Lord Beaverbrook, "It's a pleasure to meet a fellow Canadian." the Minister of Aircraft Production, spoke in a dry nasal tone.

"The honour's all mine sir," Andy responded gallantly. "thank you for supplying us with Spitfires and Hurricanes, without them I'd be out of a job"

"That's a good one Andrew," Tony Smith-Barton chuckled.

"Yes indeed Duncan, but without you 'few', as Winston calls the brave pilots of the RAF, we'd all be out of work."

"Uncle Max," Emily squeezed Beaverbrook's arm. "you're becoming quiet a wit these days."

"Emily my dear child, I'm always flattered when you call me uncle. She's a charmer as you've obviously noticed Duncan."

"Indeed she is sir, and Lord Anthony you have my word that I'll take good care of her." Andrew James affirmed, a lump forming in his throat.

"Andy, I can't tell you how happy it makes me to see Emily so full of life again. As you know, she's had some rough years, and thank God they're over."

"Tony," Beaverbrook interrupted, "aren't we forgetting our other special guest?"

"Yes we are Max, and thank you for reminding me," the name on Beaverbrook's birth certificate was Max Aitken,"if you'll excuse us for a moment darling we'll take Andy down to the billiard room."

"Of course Daddy, but not for too long." she smiled boldly at Andrew James.

Anthony Smith-Barton led Andy and Beaverbrook into the kitchen. He then entered the large panty. Hidden behind a plain looking door was an elevator. The three men stepped into the elevator and it started to move. Andy had never seen this part of the house before and was becoming apprehensive as the lift wound slowly downwards.

As soon as the door opened, Andy mouth agape, immediately recognized the person sitting in an over stuffed leather chair on the far side of a finely crafted billiard table.

Winston S. Churchill rose slowly to his feet, placed a half-smoked Cuban cigar in an ashtray by the chair and approached the trio who'd just gotten off the elevator.

"Congratulations on the DFC Duncan," Churchill rumbled. "the Empire and the free world will forever be in debt to you glorious airmen."

Andy grasped the out stretched hand and shook it. Everything had taken on a dream like quality and he fought off an urge to pinch himself to find out if it were real, "Sir, I-I think your fine speeches have been just as important."

"Very kind of you to say so Duncan and I believe the tide has finally turned on Hitler. It's not the end or the beginning of the end but I do think we've turned a corner."

"Poor London's suffering Winston, but I suspect when the history books are written this change in Nazi tactics from airfields to reprisals will be recorded as a key element in our ultimate victory." Tony Smith-Barton orated.

"My goodness Tony, you should start writing Winston's speeches. That's brilliant." Beaverbrook snorted.

Churchill cleared his throat before saying. "Maybe you should go into politics Tony, and Max, you'd make a fine P.M. someday."

"Good God no, I want a real job." Max Aitken kidded the Prime Minister.

"It may come as a surprise to you Duncan," Churchill began after the laughter had subsided. "but I knew your father during the Great War."

"That's strange sir, because my dad never mentioned meeting you or anyone else for that matter. I was really astounded when the King told me about his father presenting medals to Pop."

"I take it that the Major never talks about the war." Lord Beaverbrook interjected.

"Never is an understatement sir," Andy stated flatly, "to my dad, his days in the RFC are a closed book."

Churchill frowned before saying, "I spent several rather unpleasant months on the Western Front as a Colonel."

A fleeting glimmer of terror mixed with grief showed in the eyes of Winston Churchill and he wiped away a tear before continuing, "I can truly understand the reluctance on the part of Major Duncan. He was a true warrior, but he's wise to keep events prior to the Armistice in a tightly locked cupboard."

The Prime Minister of Great Britain was greatly relieved to hear Andy's comments for a very good reason. Towards the end of the Great War, Jimmy Duncan, had flown a secret agent behind enemy lines. The spy's mission was to contact Kaiser Wilhelm and persuade him to give up his throne. The reward was political asylum for the German Monarch in Holland, and the guarantee that he would never have to face charges as a war criminal. The Kaiser agreed and abdicated on November the 9th, 1918. Two days later the German government accepted the terms of an Armistice and the First World War was over. Churchill, following the orders of King George V, had helped to plan the covert operation and didn't want it to become public. The wise old statesman knew that the British people would not be happy with anyone who'd made a deal with Kaiser Bill. Nearly one million English soldiers, sailors and airmen had been killed in the conflict and the British populace would've cheered loud and long if the German King had of been executed.

"Well now Duncan, if you'll excuse me I have to get back to the war room and meet with the King." Churchill smiled, while again offering his hand.

"I really liked the King sir, and please send him my regards." Andy beamed.

"I certainly will Andrew," Churchill called over his shoulder, as he hurried to a set of stairs that led to a laneway at the back of the townhouse. George VI and the Prime Minister would compare notes on their individual meetings with Pilot Officer Andrew James Duncan and conclude that Royal Flying Corp Major James Angus Duncan had, as he promised, remained silent about the Kaiser Wilhelm affair.

The guests didn't stay late. Beaverbrook and Tony Smith-Barton left early as well. They worked fourteen hour days and needed a good nights rest. Lady Smith-Barton, Emily's mother, was at their estate near Foreness. Lord Anthony considered it safer for his wife to be home managing things while London was under attack.

The early departure of family and guests allowed Andy and Emily a short period of time together before the young pilot had to leave for Stonecroft. He'd borrowed the Squadron's Austin, the legacy of Turnip and Rosey, so he'd be able to drive back to the base and hopefully arrive before midnight.

"Daddy thought you were smashing Drew." Emily sighed.

"Yours father's a wonderful guy and does he ever work hard. There's no way I'd be able to keep up with him and the Beaver."

"Yes, their efforts in keeping fighter production at high levels will certainly help us to win the Battle." Emily stated proudly.

"Hey, enough about the war. Can we go up to your bedroom? I'd like to show you my DFC."

"Drew's Fantastic Club, is that what you mean darling." Emily smiled wickedly.

"I-I m-meant, boy you sure have a way with words Lady Smith-Barton."

"I ain't no lady tonight cowboy." Emily purred enticingly, anticipating a joyous joining with Andrew's very exclusive club.

A sleepy Pilot Officer Duncan was an hour late in returning to the base but Burnsey, in a forgiving mood, gently admonished Andy by saying, tongue-in-cheek, the next morning, "I suspect old boy that your tardiness was likely due to cockpit problems."

32

*

27 September, 1940

The sun was shining and the RAF meteorological boffins had proudly announced that ceiling and visibility were unlimited. Kesselring, given the same information by his Luftwaffe weather guessers, launched a major raid on London. It was approaching high noon when the coastal radar stations began reporting a build-up of two-hundred plus over the *Pas de Calais*. The Panthers were about to sit down to lunch when the order to readiness came through. Reluctantly they left a table heavy with thick roast beef sandwiches and walked towards dispersal where the pilots waited to be scrambled.

"Jerry's no bloody manners mate," Knobby complained loudly. "you'd think those bleedin' Nazi mothers would've brought them up better, so they wouldn't interrupt a blokes lunch."

"Oh come on Knobby, their mothers are just like anybody else's. There's no way they're all card carrying Nazis." Billy retorted.

"Yeah, and they're all good at making, sauerkraut, wiener schnitzel, apple strudel and all those other German dishes." Andy added to the banter.

"Quite right dear boy and in the summer the men all wearing lederhosen and yodel, or perhaps that's the Swiss." Burnsey continued to stir the pot.

"Never met a dead Nazi I didn't like, I think." Woody put in his two cents worth.

"Aye, we've managed to send a few to their wee Valhalla." Gus led them on.

"Excuse me sir, but I think that's where the Vikings go." Pup Barker made an attempt to correct Gus.

"Pup's right sir," Birdie chipped in. "they use an old boat and burn it up at sea instead of burying their warriors."

"Better than being a flamer in a Spit." Rex said brightly.

"My God sir, that would be horrible way to go."

"Always have a Webley tucked in your flight boot Pooh." Paddy advised solemnly.

"Hey cut it out you guys we've gone from Jerry's poor manners to blowing your brains out." Billy was suddenly serious.

"Relax Alley, Paddy isn't that far off base. As a matter of fact, I just about pulled that stunt when I figured my Spit was going to burn." Andy cringed at the memory.

"Bloody cherry stuff mate, now let's talk about Shielas."

"Well in that case old chap there was this terrific popsie I used to know at Cambridge. She had the biggest pair of...." Before Burnsey could finish the scramble call was sounded and the Panthers sprinted for their Spitfires.

*

"Fox-trot control, Panther leader, climbing through angels six."

"Panther leader Fox-trot control. I have trade for you, vector one-zero- zero, forty plus bandits at angels fifteen."

"Roger fox-trot control. Red leader to all sections, battle climb now."

*

Ten minutes later Paddy's excited voice punctured the airwaves, "Red leader, Red two, fifty plus Ju 88s at twelve o'clock low."

"I see them Red two. Has anyone spotted the escorts?"

Twelve pairs of eyes searched the skies for several seconds before Andy spoke into his oxygen mask mic," Red leader, blue two, no snappers anywhere."

Andy was credited with the sharpest eyesight in the Squadron and his report was all that was needed,"Roger blue two, all sections Tally Ho!" Burnsey trumpeted over the static.

The Panthers were the first to intercept the bombers and made a head-on attack. This, as usual, had the effect of breaking up part of the formation as well as damaging several of the lead aircraft.

"Mine on the right Alley." Andy shouted over the R/T.

"He's all yours pardner," Billy acknowledged.
Andy squeezed the red firing button and gave the bomber, that was growing large in his wind screen, a four second burst. Andrew watched intently as a flood of tracers hammered the cockpit of the 88. At the last moment he jammed the stick forward and howled below the stricken German aircraft. Billy and the rest of the Panthers had duplicated Andy's tactic and the Junker formation began to disperse.

By now several Hurricane squadrons had arrived and they were able to pick out isolated targets. Many of the Ju 88s jettisoned their bomb loads before trying desperately to escape the angry British fighters. The attempted raid on London had been thwarted and the fast Luftwaffe bombers were forced to abandon their mission.

It would have been an absolute slaughter if the 109s and 110s had not made a belated appearance.

*

"Break left Twist." Knobby warned.

The young Sergeant Pilot wasted no time in reacting to his section leaders command. He slammed the agile Spit into a vertical bank. When his greying vision cleared Twist was able make out an Me 110 in front of him. He pulled the plug for full emergency boost and several heart beats later his Spitfire shuddered under the recoil of eight browning machine guns. The *zerstoerer* began to belch white glycol smoke and started to dive away. Twist immediately gave chase and poured a river of lead into the engines of the Messerschmitt. It pulled up sharply then fell off into a spin. Twist knew better than to watch it crash into the fields below, instead he kept scanning the skies.

The English squadrons now had their hands full with the German fighters and the bombers were able to make their escape. One by one, however, the 109s had to leave the air battle due to low fuel reserves. The Me 110's, no match for a Hurri or Spit, soon followed suit. It was a decisive victory for the RAF.

Fifty-five German aircraft, nearly all bombers, had been destroyed for the loss of twenty-eight Hurricanes and Spitfires. Many of the RAF pilots were able to safely bail out and return to their bases.

*

One of the Hurri squadrons that had joined the Panthers in the attack on the Junkers was No. 1 Canadian. They had their best day so far with seven confirmed victories. There would be a raucous thrash in their favorite Northholt pub that evening. Ernest Archibald McNab and his squadron mates from across the pond had come a long way since the last week in August. The pilots from Canada had every reason to be proud as the Royal Canadian Air Force was the only air force other than the RAF to take part in the Battle of Britain.

*

The last day of the ninth month saw the determined Luftwaffe try again. Shortly after 9:00 a.m. Rye radar reported a large formation gathering across the Channel. When the raid reached the coast of England, Park was informed by the Royal Observer Corp that it was a massive sweep of 109s. The Air-Vice Marshall concluded this was a diversion and refused to release his fighters. By 10:00 a.m two *Gruppen* of Ju 88s had gathered over the continent and set course for London. Once again their escort failed to join them on time and the Junkers were set upon by 150 Spitfires and Hurricanes above the Kent and Sussex countryside. The English fighters had a field day shooting down a dozen bombers. The rest of the Junkers dropped their ordinance where ever they could and fled for home. Things changed drastically, however, when the snappers finally arrived to protect the retreat of the 88s.

"Behind you Dunc!" Billy screamed over the R/T.

Pilot Officer Andrew James Duncan was too late in reacting and the Me 109, that had plummeted out of the sun, pumped a stream of cannon shells into the tail of his Spit. The badly damaged kite slammed into a vertical dive, but Andy managed to fight his way out of the cockpit.

Without thinking he pulled the ripcord as soon as he was clear of the Spitfire. The parachute deployed quickly and Andy began a floating descent towards mother earth. His blood ran cold when he heard the roar of a Daimler-Benz engine coming from behind. Andy braced himself for the deadly spray of 7.9 mm slugs that would end his life. The chatter of the guns was horrifying and he knew in a mirco-second it would all be over.

Two short gasps later, and still part of the living world, he marvelled at the roiling orange-black cloud expanding before him. Billy had followed Andy down, and just before the German pilot opened fire, the kid from Saginaw blasted the snapper with his eight Brownings. A multitude of de Wilde incendiary rounds ripped apart the main gas tank of the 109, transforming it instantly into a raging fireball. Billy flew wide, sweeping circles around his best friend and only left when Andy had safely landed in a Sussex farmyard. Alley performed a victory roll, then zoomed low over the farm, waggling his wings, before setting a course for Stonecroft.

Andy had landed beside a thatched roofed, fieldstone farmhouse and was immediately greeted by the farmer and his wife. The large, rawboned man of the land brought a chair out of his parlor and placed it near the steps to his home. He suggested that Andy would be more comfortable in the fresh, warm fall air than in their stuffy house. His pleasantly plump, rosy cheeked wife conjured up a cup of tea and several shortbread cookies for the downed aviator, and when Andy started to relax, he began to feel like a Lord of Sussex.

"Get any of those Nazi devils?" the wife asked.

"One Junkers won't be home for lunch." Andy grinned.

"That's bloody marvelous lad. You're on Spitfires then?" the farmer beamed, as if he'd gained the victory over the 88.

"Yes sir, out of RAF Stonecroft."

"I take it by your accent young man, that you're an American. I can tell by the flicks I've seen." the wife stated proudly.

"You're close ma'am, I'm from Canada."

"You were a Mountie before the war then lad?" the farmer folded his arms across his chest, now very sure of his geography.

"No sir," Andy chuckled. "I was going to go back to school to become a doctor.

"From Canada are you?" the wife said. "you'll know my cousin Daisy in Toronto then."

"Sorry, I'm from Vancouver Island, it's about twenty-five-hundred miles west of where your cousin lives."

Andy could see that the farmer and his wife were having a hard time comprehending such a distance and was about to explain further when two Home Guard officers came charging down the lane.

"Saw your Spit crash." the Home Guard Lieutenant said, while pulling a flask from his jacket.

"Saw your parachute come down." the Home Guard Captain said, looking pleased with himself.

"If that's tea you're drinking lad, I think whiskey's best for shock." the Home Guard Lieutenant offered his flask.

"I'm just fine." Andy protested, but he politely took a swig anyway.

"And have a nip from mine as well." the Captain said, while extracting a pint of brandy from his coat pocket. "Brandy in my opinion is preferred for treating shock."

Andy took a hefty mouthful of the rough liquor and smacked his lips appreciatively, "Thank you sir, I feel better already." Andy smirked, his head begining to assume a slow breast stroke.

"Here, stop that you two. You'll get the poor lad drunk." the wife protested.

"Time to get him to headquarters Mildred." the Captain nodded authoritatively.

"Good luck then lad." the farmer said, while shaking Andy's hand.

"Thank you sir and you too ma'am." Andy slurred his words slightly after downing another shot of single malt.

Headquarters turned out to the local pub and Andrew James was greeted as a conquering hero. Having been plied with food and drink, Andy was roaring drunk by the time an Army truck arrived to take him back to Stonecroft. This was the best bail out he'd had so far, and he was extremely grateful to be alive.

*

It had been another bad day for the brass hats back in the Third Reich. The tally sheet at Luftwaffe headquarters showed forty-six aircraft had failed to return. Kesselring in conference with Goering added up the figures for the 27th and 30th. One-hundred and one destroyed stood out like a Union Jack in Berlin and the conclusion was obvious. The losses were unacceptable and if they continued, in time, the Luftwaffe would be severely weakened. Goering therefore issued an order that put an end to daylight raids by twin engined bombers. They would instead, concentrate their bomber forces on night attacks.

*

The Royal Air Force had yet to perfect airborne interception radar and the few Blenheims that carried the AI sets were two slow to catch the fast German bombers, even if they showed on the British airborne radar screens. The Spitfire and Hurricane night fighter pilots, based on combat experience, had found that locating a bomber in the dark over London was like searching for a virgin in a Soho brothel.

The anti-aircraft guns were not assisted by altitude determing radar, and the best they could do was to put up a continual barrage with the hope of a lucky shot. The sounds of the guns repetitive firing was also thought to be a morale booster for the beleaguered citizens of the Capital. If an enemy aircraft was illuminated by a searchlight beam for a minute or two then ack-ack crews had a chance, but mostly they were firing blind. The Germans would rule the night skies for several months yet to come.

33
*

6 October, 1940

Burnsey had been requested by Group to assign one of his sections to night fighter duties. Because Pilot Officer Andrew James Duncan was known to have exceptional vision, Robert Daniel Barnes ordered Blue section to volunteer for the task.

"Let me get this straight mate," Knobby seemed flustered. "you're giving us over to night work."

"Well after all old chap, I know you would have likely volunteered." Burnsey lit up a Woodbine.

"Come on Burnsey," Andy looked amazed. "this is a railroad special pure and simple."

"Quite right old boy, and following an old RAF tradition, I'm informing you that you've been selected by a higher authority to volunteer. King and Country, as they used to say in the Great War."

"Don't we get a vote or somethin'?" Billy groused. "I thought that England had a Parliament and all that."

"Indeed she does old bean, and yes you could vote, but remember, by the good graces of the mob, my vote is the only one that counts."

"The mob being the Royal Air Force sir?" Twist groaned.

"Spot on Oliver, good fellow that you are." Burnsey inhaled a lung full of acrid smoke.

"Burnsey, I hate to say it mate, but you're turning into a Pommie bastard."

"It's lonely at the top dear boy." Burnsey smiled, knowing that the big Flight Lieutenant from down-under had accepted his decision to volunteer Blue section.

*

The weak light from the Glim Lamp flare path looked like a series of under fueled coal oil lanterns from a circuit altitide of one-thousand feet. Andy was on a base leg for Stonecroft in his Spitfire, which had recently been painted black.

Andrew James banked slowly and set up his final approach. He had excellent night vision and was able to make a respectable three point landing on the dew soaked, grass runway. Billy, two minutes behind made a three bouncer but stayed down. Knobby, Twist and Wing Commander Stevens were waiting for them on the flight line.

"Damned fine show. You all seem to be ready." the Wingco blustered, after salutes were exchanged.

Knobby knew there was no use in pleading for more time to train and said,"Bloody great stuff this night flying sir."

"Yeah, real wizard." Billy piped up.

"Glad you chaps think so, you're on ops tomorrow."

"Jeez, that's terrific sir." Andy forced a smile.

"It'll be a full moon sir." Twist noted, trying to sound upbeat.

"Jolly great fun this Hun hunting after dark." the Wingco burbled, before about facing and marching smartly back to his office.

"Jolly good way to get your ass in a sling." Billy mimicked, when Stevens was out of earshot.

*

The searchlights from below reminded Andy of the newsreels he'd seen in movie theatres of a Hollywood opening. A smear of broken, dark cloud at three thousand feet occasionally interfered with the powerful beams projected upward by the intensely bright, one-eyed monsters. Andrew James had been alerted by sector control to be on the lookout for a bandit that was somewhere near his current position. Twist had been right, it was a full moon and the visibility at this altitude, Andy guessed, was a mile or more in any given direction. Andy continually scanned the dimly lit instrument panel and the skies around him. He was getting tired when his eyes passed over the fuel gauges. A quick calculation suggested fifty minutes of flying time remained.

Looking upwards, and to the left, something stuck in his peripheral vision.

Andy blinked his eyes several times and tried to focus on what appeared to be a ghostly smudge in the star loaded sky. Instinctively he increased power and pulled back gently on the stick. The powerful Merlin responded immediately and the Spit climbed quickly towards the drifting blot above.

Andy peered forward through the eerie blue glow of the manifold exhaust that impaired his night vision. Bit-by bit, the ghostly image of an airplane started to coalesce in the moon bright darkness. As the aircraft slowly took shape Andy's heart began to hammer against his rib cage. It was a Henikel bomber flying straight and level on a track that would take it to the coast. Andy steadily gained on the He 111, keeping the Spit below and to the right side of the twin engined aircraft. Since he hadn't been spotted by the Luftwaffe crew, Andy approached to within one-hundred yards and carefully elevated the nose of the Spitfire until it was pointing at the starboard engine of the unsuspecting Heinkel. He inhaled deeply, then applied steady pressure to the firing button mounted on the control column. The Supermarine fighter shook like a dog ridding itself of excess water as a thousand sparkling de Wilde incendiary rounds pummeled the naked power plant of the Luftwaffe war machine. For several seconds the big bomber flew on apparently untouched. Suddenly, as if someone had soaked the starboard engine with gasoline and struck a match, flames shot skywards giving the vault of broken clouds above the appearance of a dull sunrise. The Heinkel, now a burning brand below the firmament, began an accelerating roll to port that ended in screaming vertical dive. Andy watched the man-made shooting star tumble downwards until it smashed into the darkened English countryside. Andrew James uttered a silent prayer of deliverance for anyone who might be near the crash site.

*

"It was pure horseshoes Holmes," Andy suppressed a yawn. "even under a full moon it's needle-in-the-haystack time up there."

"Dunc's right mate. Fritz has it all his own way at night." Alley and Twist, who were standing close by, nodded their heads vigorously at Knobby's assessment.

"But dear boy, congratulations are in order. After all, you did flame one of those Jerry bastards." Holmes spoke with more emotion than usual. His parents' house on the outskirts of London had been badly damaged by a bomb that had exploded in their backyard.

"Come on Holmes, "Billy stretched his arms. "we'd like to get some chow and a couple of shots before the sandman pays us a visit."

"Off you go then chaps," Sherlock Trowbridge heaved a deep sigh, as he began to put the finishing touches on another after action report.

*

The Germans were relentless in their nocturnal attacks. One of the reasons for the enemies continued success on cloudy or stormy nights, other than the obvious difficulties of interception, was a radio beam guidance system code-named *Knickebein*. A transmitter and antenna located in a fixed location on the continent produced two powerful high frequency overlapping radio signals with Morse dashes radiated in one and Morse dots in the other. A steady note was produced where the two beams converged. The pilot of a German bomber would fly along the constant whistle like-note and release his bombs when he detected a similar tone from a second transmitter which intersected the first signal over the target. If the pilot was left of his course he would hear Morse dots and to the right Morse dashes. A steady high pitched hum told him that he was on the beam. The system was accurate to within one square mile. This was good enough to hit most major centres in Great Briton. The Germans were no longer attempting to destroy military targets. It was strictly terror bombing, whose primary purpose was to kill and injure civilians. Hitler was extracting his revenge for the RAF raids on Berlin and delighted in viewing photographs of bomb damaged London.

British Intelligence led by the brilliant scientist Dr. R.V. Jones deduced that some form of guidance system was being used by the Germans and eventually discovered the radio signals. The RAF formed a dedicated group known as No. 80 Wing which developed specialized equipment to jam the beams. It was partially successful and not all Luftwaffe aircraft were able to complete their 'blind' bombing missions.

34
*

15 October, 1940

Blue section had been taken off night work. A full squadron once again, the Panthers latest task was to intercept Me 109 and Me 110 fighter-bombers that were attacking London. The tip-and-run raids, as Park called them, were all from altitudes of twenty-five thousand feet or greater. To have any hope of defeating these sky-high incursions, 11 Group was forced to mount standing patrols of Spitfires and Hurricanes. It took a Spit twenty-two minutes to reach angels twenty-five and only seventeen minutes for a snapper to reach the outskirts of the Capital, after the German fighter was detected by radar. Therefore, the Supermarines maintained fifteen-thousand feet during their watch over England. Three mile high patrol lanes were the maximum allowable without the pilots having to tap into their limited supply of oxygen. To make things more interesting 109s, unfettered with an external bomb loads, escorted the fighter-bombers. The bombing was inaccurate and did little serious damage, but Fighter Command was under tremendous pressure from the government to do something to stop this latest threat to the city on the Thames.

*

"Blue two to Red leader, bandits at three o'clock low." Andy's dry voice tickled the airwaves.

"Roger, Blue two, right where sector control said they'd be." Burnsey suppressed a cough. "Has anyone spotted the escort?"

"Too right mate, coming out of the sun now."

"Break," Burnsey ordered.

Six pairs of Spitfires peeled off in different directions. The combination of leader and wingman was the most effective way of dealing with being bounced from above. Andy and Billy soon found themselves hotly pursued by three snappers.

"On your tail Dunc," Billy hollered into the mic.

Andy saw the speck in his rear view mirror and slammed the kite into a vertical right bank. One of the 109s attempted to stay with the tightly turning Spitfire but slowly lost ground. Andy vision greyed under the heavy G-forces but he managed to remain conscious. The pilot of the Me, however, blacked out and went into a spin. Andy dove on the twisting Messerschmitt—a voracious eagle, talons extended. Andrew waited until the 109 filled his reflector gunsight before peppering the cockpit of the German fighter with a four second burst. The pilot was savaged by a torrent of high velocity chunks of lead that punctured his body like pins jabbed into a balloon. Andy could see that the Jerry was done for and began to rapidly rotate his head in order to spot Billy.

Pilot Officer William Allison had tried every trick in the book, and some that weren't written down, to shake the snapper that seemed to be attached to his rudder by a long elastic band. Billy let out a whoop of joy when he caught Andy's Spit in his peripheral vision.

Andrew James attacked the Messerschmitt from behind and below. A prolonged five second blast from the eight, wing mounted Brownings caused the engine of the 109 to emit a dense stream of black smoke. The damaged snapper immediately peeled off and fled east. They were over the coast by now and Andy, despite orders not to, pulled the plug for emergency boost and followed the German fighter out over the Channel. Billy did the same and the pair of Spitfires quickly closed on the Messerschmitt. Not realizing he was being chased by two British fighters, the 109 tried a half-roll off the top of a loop hoping to get on Andy's tail. Billy had the German square in his sights when the Luftwaffe pilot leveled off. He wasted no time and pummeled the wounded 109 with a deadly barrage of de Wilde incendiary rounds. The Me, its dead pilot slumped over the controls, pulled up sharply before plunging downwards into the sea.

The RAF pilots didn't have time to celebrate their victories as six 109s appeared suddenly out of the hazy, high overcast.

Andy and Billy, both out of ammunition, put their noses down and dove for the English coast. The snappers had divided up, three chasing each of the Spitfires. Andy jinked, twisted and turned in a desperate attempt to stay away from the lethal guns of the Messerschmitts. During a desperate side-slip maneuver he had a chance to glance at his rear view mirror. It was a short, horrifying moment that would haunt him for the rest of his life.

Billy's Spit had been hit in the gas tank directly in front of the cockpit. A dozen white phosphor cannon shells had ignited the highly flammable 100 octane gasoline and within the blink of an eye the Supermarine fighter was turned into a raging funereal pyre. Andy wiped his eyes with the back of his hand hoping that the nightmare would end, but it wouldn't go away. His best friend had just been cremated at four-hundred miles per hour.

One by one the snappers turned back to France as their fuel supplies ran low. Andy had taken several hits, but the Supermarine, throttle to the gate, was still airborne and heading towards a friendly coast. Just as Andy spotted RAF Hawkinge the remaining 109 fired, hitting the engine and radiator of the Spitfire. The snapper, now running on the fumes, turned one-hundred and eighty degrees hoping to make Calais before his tanks ran dry.

*

Andy had made it over the boundary of the grass runway and blew down his wheels. The aircraft was flaming and smoking—a fire-engine racing alongside as it rolled out. The Spitfire was still in motion when Andy jumped out of the cockpit and hurled himself onto the ground. The fire-truck followed the Supermarine fighter and sprayed it with foam as soon as it came to a stop.

*

"Come now sir, you've got to get a hold." a pimple faced, gap-toothed Flight Sergeant pleaded, trying for a second time to get Andy up off his knees.

"He was my best friend Flight," Andy sobbed.

"There, there sir," the NCO spoke softly. "let's get you over to the NAAFI for a nice cuppa char."

"He just blew up Flight," Andy chocked on the words. "one second he was there, and then nothing but a boiling, black hole in the sky."

By this time a Royal Air Force chaplain, who held the rank of a Flight Lieutenant, had arrived to assist the flustered Sergeant. The padre had witnessed Andy's landing and sensed that his services might be required before the young pilot reported to the I/O. Andy, now taking deep breaths and beginning to get his control back, told the chaplain what had happened.

"That's a tough one lad," the middle-aged minister comforted. " but you can be assured that your friend is now in a better place."

"Maybe so sir, but it was my fault. I should never have chased those Jerrys."

"You did what you thought was right lad and that's all that matters."

"What matters is; I'm responsible for the death of my best friend." Andy snarled.

"If you keep on that track old chap, it'll eat away at your soul." the chaplain stated firmly.

"Then I'll rot in hell!" Andy raised his head back and yelled at the heavens. "I'll rot in bloody hell!"

35
*

Andy, after reporting to the Intelligence Officer, was able to travel back to Stonecroft as a passenger in a Miles Master. The pilot, on a training flight, had gotten lost. He'd sense enough to fly as far as the coast and then parallel to the Channel until he spotted an airbase. After dropping Andy off, he would continue to his Service Flight Training School. Andy said very little on the short trip and let the sprog do all the flying and navigating. It was late afternoon when the sturdy trainer rolled to a stop at the flight line. Andrew James thanked the young pilot then walked quickly to the Nissen hut where Holmes had his office.

*

"I'm terribly sorry dear boy," Sherlock Trowbridge's voice broke, while wiping his glasses. "Billy was one of the best."

"At least in was quick Holmes." Andy had gotten over the shock and was trying his best to rationalize the events of the day. "It all happened so fast; Alley never knew what hit him."

"Yes, there is some comfort in that old chap."

"If you'll excuse me, I'll tell Burnsey before he goes to the mess."

"On your way then Andy. This war does have it's moments." Holmes rasped, as Andrew James got up to leave.

On the way to see Squadron Leader Barnes Andy was stopped by WAAF Corporal Jane Snowdon, a good friend of Emily's, "There you are," she smiled brightly. "I've a note from your fiance."

"Thanks Jane," Andy managed a sheepish grin while looking at the piece of paper that Corporal Snowdon had handed him.

"I hope you and Billy can make it to town then." she said, before hurrying to the control tower to work the evening shift.

*

It crossed Andy's mind to tell her about Billy, but Jane was gone before he could say anything.

The short message was to inform Andy and Billy that Emily and Margot would be at the townhouse for the night and if they could get a pass, then come on over. Andy crumpled the standard issue RAF page and stuffed it into the left breast pocket of his flight jacket. Normally he would have been over joyed at the prospect of spending time with Emily but Andy knew the news he bore would be earth shattering.

*

"A-Alley you say old sport," Burnsey was stunned and fought to keep his composure. "there's no justice in this bloody war. So many good chaps getting the chop."

"I-I need to borrow the Austin Burnsey," Andy sputtered. "Maggie and Emily are in London and it would be better if they found out about Billy from me."

"Yes, of course Andy," Robbie Barnes cleared his throat before lighting up a Woodbine. "I'll write you a twelve hour ticket. Forgive me old bean that's the best I can do, we'll be on standby at first light. These tip-and-runs are a bloody nuisance."

"No problem there Burnsey," Andy said calmly. "I'll look forward to a dogfight. My father used to say, if someone did you wrong; don't get mad, get even."

"I pity the poor Jerry that comes anywhere near your kite Dunc." Burnsey grimaced, before shaking Andy's hand.

*

Andrew James was able to get the well travelled Austin sedan to within a half mile of Berkeley square. He parked the car in an alleyway and walked carefully through the bomb damaged streets. The city was blacked out and he lost his way several times. Andy finally recognized a familiar landmark and knew that Emily's house was just around the corner. After entering the square, he peered through the darkness trying to spot the townhouse. It had disappeared. Andy raced towards where the building should have been, and as he got closer things began to take shape. The high rent dwelling had been transformed into a smoldering mound of rubble.

Jerky flashlight beams danced above the wreckage as a group of firemen searched the debris.

"Nothing over 'ere sir," a voice echoed in the darkness.

"Not bloody likely to find anything either." another voice answered.

"Don't be too sure about that sir, I've found something under a brick." a third voice reported

"Bring it 'ere then lad." the second voice ordered.

By this time Andy had made his way to what was left of Emily's London residence. As if one, the three London firemen turned towards the crunching footsteps that sounded behind them. The leader of the group shone his flashlight in Andy's face then slowly downwards.

"RAF?" the fireman lowered the flashlight.

"Yes sir, my fiance lives here," Andy croaked, fearing what was to come.

"You'd better get a grip then lad," the fireman, so used to death and dismemberment, stated blandly." because I've something to show you."

"No! Oh my God no!," Andy cried, instinctively staggering backwards.

The fireman had held up a charred hand. On the second finger of that badly deformed appendage was Emily's engagement ring.

*

Andrew James sick with grief and sorrow made it back to Stonecroft that evening well before midnight. There was nothing he could do to help the firemen and he knew an important phone call was necessary. Andy finally reached the residence of Anthony Smith-Barton, and in a voice strangled with emotion he told Emily's father what had happened. There was silence for a long moment at the other end of the line then in a stiff-upper-lip tone the broken hearted father said that he'd take care of everything and would get back to Pilot Officer Andrew James Duncan as soon as possible. Andy found out later that they'd searched all night but found nothing else.

There was no trace of Margot Cooper and the ring positively identified Emily as the a victim of a direct hit. True to his word, Lord Smith-Barton got in touch with Andy. The funeral would be held in London the following week.

*

Sometimes they're blown to bits. I try to identify the pieces so there's something to put in the coffins. All the Kings horses and all the Kings men. These gruesome memories, from his meeting with the nurse at the community centre, kept rattling around in Andy's numbed brain. They were at the grave site and the caskets had just been lowered into the ground. Lady Smith-Barton, a kind and generous woman, insisted that Margot be buried alongside Emily. The Smith-Bartons, realizing that Maggie had no living relatives, also ordered a gravestone for their daughter's best friend. Andy knew there was nothing but sandbags in the expensive oak boxes, but it looked better to those attending the funeral to see that the pall bearers were straining to lift a substantial weight.

When the service was over Anthony Smith-Barton approached Andrew James and patted the grieving Pilot Officer gently on the back before saying, "She loved you very much Andy and I know she'd want you to have this." Emily's father then handed Andy the engagement ring.

"Thank you sir, I'll treasure it forever."

"God's speed Andrew." Tony Smith-Barton croaked, as he left to comfort his wife.

*

2 November, 1940

The Panthers had been ordered by Air Chief Marshall Hugh Dowding to leave Stonecroft and set up shop at RAF Digby a much quieter sector station in 12 Group.

It was to be considered a rest for the battle weary fliers of 689. There were very few tip-and-run raids in this part of England though the Luftwaffe had attacked Birmingham several times, but usually at night. There was the occasional reconnaissance flight to intercept but this type of sortie was like a holiday compared to the shooting gallery over the Capital.

Andy was at first unhappy because he wanted to get even for what the Germans had done to Emily and Billy, but the relatively peaceful life at the new air base gradually began to agree with him. He would never forget the lovely Lady Smith-Barton and his best friend, but he realized that he'd have to get on with his life. Besides, from all signs, it promised to be a long war and Andrew James knew his chance would come again to settle the score with the airmen of the Third Reich.

*

"I think the air's better up here mate." Knobby said to no one in particular.

"If you're talking to me sir, I'd have to agree." Sergeant Pilot David Thompson Davis, a slim, beak nose, grey eyed, Londoner whose floppy, long brown hair lifted occasionally in the early morning breezes, smiled brightly. Gunner Davis was the replacement for Billy

"Yes, indeed Knobby old chap, the smoke from town did tend to foul the air around Stonecroft." Burnsey patted his pocket to make sure he had a full pack of Woodbines.

The Panthers were grouped around the big Australian's Spitfire awaiting a signal from Group to intercept a bandit that had just been reported by West Beckham radar.

It was likely a meteorological flight.

"Aye, it's a bonnie wee place this Digby, but my heart aches for the glorious Loches of the Highlands." Gus lamented poetically.

"We're all a touch homesick, I think." Woody added.

Before anyone could reply the Tannoy clanked on, and the scramble order ended the idle chit-chat.

*

"Red leader, blue two, he's just above cloud at one o'clock." Andy called over the R/T.

"Roger blue two, battle climb now." Burnsey ordered calmly.

When the twelve Spitfires had reached a position above and behind the Dornier Robbie Barnes toggled his mic, "Anyone spot an escort?"

"Eight 110s at twelve o'clock high mate." Knobby reported.

"Blue and Green take the fighters, Red follow me." Burnsey coughed loudly before lowering his goggles.

*

Gus, acting as Burnsey's wingman, followed his leader in a beam attack on the Do 17. Squadron Leader Robert Daniel Barnes squeezed the firing button and counted slowly to four. The concentrated cone of .303 rounds damaged the port engine of the bomber and it began to spew a sticky, black stream of oil. Gus right behind Burnsey's Spit hammered the port wing of the Dornier and seconds later flames could be seen along the trailing edge. The ventral gunner of the flying pencil, one of the best in the Luftwaffe, blasted Gus' Spitfire with a deadly river of machine gun rounds. One of the high velocity lumps of lead slammed through the folding door and hit Gus in the thigh. It missed the bone and a vital artery but remained lodged in muscle tissue. Gus was bleeding profusely but managed to apply pressure to the wound with his left hand.

"Red leader, Red one, got it in the leg, returning to base." Gus' strained voice penetrated the static on the R/T.

"Roger Red one, I'll be off your starboard wing." Burnsey said as he formed on Gus.

The Me 110s wanted no part of the eight Spitfires that were climbing to the attack and dove towards France. The crew of the Dornier had bailed out and the bomber was heading out to sea. It would eventually crash into the Channel. The weather report had been radioed to Kesselring's headquarters, but the bomber's crew would spend the rest of the war in a British prison camp.

*

Gus was weakened by the loss of blood but was still conscious when Burnsey and Woody helped him to a waiting ambulance. An RAF medic took charge and field dressed the wound on the way to the Royal Victoria Hospital in Nottingham. Gus would need surgery to remove the bullet and a period of rest in the wards to recover from being gunshot.

"Don't worry old sport," Burnsey soothed, before the door of the blood wagon had closed. "the chaps will be over for a visit as soon as you're up to it."

"Aye, Robbie that's very kind and tell the wee laddies that Scotch whiskey is the best for pain." Gus smiled thinly.

Two days later Andy caught the morning train to Nottingham. The hospital had reported that Gus was resting comfortably and was looking forward to seeing someone from the squadron. Burnsey, overwhelmed by paperwork, had asked Andy if he'd like to visit the popular Scotsman. Pilot Officer Andrew James Duncan was happy to oblige.

"And who might you be looking for?" An Army nurse smiled at Andy, who was having a hard time finding his way around the unfamiliar surroundings of the Royal Victoria.

"Flying Officer Augustus McGregor ma'am." Gus had been recently promoted.

"The young Scotsman?"

"That's the one." Andy nodded.

"Ward C, down the hall and to the right. There's a sign over the door."

Andy thanked the nurse and was soon in a twelve man ward. He spotted Gus in the sixth bed at the end of the room and gave a friendly wave.

"Does it hurt much?" Andy frowned.

"Aye laddie, but only when I laugh," Gus chuckled.

"No jokes then eh?"

"And what's that in the paperbag?" Gus raised up on to his elbows.

"Just some of that Highland nectar you're always talking about." Andy grinned, as he lifted a bottle of Johnny Walker Black Label from a brown bag.

"Quick, under the wee bed Andy. I do no want the nurses to see it."

"Yeah, I thought they might not allow booze in here, but you can take a belt or two at night when things are quite."

"Aye, that I will, and glady too."

They talked for an hour about the squadron, their times at Stonecroft and what they were going to do after the war. Andy could see that Gus was starting to labour and said he'd be back tomorrow morning for a short visit before catching the eleven o'clock for Digby. Andy had booked a room at a hotel near the Royal Victoria and after a tour of the town and a sumptuous dinner, in the dinning room of the Robin Hood Inn, he retired for the evening. Andrew James was glad to be away from flying, even for a brief period, and was very tired. He was asleep before the pillow warmed up and for a change his dreams were pleasant ones.

*

Andy easily found his way to the ward where Gus was recuperating and entered the large room just after nine the next morning. He looked around and was completely disorientated. The room was filled with a dozen female patients.

"Here, what do you think you're doing?" a stocky Army nurse demanded accusingly.

"L-Looking for Flying Officer McGregor ma'am." Andy stammered.

"Oh, I see," the rotund nurse softened. "he's been moved to Ward E on the third floor. We need this space for ladies who are recovering from head injuries."

Andy heard a moan coming from the bed behind him and reflexively turned around, wanting to help if he could. A woman, head covered by bandages, lips displaying obvious lacerations, eyes blackened and a broad piece of adhesive tape strapped across her nose, groaned again. It was the eyes! Andy walked towards the figure in the bed, staring intently at the azure blue eyes.

"What the bloody hell," the nurse fumed. "get away form there. That one's been in a coma since she arrived from London, but I think she may be coming around."

Andy completely ignored the nurse and reached out for the left hand that was resting on the injured woman's rib cage, "Emily," he murmured.

The woman on the bed blinked several times before whispering hoarsely, "Drew I-I, is Margot all right?" Emily sluggishly closed her eyes and seemed to be sleeping again.

"You know her then?" the nurse asked gently, while glancing over Andy's shoulder.

"Yes, I do." the tightness in his throat making it difficult for him to speak. "She's my fiance and I thought she was dead."

"It's a miracle then sir," the tough Army nurse sighed, she too had been moved by what had happened. "If you'll excuse me I'll fetch the doctor. Be careful of her other hand sir, the right arm's broken and in a cast."

37

*

Emily opened her eyes slowly and looked at Andy, "Is there something wrong darling?" she croaked, seeing tears streaming down his cheeks.

"Absolutely nothing Corporal Emily. This is the happiest day of my life."

"W-Where am I?" Emily looked confused.

"At a hospital in Nottingham. You must have been evacuated here after the bomb hit your townhouse."

"I remember now," she said weakly. "Margot was saying that her ring band was too small and she'd like to get a new one. I told her to try mine on for size and it fit her perfectly."

"Easy now Em' go slowly." Andy soothed, as the memory of the charred hand hit him like as belly blow. It was obviously Maggie's.

Emily looked around suddenly frightened. "Is Margot here?" she rasped.

Andy took a deep breath before saying. "She was killed when the bomb hit. I'm sure it was instantaneous."

Emily began to cry and Andy let her get it all out. Several minutes later she was able to tell him more. "I-I was standing by the window and I saw a little girl wandering around on the street. The siren had just sounded, so I rushed out to get the child and take her down to the billiard room. That's all I remember."

With the help of the doctor, who'd just arrived and was taking Emily's pulse, they were able to piece things together. Emily was found unconscious on the street in front of her home by an air raid warden. She'd been struck in the head by a flying brick and shattered pieces of glass had cut her lips badly. Her nose was fractured and her right arm was broken above and below the elbow. Emily was taken by ambulance to an over worked London hospital where she was given first aid. The attending doctor knew there was no room, so he arranged transport for her to Nottingham.

Emily had no identification on her person—a purse crushed by the bomb blast lay buried beneath the rubble of the townhouse. She was treated at the Royal Victoria and had been in coma for twenty days.

"You thought I was dead then. Oh my God, Mummy and Daddy." Emily looked terrified.

"I'm on my way to the phone darling," Andy called over his shoulder, this calmed her down and she sank back on to the pillow.

*

Andy was able to contact Lord Anthony Smith-Barton at the Ministry of Aircraft Production a gave him the stunning news. He remained speechless for a moment, then between sobs of joy he said,"Bless you Andy, bless you. I'll call her mother immediately."

*

When Andy got back to the ward Emily was resting peacefully and the nurse was sitting by her bed, "Just a few minutes more, then we should let her sleep."

"Yes, ma'am and in the meantime would it be okay to leave us alone?"

"Why certainly!" the nurse smiled.

When they were alone Andy kissed the back of Emily's left hand and told her he'd called his Lordship and that Lady Smith-Barton should have been informed by now.

"How did Billy take the news of Margot's death?" Emily asked in a weak voice.

Andy tried to say something but a clamp-like restriction in his vocal chords made it impossible for him to speak. Emily saw the look of anguish in Andy's eyes and realized what must have happened, "N-not Billy too." she stammered.

Andy was able to nod his head but that was all. Slowly he pulled a gold chain over his head and removed the ring that was attached to it. He placed the ring carefully into the palm of her hand. Emily, her eyes sparkling like the diamond she cradled in her cupped fingers, whispered softly, "I'll always love you Drew."

Two months, to the day, after Andy found Emily alive in a Nottingham hospital they were married at St. Paul's in London. Churchill, Beaverbrook, George VI and the Panthers attended the wedding. The rest of the guest list looked like a who's who of British society. It was a heart warming social event for the ravaged Capital and seemed to give many people hope.

The Luftwaffe, however, raided every night and this would continue until May of 1941. Thousands of Londoners would never see the flowers blooming in Hyde Park that spring, but Bomber Command was slowly picking up strength and Nazi Germany would eventually be taught a lesson as old as the Bible: "They who sow a wind shall reap a whirlwind."

Historical Note

In this work of historical fiction, I have attempted to present the Battle of Britain as accurately as possible within the requirements of the story. The official dates for the Battle according to the Royal Air Force were: 10 July, 1940 to 31 October 1940.

All the pilots and ground crew of 689 Squadron and RAF Stonecroft are fictional. The Canadian pilots: William Lidstone McKnight, Mark Henry Brown, Ernest Archibald McNab, John Alexander Kent and Fowler Morgan Gobeil are real and their accomplishments are as presented in the novel—although Ernie McNab did not fly with a Spitfire squadron before No. 1 Canadian became operational. The Commonwealth pilots: Edgar James 'Cobber' Kain and A.G. 'Sailor Malan' were also real.

The Royal Canadian Air Force represented by No. 1 RCAF was the only air force other than the RAF to fight in the Battle of Britain. I make this point because several of the history's I researched for *Spitfire Sunrise* claimed, that on the British side, the RAF was the only air force to take part in the Battle.

Churchill's speeches have been edited to fit the story line but they are his words. Beaverbrook, Dowding, Park, Leigh-Mallory, George VI and Douglas Bader were of course amongst the larger than life figures involved in the Battle. All the German leaders are non-fictional.

I found it incredible that in November of 1940, the Air Ministry took Dowding and Park to task for their handling of the air war. Their tactics clearly won the Battle of Britain but political in-fighting and petty jealousies carried the day. Dowding was forced to retire and Park was relegated to Training Command. Leigh-Mallory took over 11 Group and his 'Big Wing' concept was accepted in theory.

Later in the war Fighter Command staged a war game in order to prove that the 'Big Wing' would have, in fact, been successful. Leigh-Mallory directed the fighters of 11 Group against a make-believe raid on RAF air bases.

The exercise proved to be a shambles and the military judges declared that Kenley and Biggin Hill would have suffered serious damage before the 'Big Wing' had actually taken off.

The flying experiences encountered by Andy Duncan were based on the personal combat records of various Battle of Britain pilots. The Edward R. Murrow broadcast is exactly as given by the famous American war correspondent and journalist.

How important was the Battle? Even if Hitler had not invaded, but was able to destroy the Royal Air Force, the subsequent uncontested bombing of major British cities would have eventually driven the British government to sue for peace. Hitler would then have had a free hand in his attacks on the Soviet Union and developed jet aircraft in time to make a significant difference to the war. The German rocket scientists would have perfected the V-1 and V-2 ballistic missiles and, given the resources, an intercontinental missile aimed at the United States. It is not unreasonable to assume that the Germans would have also developed an atomic bomb.

Without an English base for aircraft and armies to use for attacking the countries occupied by the Nazis war machine, D-Day or the strategic bombing of Germany would never have happened. The list of possibilities and ramifications are large indeed. I would encourage each and everyone to consider Churchill's words one more time: "Never in the field of human conflict was so much owed by so many to so few."

This novel is from a Canadian perspective but it should be noted that the Battle of Britain was primarily a British show. Yes, the Commonwealth nations, the Poles, Czeches and Americans serving in the RAF did make a difference, but over eighty percent of the pilots came from the United Kingdom. On the British side, all the aircraft that participated in the Battle expect for the Canadian built Hurricanes were manufactured in England.

It will prove to be a long war and Andy Duncan will once again pilot his Spitfire and other British fighters in the skies over Great Briton and Europe.

BIBLIOGRAPHY

Bickers, Richard Townsend. *Ginger Lacey: Fighter Pilot.* Oxford: : ISIS, 1998.

Bishop, Patrick. *Fighter Boys: the Battle of Britain, 1940.* New York: Viking, 2003.

Deighton, Len. *Battle of Britain.* Toronto: Clarke, Irwin, 1980

Gelb, Norman. *Scramble: a narrative history of the Battle of Britain.* San Diego: Harcourt Brace Jovanovich, 1985.

Haining, Peter. *Spitfire Summer: the people's-eye view of the Battle of Britain.* London: W.H. Allen, 1990.

Halliday, Hugh. *No. 242 Squadron, the Canadian Years: the story of the all-Canadian fighter squadron.* Stittisville On: Canada's Wings, 1980.

Hough, Richard and Richards, Denis. *The Battle of Britain: the greatest air battle of World War II.* London: Norton, 1989

Kershaw, Alex. *The Few: American "knights of the air" who risked everything to fight in the Battle of Britain.* Cambridge Ma: DaCapo Press, 2006.

Korda, Michael. *With Wings Like Eagles: a history of the Battle of Britain.* New York: Harper, 2009.

Mosley, Leonard. *The Battle of Britain.* Chicago: Time-Life Books, 1980.

Overy, Richard. *The Battle of Britain.* London: Penguin Group, 2000.

Parker, Matthew. *The Battle of Britain.* London: Headline Book Publishing, 2000.

Price, Alfred. *Battle of Britain*. London: Arms and Armour Press, 1990.

Ralph, Wayne. *Aces, Warriors & Wingmen: first hand accounts of Canada's fighter pilots of the Second World War*. Mississauga On: John Wiley & Sons, 2005.

Ralph Wayne. *Barker VC: the life, death and legend of Canada's most decorated war hero*. Mississauga On: J. Wiley & Sons, 2007.

Townsend, Peter. *Duel of Eagles*. Norvato Ca: Presidio Press, 1991.

Willis, John. *Churchill's Few: the Battle of Britain remembered*. New York: Paragon House Publishers, 1987.